THE DILEMMA

SARAH HAWTHORN

BLOODHOUND
— BOOKS —

www.bloodhoundbooks.com

Print ISBN 978-1-5040-7273-1

For my parents, with love and gratitude

ESME

LONDON, JUNE 1958

*T*he Chelsea flat hadn't been disturbed at all. Why would it? No one had been here in weeks. Not since the charlady had raised the alarm and then all manner of people had turned up: neighbours, police, ambulance crew. That day, Esme had arrived to be greeted by unfamiliar faces and a babble of voices. When she'd walked into the sitting room everyone had gone silent, the sort of ghastly hush which means you're the star of the moment, the one who's going to set the scene for whatever comes next.

The charlady had bustled over, all important with a look of excited sympathy, and taken her elbow. "It's your mother, dear. Quite a shock it was. I found her, you see. Lying on the floor by her bed, clutching the blanket." Esme had looked around then to see several pairs of eyes fixed on her.

Before she could react, Dr Blair – stooped with scoliosis, and blessed with fascinating bushy white eyebrows – had ushered her through the nearest door into the kitchen. He'd flapped his hand at the waiting audience. "There's nothing to see here. Please leave."

Esme had leaned against the pale-blue cabinetry while he

opened and closed his mouth, making incomprehensible words. Something about a weak heart and a massive stroke. She hadn't really taken it in, too shocked at hearing her mother had *died*. Only the day before, she'd received a letter from her, asking to meet for afternoon tea at The Ritz. *It's been too long. I've something to tell you, darling, before it's too late.* Had her mother known? Or experienced a premonition?

Now, in the aftermath of her funeral, Esme paused in the hallway, taking in the stale odour of shut-up rooms and the dead silence of a lifeless home, feeling like an interloper. She'd never even had her own key, and yet she had the intimate task of going through her mother's belongings. Irrational anger welled at the unfairness of this untimely burden. Arcadia had always seemed so invincible, one of those women who by raw power and force of personality would grip onto life with fierce intensity. People such as Arcadia didn't die young. They outlived their contemporaries in grand, arrogant style until old age made its final demand.

A knot of panic twisted in Esme's stomach at knowing any chance of mending their fractured mother-daughter relationship had now passed. With a sigh, she made her way to the kitchen and opened the cupboard over the sink. Four plates, four cups and four bowls were arranged side by side. In the next cupboard, a few tins: corned beef, baked beans, carrots, tomato soup, new potatoes. At least tidying up shouldn't be too much of a drama. When Arcadia had moved here after the war, she'd made a point of 'cleansing' her life. "Possessions are of little importance," she'd said, when what she really meant was the new flat was so small, she couldn't fit much in.

Bracing herself, Esme ventured into her mother's bedroom but the charlady had stripped the bed and tidied away any lingering signs of life: no bedside water glass, discarded clothes, or slippers waiting to warm up cold feet. Only a sad collection of worn clothes graced the drawers and small wardrobe. Arcadia's once extensive collection of designer ball gowns and outfits for every occasion had been mothballed long ago, useless once the war was over and her social life had become moribund. Esme took just her mother's jewellery case – everything else could be boxed by the removers – and firmly closed the door, glad to leave the room.

She strolled into the sitting room, noting that her mother's life was a little less spartan here. Her collection of avant-garde paintings – vivid splashes of daring colour and movement – relieved the dull spread of off-white dust sheets. A bookcase adorned one wall, its shelves filled with Arcadia's library of vanity-published books neatly stacked by publication date, with at least six copies of every title. She uncovered Arcadia's prized chaise longue, the one on which her mother always claimed her best inspiration came. Perching on the end of it, she opened the jewellery case. Only costume pieces remained; imitation pearls, crystals and strings of coloured beads. Gone were the diamonds, rubies and sapphires, sold to pay the bills, no doubt. She lifted the tray of trinkets and underneath found two photographs, faded and crinkled; one of a baby, another of a young soldier. Neither carried a date or name on the back, but the baby must be her, or even Arcadia, she supposed. The soldier, however, bore no resemblance to her father. The pictures had probably been secreted there for years, forgotten. All the same, Esme's curiosity was piqued.

She put the box aside to consider its contents later and crossed to the mahogany roll-top desk. The drawers were filled with old bills, bank statements, diaries detailing every dinner party Arcadia had held (the guests, the menu, the flowers, the seating plan), and piles of notebooks where Arcadia jotted ideas for her novels. On the desktop was more recent correspondence, writing paper, pens, stamps and a cheap exercise book, filled with her mother's loopy scrawl, which appeared to be the draft of her current work in progress, *The Art of Artifice*. Esme's heart sank. It felt like a clarion call, a final request from the grave. She sighed, irritated at being burdened with such a task. She'd read it when she had time, and if it had merit she'd get it published as homage to her mother. A clearing of the decks.

Time marched and the removers were due in an hour. Despite Arcadia's minimal belongings, Esme still had to sort her possessions into piles for the auction house, various charities, and those to throw out. She'd keep a selection of her books, although as a shy teenager she'd dismissed Arcadia's work as romantic rubbish after being made to read a passage from *Sunrise Over Heartache* at a private 'at home' event. Standing before the assembled throng, Esme had blushed scarlet and stumbled her way through several blue paragraphs about a schoolgirl frolicking in the woods looking for butterflies and grubs, but finding only the farmer's son.

Perhaps her mother's voracious output would stimulate Esme's creative juices. An injection of her mother's purple prose might be just what she needed to put the demons to rest. Although Esme's first novel, *The View From Here*, had garnered positive reviews, she'd since suffered crippling self-doubt. Arcadia, who had a powerhouse of belief in her own dubious talents, had merely chivvied her along, saying, "Harden up, Esme. You'll never be a successful author if you buckle under criticism."

From the bookcase, she pulled a novel at random, *Love on the Farm*, and read the overblown notes on the flyleaf. *Arcadia Fanstone, renowned for the passion and romance of her works, once again enthrals with this sweeping saga, the second in her Farm trilogy...* Another caught her attention: *We Will Overcome*. She smiled. Really, her mother's imaginative flair knew no boundaries. *In war-torn England, amidst the bombs and the blackouts, love conquers all opposition to freedom.*

She closed the cover. About to push the book back into its designated slot on the shelf, she noticed an envelope had fallen into the gap between its neighbours. Postmarked *Guernsey, 6*

October 1945, over red and green postage stamps, it was addressed in a barely legible script to *A Fanstone, c/o Knightsbridge P.O.* Esme pulled out the single sheet of flimsy, lined paper. There was no address at the top, just the same date: 6 October 1945. The handwriting was spindly, punctuated by ink blots.

Dearest–

It's been the most terrible two days. I so hoped to sort everything quickly and not bother you but things go from bad to worse. C has got into the most awful trouble and landed in jail. Now there's talk of an attempted murder charge. C's gone all mute and sullen and won't speak to any of us. You must get over here as soon as you can. The ferries are running again though Lord knows how reliable they are.

Love, in haste, M.

Esme stared at the sheet of cream airmail paper and frowned. Who was C? Or, come to that, M? Not relatives because her mother had been orphaned as a child and had no siblings. She knew Arcadia had been born in Guernsey, a little-known island until the Germans occupied the Channel Islands during World War II; Hitler's prized possession, his one piece of Allied territory. But Arcadia had left decades earlier, before World War I broke out, sent away to a spinster aunt in the north of England after her mother contracted tuberculosis. As a young girl, Esme had been fascinated by this tale of childhood trauma, desperate for details, but her mother always sidestepped talk of Guernsey. As for the spinster aunt, Arcadia had shut down the conversation, saying, "Oh her. She was a stick of a thing and not very kind to me."

She scratched her memory for anything Arcadia had said about her parents. When pressed, Arcadia had described her mother as beautiful but distant; a sickly woman who largely kept to her bed. As for her father, Arcadia claimed hardly any memory of him, except to say he was a strict man who stayed in his study poring over his stamp collection. He'd later served in the Great War and never returned. There was frustratingly little else, and Esme wished she hadn't been so cavalier, sure in her belief that one day – when she felt less resentful of her mother – she'd find out more about Arcadia's side of the family, her childhood spent growing up on Guernsey, and whether any distant relatives still lived there. Now there'd never be a chance to know how it was for a little girl to be ripped away from all she knew, sent to live with a fearsome aunt in a foreign land, and at some point to learn – presumably via telegram – of her parents' deaths.

So this letter was extraordinary, popping up out of context, seeming to infer Arcadia had retained links to her birthplace. Or was Esme reading too much into it? Arcadia was forever going off on 'reconnaissance trips', as she called them, scouting for new locations or story ideas for her next book. Perhaps she'd had a yearning to revisit the place of her early years, and whilst there become involved in the lives of M and C. But why never mention it?

Esme slipped the letter back into its envelope. She'd tell Hugh about it later, over dinner, and ask him what he thought. He enjoyed the challenge of solving crossword puzzles and ciphers, so maybe he'd be able to unravel these scant clues and come up with a clever answer.

2

JANE

GUERNSEY, AUGUST 1914

*O*n 5 August 1914, my childhood ended. Not just because we learned of the looming threat of invasion and feared losing our men in the mud-soaked trenches of France – us girls never thought of such things. No – something far more sinister occurred in our household that day. Looking back, I think being the youngest meant until then I'd been somehow sheltered from the ugliness. Or perhaps I didn't notice until my nose was pressed firmly against the reality of what went on under our roof. Or maybe I blithely believed the people who said: *How lucky you are to be the daughter of the headmaster! What a wonderful education you and your two sisters must have! How marvellous that the three of you are such good friends!*

That particular Wednesday, my eyes were opened to injustice, jealousy and something darker that changed all of us, and which we refused to expose, preferring to bury our secrets under a veneer of family happiness. And I learned that love has the power to not just bring joy, but to destroy too.

Father had attended the announcement at Town Square that afternoon. The school bursar had urged him to go, telling him as headmaster he must be sure to have the facts so he could relay the news accurately to both the teachers and the boys. And now it was our turn. My sisters, Ginia and Mavis, my mother and I were seated around the dining table, gazing at the unusual sight of Father standing behind his chair, a grave look on his stern face, holding the Bible.

"It is my solemn duty to advise you that yesterday the King declared Great Britain is now at war with Germany, after that country's failure to withdraw its military might from Belgium. Praise God," he said, tapping the Bible, "this madness will last only a few weeks. In the meantime, we must carry on as normal."

The rumours had been rife and the news not unexpected. Nevertheless, my heart thumped in anxious beats. "Are we in danger?" I asked.

Father opened his mouth, but Ginia interrupted. "Of course we are. Guernsey is far closer to France than Britain and therefore we are at risk of German invasion."

"Virginia, don't presume to talk of things you know nothing about." He ladled soup from the large blue-and-white-striped-china tureen, lips drawn in a tight line.

"Because I'm a woman?"

"Hardly a woman. A child." A tic flickered in his left temple. Mother passed the bowls around the table and nodded at Mavis to hand out the bread basket.

Ginia wouldn't be silenced. "I'm old enough to know this war was avoidable. If women had the vote, then the liberals would be in power and this would never have happened."

Father threw the silver ladle into the tureen. The sudden clatter made us all jump and spurts of oxtail soup landed on the white tablecloth. "You–" he pointed his finger at Ginia, "are an impudent, ignorant *child*. The mere notion of women having the vote is preposterous and let me tell you, my girl, were it to ever happen, God forbid–" he looked skywards to his ever-present Lord, "then your husbands would have to tell you which party to vote for."

"How dare you? *How dare you?*" Ginia's eyes bulged in fury. "Do you really set yourself so far above us, all of us, your daughters, your wife..." She gestured at us sitting around the table, wide-eyed and fearful. "Do you seriously believe you know what's best for us? That politics are the domain of men? Those very men who have served this country so poorly whilst women have borne the brunt of their cruelty and dominance, without ever having a voice of their own?"

She was truly admirable, facing down Father and letting fly without blinking or trembling.

"Go to your room." Father's voice was ominously low.

Ginia scraped back her chair, flung her serviette into her bowl and exited without a word.

Mother squeezed her hands together, and with frantic eye movements urged Mavis and me to remain silent, as she always did when Father's black mood exploded. She'd retreat, not physically, but quietly into herself, as if she were trying to shrink into a shell and become invisible.

The only noise in the room was the clinking of spoons against china, and Father chomping on his bread. Mavis and I grinned at each other from under hooded eyes. Father's moods never lasted; he'd eat his supper, tell us to go to our rooms, do our homework and not come down again, and then say he and Mother weren't to be disturbed. I concentrated on not slurping my soup and mulled over Ginia's outburst. At fifteen, I'd not considered what came next, after school, but she had a point. Did I want the rest of my life decided for me, at the whim of my father or a husband?

Father finished eating, wiped his mouth and with fists clenched, he leaned on the table and raised himself up. "I'm going to deal with Virginia. She needs to be taught a lesson." In three large strides, he crossed the room.

A look of agony passed over Mother's face and she flew after him. "*Frank. No.*"

The dining-room door banged behind her. Mavis gasped in that easily shocked way she puts on. "Goodness."

"Shhh." I tiptoed to the door and pressed my ear to the woodwork. Raised voices hissed in a vain effort not to be overheard. I pictured Father halfway up the stairs and Mother clutching his sleeve.

"Mind your own business," I heard Father say.

"It *is* my business. She's our daughter. Don't Frank, please, don't," Mother pleaded, tears in her voice. "Don't touch her."

"Let go of me." His voice was cold. "Stay with the girls until I return."

"If you lay a finger on her, I'll... I'll–"

"No, you won't. Not if you know what's good for you." His footsteps landed in heavy thuds on the stairs. A door opened and closed. My mind whirling, I sat back at the table. Mavis gave me a questioning look.

"I think she's in for the birch," I said. Father never beat us, saving that punishment for the boys in his care, but he seemed angry enough to break his own rule. "Mother sounded–" but I never got a chance to say, *Mother sounded frightened*, because just then she entered the room, wearing a distracted frown and wringing her hands, the way she did when wrestling over how to stop milk curdling, or how to stretch supper to feed extra guests.

"Go into the garden," she said. "I'll clear the dishes."

Mavis started to object but I waved her outside. Clearly, Mother wanted to be alone.

We sat on the stone wall that ran alongside the front garden. Mavis twiddled with the head of a snapdragon, opening and closing its mouth in the way we'd done as children, playing with them like miniature puppets.

"How was orchestra practice?" she asked.

What she meant was, how was Charlie? He plays the cello while I sit at the back waiting to strike my triangle, covertly watching him. Mavis has a monumental crush on him, but it's me he smiles at and tells his dreams to. He wants to be a professional cellist but his parents insist he goes into the family business when he leaves school. Charlie has no interest in growing tomatoes. Today, I told him about my dream of living in France one day. He didn't laugh. He actually said he'd like that too.

"Charlie walked me home." I knew that would annoy her and I was right. Her face darkened.

"He's a monitor, in sixth form," she said, as if this meant I had no right talking to him. "You're too young. He's my friend."

I shrugged. Something miraculous occurred today when I was with Charlie, something I wasn't about to give to Mavis.

"I'll tell Father," she said. "And it will be worse than the birch, mark my words."

I ignored Mavis's burning jealousy. Of course, a nice sister would drop all hopes of winning Charlie, and sacrifice him to Mavis, but I knew that I wouldn't. And why should I, if Charlie preferred me?

Mother called to us from the front door. "Homework time. In your own rooms."

Mavis lowered her head and pushed past me. I followed her in and saw Father, flushed and smiling, with a proprietorial hand on Mother's shoulder. I ignored them and ran up the stairs in time to see Mavis disappear into the bathroom, her back rigid with disappointment. Ginia's door was closed, so I knocked.

"Are you all right?" I asked.

"Yes." She didn't sound all right.

"Can I come in?"

"Not now. I'm... I'm reading."

If she was reading, then everything must have calmed down with Father, and I could pretend to study whilst thinking about Charlie. "Night night then."

She didn't reply, and I ignored my tick-tock of concern for her. It's all this news about war, I reassured myself, it's got everyone in a state. As Father said, we must act as normal.

~

GUERNSEY, SEPTEMBER 1914

Ginia and I were in the kitchen – me doing geography home-work, Ginia peeling potatoes – when Father interrupted us. He filled the doorway, wearing his militia uniform, all stiff khaki and brass buttons, and waited until we gave him our full attention before he spoke.

"Anyone else at home?" he asked.

"Mother and Susan are at a Red Cross meeting with Mavis," I offered. Susan was Mother's best friend.

He circled the table, running his fingers along the edge. "I forgot to pick up the evening paper. Off you go, Jane."

I sighed. "Why can't Gin–Virginia?" Only I called her Ginia. Father abhorred short forms, said it was common.

"You're the youngest."

As I trudged to Carr's Store, I couldn't erase from my mind the look on Ginia's face when I left: a funny mix of fear and determination. There had been no further sign of Father admonishing her for outspokenness, and yet her expression scared me, and I couldn't work out why.

In the weeks since war was declared, there's been this dark cloud over the house. Everyone's jittery. Mavis is forever bursting into tears and does her darnedest to ignore me, still in a sulk about Charlie. Ginia is even more obsessed with the suffragette movement, if that's possible. Mother spends more and more time whispering with Aunty Susan. Father lectures us about 'being prepared' and brooks no discussion. And Charlie, dear Charlie, says he's going to sign up for the militia as soon as he's old enough. Of course, the war will be over by then, but I'm sickened at the mere *thought* of us being apart. I think about him all the time. I can't help it. There's a constant picture of him in my mind. The way he plays his cello with furious intensity:

brows knotted and long, bony fingers pressing the strings as he draws the bow back and forth. I love to watch him. Or listen to him talking. His voice has a melody to it, his sentences are always perfectly formed and he never speaks for the sake of it.

The tinkling of the bell as I entered the shop interrupted my musings. Waiting at the counter to be served, I replayed the note Charlie sent me today: *Margaret Ann Neve was the oldest woman in the world until she died in 1903 aged 110. Imagine living across three centuries! Will we still be alive to find out? In 2001, you will be 102 and I'll be 104.*

"Wake up, ducks." Mr Carr, rotund and bellicose, hooted with laughter. "Here's your dad's paper." He handed me the *The Guernsey Evening Press* and I hurried out to avoid being pincered by his childish jokes and having to politely laugh at them for the umpteenth time.

I quickened my pace, still uneasy about Ginia. I had the feeling I should get back to check everything was all right – although I'd have to make some excuse, because Ginia, being the eldest, couldn't suffer what she called 'namby-pambying'.

I'm not sure why, but when I reached our back door, I made a big to-do about slamming it closed, and loudly kicked off my boots. I heard a scuffling noise overhead and walked to the bottom of the stairs. "I'm back," I called out, then crossed the hallway and knocked on Father's study door.

His voice made me jump. "You can give that to me, Jane." I swung around and saw him coming downstairs, straightening his tie and smoothing back his hair. He held out his hand for the newspaper and beckoned me to follow him into his study. Oh blimey, what had I done now?

He shut the door and strode to the front of his desk. He didn't ask me to sit down. "What's this I hear about some boy sniffing about?"

How on earth had he found out about Charlie? Mavis, proba-bly. She'd been in a huff ever since it became clear Charlie's interest lay with me, not her. She doesn't know the half of it. Imagine if I told her about our walks, how we hold hands and talk about the future, our dreams and ambitions. How Charlie wants to play in an orchestra and how I want to travel the world. How I tremble when he touches me and the yearning I feel when he kisses me.

I looked down at my feet and set my jaw. "Nothing."

"You've been seen together. I won't have a daughter of mine disgracing our name. And look at me when I'm talking to you." He clenched and unclenched his fists, his face getting redder. "Come here." He began to unbuckle the wide belt around his jacket.

My heart gathered speed, pumping hard in my chest.

"Bend over," he said.

Terrified, I did as he commanded. His hand came up my skirt and grabbed the top of my knickers, his breathing heavy and laboured. Tears streamed down my face and I tensed for whatever came next. I heard the door fling open and Father yelled, *"Get out."*

A hand grabbed me. "You promised," screamed Ginia. "You promised." She placed her body between Father and me.

"Then be a good girl," Father said. "You know the rules."

Ginia pushed me from the room. "Get upstairs."

The door clicked shut and I was left, alone, in the hall.

I ran, shaking, up to Ginia's room and sat on the end of her bed. The house was eerily quiet, the only sound a soft, rhythmic banging from somewhere down below. I concentrated on sending my thoughts to a happy place – to Charlie, the little tilt of his head when I say something funny, the tiny mole on his earlobe, his fondness for hedgehogs – and when they veered back to Father looming over me, his hands rough on my skin, I closed my eyes and recited the names of Latin poets. But despite my best efforts, my mind kept pitching into shadowy places.

A few minutes later, I heard footsteps and Ginia darted in,

wild-eyed, her hair half-loosened from its ribbon. I stared warily at her, not sure what to expect but she came and put her arm around me. "Are you all right? Did he hurt you?"

I shook my head. I dared not ask the same question back again, afraid of her answer; that Father had done to her what he'd intended for me.

"Listen, Jane." Ginia glanced to the door. "You mustn't tell anyone what happened today. Do you understand? No one. Not Mother and especially not Mavis. It's our secret. You and me."

She didn't need to tell me to say nothing. I wanted to forget this afternoon ever happened. As for Mavis, I'd hardly be having a conversation with her any time soon.

She squeezed my hand. "If ever anything happens which confuses or frightens you, come to me. You hear me?" She sat up straighter and took a deep breath. "And I'll decide what needs to be done."

We heard Mavis rattling up the stairs and all of a sudden, Ginia burst into song, 'Keep the Home Fires Burning'.

Mavis poked her head around the door. "Oh, do pipe down."

Back on familiar territory, bickering with my sisters, eased some of the tension. "That's typical of you, Mavis. Ginia's just being patriotic," I said.

Mavis glared at me. "It's not Ginia. It's Vir-ginia."

Ginia stopped singing. "Actually, dear sister, I'm exercising my right to make my own decisions. Women's voices have been stifled for too long. If I choose to be called Ginia, there should be no opposition. If I want to work in a factory so men can go to war, so be it. Emmeline and Sylvia aren't lawbreakers, they want to be lawmakers and give us women the vote. That's what the suffrage movement is all about."

Mavis pursed her lips. For a girl of seventeen, she'd perfected the look of a spinster schoolmarm. "So you keep telling us but there's no need to be so pompous about it."

I watched the verbal ping-pong with glee. Mavis had a point.

Our older sister did carry on as if the Pankhursts were personal friends. But I agreed wholeheartedly with Ginia; I didn't want to be tied to a life of domestic drudgery, under the thumb of a man, being told how to think and behave. Unable to complain or voice an opinion.

I didn't hear the rest of their argument, too absorbed in considering my future if nothing changed. Married to someone like Father, unable to make my own choices. Having to stay silent when I wanted to speak out. I made a vow right there and then, sitting on Ginia's bed with Mavis squawking like a chicken, that whatever happened I'd never allow myself to be bullied, forced to settle for a mundane existence. As soon as I was able, I'd make my own way and defy anyone who tried to stop me.

3

ESME

LONDON, JUNE 1958

*E*sme hadn't expected it to take so long to sort her mother's things, with such conflicting emotions – sadness, anger, regret – halting her progress. In the end, it was almost six o'clock by the time she returned to her West Kensington flat carrying a hessian bag containing a dozen of Arcadia's novels; her last hurrah, *The Art of Artifice*; the jewellery case; a stack of unpaid bills and that intriguing letter from Guernsey.

She dashed up the two flights of stairs to her cramped rooms, threw the bag into a corner, stripped down to her underwear, had a quick wash with a flannel at the basin and dabbed Yardley English Lavender behind her ears. She smoothed on foundation, making sure to disguise the scar that ran below her cheekbone, dabbed the sheen with powder, and being careful not to overdo it, applied pale-blue eyeshadow. At work, she kept her hair pulled back into a ponytail; tonight, she let the curls bob close to her shoulders. She'd always had long hair, preferring to wear it loose when she went out so she could hide that side of her face and not be stared at by strangers. But she really liked some of the newer styles coming into vogue, short with soft waves cut into the nape of the neck. Sophisticated yet practical. Dare she?

Thank goodness she'd polished her shoes and ironed her dress earlier. In a hurry now, her fingers trembled as she buttoned up the front, and she almost discarded it in favour of one with a back zipper. But the wide red belt, cinched at her waist over a flared white cotton skirt, flattered her figure, so she persevered with the troublesome rose-shaped buttons.

Standing back from the mirror, she checked the effect. Satisfied, she stepped into the final touch: a pair of high heels, rather than her usual sensible brogues. After so many years of waiting for Hugh to take her on a date, she wanted to make a big impression, wow him.

He was taking her to a new Chinese restaurant in Soho. Hugh said Mr Chong's was all the rage, and he wanted to try it out before taking a potential new advertiser. She'd only ever eaten Chinese food once, and had struggled to make much of it, mostly because getting rice and noodles from the bowl to her mouth with chopsticks proved harder than she'd imagined. Yet millions of Chinese ate that way, so it couldn't be too impossible, could it? Esme prayed she wouldn't make a fool of herself and drop fried rice and chop suey down her white frock.

She draped a cardigan over her shoulders, popped her keys and a comb into her clutch bag, briefly considered – and then dismissed – taking an umbrella, and closed the door on her rooms. She ran lightly down the stairs, keen to avoid being cornered by her nosy downstairs neighbour, Mrs Smithers, and was out of the front door breathing in the evening air.

They'd arranged to meet at seven o'clock and although she was tired after packing up her mother's flat and would prefer to catch a black cab, she couldn't afford it, so she set off for the Underground. The shoes slowed her down, but Esme was damned if she'd turn up looking anything less than glamorous.

The carriage was half empty, but even so Esme was certain the old man seated opposite and the young couple who silently held hands could sense her nerves. The girl gave her a shy smile, as if to say, 'Courage'. Fine for her, with her glinting ring, secure in her fiancé's affection. Esme, on the other hand, was on the cusp. She clenched her palms together, clammy in her lap, and her stomach tightened. She had waited so long, dreamed of the moment when her years of loyalty and love would at last be recognised. And now, tonight, here it was: her chance to become more than his colleague, his Girl Friday, his right-hand woman, and take a position by Hugh's side as his equal, sharing their triumphs and disappointments.

This time, she wasn't going to let happiness slip by like before. She was quite capable of speaking her mind and making her feelings known. She'd even had a book published, for heaven's sake, and it may not have sold many copies or made her fortune despite one reviewer hailing it 'a literary triumph', but it had proved to Hugh she was capable of more than typing and shorthand. It was a start. She'd noticed a shift then, a bit more respect, soon followed by the promotion to copy editor.

Occasionally he'd ask if she was working on anything new and place a consolatory hand on her shoulder when she smiled and said, "Writer's block. You know." He'd say, "Patience, it will come." He never offered unhelpful comments, or made her feel inadequate, a 'one-book wonder'. That was the incredible thing about Hugh; his ability to know when silence trounced meaningless words. It was the same when Arcadia died. He gave cautious condolences and whatever time off she needed, but never probed for more. "I'm here when you want to talk," he'd said.

The train jerked to a stop at Piccadilly Circus. The old man stood and held back the doors to let her alight first. "Have a good evening," he said. Esme felt a whiff of pleasure course through her body and she almost ran up the escalator and out into the cooling air. Spring was giving way to summer; a few tourists remained but mainly workers and theatregoers were on the streets at this hour.

She walked slowly towards Gerrard Street, keen to arrive last.

The entry to Mr Chong's was easy to spot with its multi-coloured doorway made of plastic strips. Inside, lanterns hung overhead and gaudy paintings of dragons adorned the walls. Diners occupied a few tables, and in the corner, Hugh stood and waved to her. In a sharp navy suit and red club tie, he held himself with military confidence. With his newly-clipped blond hair, unwavering blue eyes and wicked moustache, he was still the handsomest man she'd ever seen.

She made her way over and he took her by both shoulders and kissed her cheek. "You look rather spiffing," he said.

She laughed. "How P G Wodehouse of you." Suddenly, she felt awkward, out with Hugh on a Saturday night, dressed to the nines. She took time to fold her cardigan and place it under her bag on the spare seat beside her.

"Everything all right at your mother's? Get it all sorted? Not too gruelling?"

She nodded, trying but failing to find words that explained the oddness of it all – the sudden absence of someone who had been so present, so vital.

Hugh twiddled the sticks in front of him. "We're going to have to go to war with chopsticks. Or we can be cowards and eat with forks." He grinned, and she was reminded of when she'd first worked for him during the war at the Ministry of Information, and he'd said, "Only cowards fight like bullies. We'll fight this war with words." Taken by his assured air and twinkling smile, she'd been immediately smitten by Wing Commander Hugh Tate.

Months later, when he asked that she be reassigned to him in the Cabinet War Rooms to help plot U-boat sightings, she'd willingly agreed. It couldn't have been less comfortable or more unpleasant, but the feeling of being in the heart of the action made it worthwhile. Even stripping down to her undies for five minutes each week, exposing the body to a lamp to temper the effects of light deprivation, and the constant smell of soot and musty air, were small inconveniences compared to helping topple Hitler. And of course, there was the added bonus of Hugh's constant presence.

A waiter came over with two beers.

"I hope you don't mind," said Hugh. "I rather thought beer would be the thing. Let's enjoy a drink before we order. Besides, I want to talk to you."

Esme's heart took a small skip, and she covered her fluster with a sip of beer.

"Good?"

"Mmm."

He smiled, leaned over, and wiped her top lip. "Froth. Very unbecoming for a lady."

Esme relaxed. It was all going to be fine. She could feel it. "We're still fighting with words, aren't we? But at least chasing the truth these days."

"D'you know, I worked out the other day that it must have been ten years ago you joined the paper."

"Eleven."

"Oh? A couple of years after the end of the war anyway." He leaned back. "Those were the days, eh? Dealing in propaganda. Much as I enjoyed being in that secret bunker rubbing shoulders with the likes of Churchill and Eden, I must say the earlier years were strangely satisfying, coming up with wild ideas to boost morale."

"Or confuse the enemy."

"Indeed."

He patted her hand. "You've been very loyal. I couldn't have done any of it without you. I want you to know that, because I think I've taken you for granted, not thanked you enough."

Esme swallowed. "It's been my pleasure."

"Yes... We've had fun, haven't we? And bad times. You've weathered those too. Not just the business ones either. Tomasina... Pippie."

His wives. The one who died and the one who fled. Both

times, Esme held Hugh's hand, managed the fallout, helped him get back on his feet and waited in the wings. Overlooked first for Tomasina, who returned after the war from driving ambulances in France to reclaim her university sweetheart. Then after her death, at Esme's suggestion Hugh holidayed in Torquay to grieve for his lost wife, and was snared by Pippie. A gold digger with a pretty face, she soon bored of life as a publisher's wife and ran off with a wealthy diamond trader.

"Tomasina used to say you were a gem. That I'd never have got the newspaper on its feet without you. You drove a hard bargain with everyone: writers, typesetters, printers, delivery boys. And look at us now. One of the most successful rags in town." He tapped his chopsticks on the table. "I'm sorry she never lived to see it."

The Monitor traded on appealing to the working man, and Tomasina – a true blue stocking – had hated some of its articles which she'd considered demeaning to women. She and Hugh often loudly fought about what she called his lack of editorial integrity, and she'd call in Esme – who knew better than to take sides – to arbitrate. Esme would watch their arguments, amazed at how badly they handled each other. Had she been Hugh's wife, she'd have appealed to his intellect, proposed an alternate path and let Hugh believe it had been his idea. At least, with Pippie, Hugh had been glad to see her go after years of tolerating her manipulative behaviour. And now it was Esme's turn. His next wife, partner for life in every way.

"It's been quite a journey," said Esme. "Shall we order?" She opened the menu and scanned the list of unfamiliar dishes: spring rolls, chow mein, sweet and sour pork, stir fry noodles. "You choose."

Again, Hugh laid his hand over hers. "Not yet."

Esme momentarily closed her eyes, relishing the feel of his hand, rough and strong. Her head went into a blind fuzz and she scrambled to find a sensible topic. "You'll never guess–" she began, keen to tell Hugh about the letter she'd found.

"Esme–"

"At my mother's, clearing out her apartment, the most unusual thing–"

"Esme." He squeezed her hand. "Esme, listen to me."

"But Hugh, it was so strange–" She looked into his face. At his intent eyes, his brilliantined hair slicked off his forehead, and full lips she longed to kiss. "Yes?"

"I'm going to America."

His words hit her like a slap. America? What could he mean? She tried to ask but her mouth just opened and closed, with no words escaping. Leaving her?

"I want you to come with me. Will you?"

This time, a punch to the chest, winding her. A glorious rush of mad excitement filled her. "Oh, Hugh..."

He leaned forwards. "It's the new world, Esme. Opportunities galore. I know *The Monitor* has done fine here but over there, in Pennsylvania, I can really make my mark. Make a fortune too. I met a man who's keen to invest and, well, what do you say? All these years we've been a team, Esme. Are you game to try it?"

His eyes glistened as he examined her face for her reaction. Words, dozens of them, tumbled in her head but she couldn't form a coherent sentence. First, though, she must be sure. "Are you proposing... are you asking–?"

A shadow fell across the table and Hugh looked up. "You've arrived," he exclaimed and jumped up. "I was just telling Esme. Come, sit here."

Esme swung around. A tall woman with an elegant chignon, dressed in a severe navy-blue suit, towered over them, looking out of place amongst the casual ambience of rice dishes, beer and chopsticks.

"Esme. Meet Miranda."

Esme frowned and glanced between Hugh and Miranda. He

held her elbow and she leaned into him. "Darling, I'm so sorry to be late. Daddy insisted. You know how he is." Her perfume, strong and heady, drifted across the table.

Esme watched the scene before her play out in slow motion. Hugh kissing Miranda's cheek. Miranda slipping onto the seat beside him. Hugh placing his arm around her shoulder. Miranda smiling. Hugh opening his mouth and saying something.

Esme blinked, caught her breath and straightened her expression. "How do you do?"

Hugh clapped his hands together. "I want you two to be the best of friends. Darling, Esme's agreed to come to America with us and help me set up the business." Esme gasped. "Esme, meet the future Mrs Tate: my fiancée, Miranda."

After stumbling home, Esme stayed in her room for two days, choked with sorrow at the loss of what she'd never had. Each morning she woke with the dead weight of disappointment pinning her down, the sound of Hugh's voice drumming in her ears: *Meet the future Mrs Tate: my fiancée, Miranda*, and the smug smile on Miranda's face. She lay curled in bed in the dawn gloom, grey light seeping through the crack in the curtains, listening to rain pound the window and the swoosh of tyres along the road below.

She was a fool. A silly, infatuated fool who couldn't tell the difference between friendship and romantic interest. Hugh had never shown her anything other than courtesy and appreciation, never indicated his feelings ran deeper, or that their relationship might develop beyond master and servant. And yet she'd hung on, taking any crumbs of hope, and twisting his words to give them meaning which suited her cause. She shifted under the bedclothes, and hugged her knees to her chest, embracing the emptiness which refused to go away.

A loud knocking on her door pulled her back to the grim West Kensington morning, and she lifted herself from the pillows.

"Miss Fanstone. You awake?" Mrs Smithers, her voice shrill with impatience, battered louder. "Visitor for you."

Before Esme could shout some excuse, she heard Mrs Smithers' footsteps retreating down the stairs to her ground-floor flat. With reluctance, she swung her legs over the side of the bed and pulled on her cotton dressing gown. Most probably it was Hugh, wondering why she'd not been in to work. She couldn't put off talking to him, so perhaps it was best she get it done and dusted. A glance at her reflection in the mirror showed puffy eyes; hair knotted, in need of a good wash and brush; and her scar leered, red and ugly. In a poor effort at disguise, she ruffled her matted hair to hang over the side of her face and applied a quick coat of lipstick.

Be brave. In bare feet, she padded downstairs. First Hugh's feet, in black lace-ups, came into view, followed by the slow reveal of his body in a charcoal suit, his hand flapping a black homburg against his thigh, and finally his face, with a puzzled, impatient expression.

"Sorry to barge in," he said. "Were you taking a bath?"

Esme frowned. A bath? "No. I–" Oh, what was the point of explaining. What could she say, anyway? That she'd been bawling her eyes out at her own stupidity?

Hugh hovered, his large frame dominating the hallway, awkward and out of place. Esme crossed her arms and waited. She could hardly talk to him outside in the street, wearing only her dressing gown. And she wasn't going to invite him up to her flat.

He fiddled with the rim of his hat. "I've been worried. You didn't quite seem yourself the other night. A bit quiet. A lot to think about, I suppose. Moving to America."

"Hugh, I–"

"Miranda liked you a lot. Said she couldn't understand why you hadn't been snapped up."

"Oh, well–"

Hugh laughed. "It wasn't a question."

There was an uncomfortable pause. Esme waited for Hugh to break the silence.

"Are you sick? Why didn't you come in today?"

Her heart thumped high in her chest. "I'm not. I mean, I'm leaving. It's best."

"What?" Hugh shouted so loudly that Esme took an involuntary step back. "You can't. That's ridiculous." He stopped. "Oh. Do you mean you're getting ready to leave? For the United States?"

Esme leaned against the bannister and closed her eyes. *Be brave.* "No, Hugh. I'm not coming with you. It's very kind of you but it's time for a break. You and Miranda will do fine without me." The effort of saying Miranda's name was a small agony.

His lips formed a thin line and a slight scowl marred his good looks. "No, we won't. I need you. Don't be daft. It's a huge opportunity. Why would you want to stay here? There's nothing in England but bad weather and yet another blasted recession."

He was right. What was there to stay for?

"I'm going to write my next book." As soon as she said it, it felt right. Yes, she must exorcise Arcadia's ghost, with its cold finger of failure wagging in front of her eyes, and prove her worth as a novelist.

"Write it in Philadelphia."

"I'm going to Guernsey." The words popped out, unbidden.

"Guernsey? Why Guernsey, for Pete's sake?"

Her heart beat faster now, but not with anxiety. With excitement. "Because there's something there for me, Hugh. Something I have to find out. I don't know what it is. Only that I must go." That letter, those photographs, the conundrum of her mother – and the opportunity to put the English Channel between herself and Hugh.

"You're talking gibberish, Esme. I think you're a bit feverish. Go and sleep it off." When she didn't reply, he snorted. "Guernsey. Really? You do realise it was overrun with Jerries during the war and nowadays it's home to tomato growers and cows?"

His dismissal was offensive. "Goodbye, Hugh. And good luck." She brushed past him and opened the front door. The noise of traffic, footsteps of passers-by and the light chatter of a group of schoolgirls wafted between them.

He stared at her for a moment, motionless. Esme watched as he battled to decide his next move. Finally, he slammed his hat on his head and with a quick nod, left. As he walked away, she thought: is this how endings are? Abrupt, without analysis or a backwards glance?

Then she spun around and ran up the stairs two at a time, fired up at the prospect of pursuing a mission of her own. Not since *The View From Here* was published had she experienced such a wave of exhilaration.

4

JANE

GUERNSEY, JANUARY 1915

a blue-sky afternoon, a frosty breeze and a heart blooming with happiness kept me company on the walk from the tram stop. I was quite elsewhere, replaying New Year's Eve, savouring every second. Singing 'Auld Lang Syne', arms crossed and holding hands with Charlie, then dashing into the garden, scrunching our way across a thin layer of snow. Charlie had stopped behind the old oak tree, a yard wide, and asked me what I thought about the announcement of Mavis and William's engagement.

"Oh, it's wonderful," I said.

What else could I say? After all, William was Charlie's best friend. Actually, I'm speechless. William Lucas is such a bore. He didn't even get down on one knee. Oh well, he's her choice. He wouldn't be mine.

"One day, that will be us," Charlie said.

It took a second to register what he meant, but before I could react Charlie stepped forwards and brushed his lips against mine. The most delicious feeling ran through me and I swayed in the warmth of his arms, the wintry cold forgotten.

I dawdled the last few steps to the house, absorbed in reliving the sensation of our kiss, bodies pressed together. Suddenly, I became aware I wasn't alone. A young boy, who couldn't have been more than ten or eleven, was snivelling by the garden gate.

"Are you lost?" I put my heavy basket of groceries on the garden wall and knelt to his height.

He looked at me with big brown eyes, circles of misery peering from under his school cap. "I've a Latin lesson," he burbled. "With Mister Robin."

"You must be one of Father's boys."

For the past few months, Father had begun giving private lessons at home because he said he got too many interruptions at the school. Mostly we never saw the boys, and woe betide any of us if we disturbed him while he was tutoring. One time, he roared at Mavis for trying to deliver a telegram, which the delivery boy had said was urgent. Mavis burst into tears (she would) but after that, we learned to stay away.

"Come along, I'll show you the way." I stretched out my hand, which he reluctantly took, and picked up my basket. "Why are you upset?"

He didn't say anything, merely clutched my hand tighter.

"I know Latin's boring," I said, trying to sound chipper. "But Fa– Mr Robin is a very good teacher."

"Will you stay with me?" He sniffled and wiped his nose on the back of his hand.

"Come now, there's no need to be a sissy." I elbowed my way into the hall, knocked on the study door and gave him a gentle push. "Try to enjoy it."

After delivering the boy to Father, I sought out Mother, who was kneading dough at the kitchen table. She had flecks of flour on her face and I couldn't help noticing how worn down she appeared. Probably all the worry of the war, even though everyone said it would soon be over. Or perhaps she'd had another argument with Father. They thought we didn't know but the last time I heard them shouting I went and listened at the door. Of all things, they were fighting about Mother's friend, Aunty Susan. Father called her, "That poisonous woman who tells lies", and Mother said, "How dare you, you're in no position to say anything".

I opened the cake tin and took out a slice of gingerbread.

"I just took a poor young lad to Father who honestly looked as if he were about to be tortured."

Mother kneaded faster and muttered what sounded like, "I hope Susan's wrong."

"What do you mean?"

She looked at me, startled. "What?"

"You said you hoped Susan was wrong."

"Did I? I must have spoken out loud by mistake." She wiped her hands on her apron. "I was thinking about something quite different. The... ah... price of eggs."

She returned to her kneading and I took my cake, unsure why she'd be bothered about the cost of eggs when we have our own chickens. Maybe they weren't laying.

As I headed to the stairs, I remembered that boy and paused at Father's study. I pressed my ear to the door jamb but couldn't hear anything, so I bent down, shut one eye, and squinted through the keyhole.

Father was sitting at his desk with his head back and eyes closed. Perched bolt rigid on his lap, the boy looked terrified and even more miserable than before. At first, I thought Father was trying to comfort him but then I saw he had his hand down the front of the boy's trousers, presumably eking out some kind of punishment. But the look of pleasure on Father's face as he pummelled the boy up and down with his fist horrified me. I turned away, disgusted Father could be capable of such a thing, and ashamed that I would even think it of him.

∾

GUERNSEY, MARCH 1915

On Sunday, as every week, Charlie came to supper with the newly-weds, William and Mavis. Mother managed it by saying, "Your father can't complain at my inviting his son-in-law's best friend, can he?" As they all served together in the militia, Father stifled his disapproval of Charlie, and they'd talk at length about duty and beating back the Huns. Lately, there'd been talk of the militia disbanding and a new army unit forming, so that our boys could fight alongside the British. But I thought it was all men's talk because surely Guernsey wouldn't get dragged into the war, and it would be over long before they'd be called up.

When I answered the door – the men spruced up in their Sunday-best suits, Mavis in a dreary grey frock and looking downcast – Charlie signalled them to go in without him, and we hung back in the shadow of the hallway.

Despite the gloom, I saw Charlie's usual calm face held lines of tension. "I could be sent for training as soon as three or four weeks' time," he said. "Can I speak to your father tonight?"

It was what I yearned for – and dreaded – and I didn't know which was worse. It hadn't occurred to me we'd marry in the face of danger, and a cold shudder ran through me. Was Charlie preparing for the worst? I'd always thought we'd have a long engagement with plenty of time to make wedding plans. I knew Charlie was itching to be in the thick of it, but I'd convinced myself he'd remain safe with me, unless the looming threat of conscription became a reality and there was no longer any choice.

He held me in his arms. "It will be a comfort. Being far from home and knowing you're my wife."

"What if Father won't agree?"

"It's different in wartime."

I wasn't so sure. Father had firm views. He'd made Mavis wait a few weeks to marry William, until she was eighteen. I was just sixteen. Why would he make an exception for me?

In the darkness, Charlie knelt. "Marry me, Jane? Forever mine?"

From inside, Mother's voice bellowed down the hallway. "Supper's ready."

"Yes, please," I whispered. "Let's have photographs taken too, so I can look at your dear face every night before I go to sleep, and every morning when I wake."

Charlie stood, hugged me and buried his face in my hair. He made a small, choking sound. "My bride-to-be, I will love and cherish you all my life."

I determined then and there to make absolutely every single second of the next few weeks count. When he went away, I wanted all the memories he took with him to be happy ones. I wouldn't let Father come between us.

We ate corned beef and the men bandied around their opinions of the war. Sitting across from Charlie, our toes touching, I thought about how life might be without him. For more than six months, whenever I could escape from Father's watchful eye, we'd been inseparable. We laughed, we danced, we read aloud, we played tennis – and when we were alone, we ached for each other with such intensity. Our kisses set my body alight. Charlie's too. I could sense his inner tussle to remain a gentleman but oh, how I longed to feel his hands stray to forbidden places. Married, there would be no barriers, making it all the harder to be apart with only letters to sustain us.

"It's for the best," said Father, wiping the last of the gravy on his plate with a crust of bread. "The militia is one thing. I should know, been with them almost twenty years. But to win, we need strength in numbers."

"I'll be in it, sir," said Charlie.

Father nodded his approval.

"It's been hell for William and me standing on the sidelines. All the chaps feel the same way."

"Hear hear," said William.

I glanced over to Mavis. Sitting there, hands clenched and with a stiff expression, I wondered if she'd sorted her problems with William yet. It wasn't something I liked to keep asking about. She'd only confided there were 'difficulties', and then burst into tears saying she was worried William would get tired of waiting for her to be a proper wife. "I can't bring myself to do it," she said. I've a suspicion I know what she means. How awful. Six weeks they've been married and it's no secret she's desperate for children. I almost feel sorry for her – and William too, dry old stick that he is.

Charlie stroked my calf under the table. "What will you girls do? With the men gone, women will be needed in their jobs."

Father snorted. "Ridiculous."

"I'm as capable as any man," said Ginia. She's off to the Belgium front any day now with the Red Cross. "We've all got to do our bit."

"What about you, Jane?" Charlie asked, knowing I wanted to do more than Mother's idea of war work: knitting socks and teaching five-year-olds how to spell.

"I've no stomach for blood and guts, so I've applied to be a conductorette on the trams. Fingers crossed I'm accepted."

"Good for you," said Ginia.

"You'll need my permission," said Father. "I'm not sure it's suitable work for a young girl."

I lowered my eyes. If I spoke, I might regret the words which would spit forth. One thing for certain, I wouldn't let him stand in my way. Neither would Charlie.

"Could I have a word, sir?" Charlie looked dead straight at Father.

Without saying anything, they both scraped back their chairs. If it weren't for the fact that I held my breath so tight, I'd have laughed at the looks on everyone's faces. Literally, Ginia and Mavis's jaws dropped open and Mother's eyebrows shot up her forehead. William acted as though nothing had happened and poured a cup of tea.

Father and Charlie stepped outside. We four women remained silent, unsure whether to carry on or wait for their return.

They weren't gone long. Barely two minutes. Charlie walked through the door first, his face set in a grim line.

Father followed, and with slow deliberation walked to the head of the table. "You can see Charlie out, Jane."

Anger churning in my stomach, I flung back my chair and led Charlie to the front door.

I faced him square on. "He refused, didn't he?"

Charlie nodded. "He said he didn't want to see his daughter a widow before she came of age. He said I was thoughtless and selfish."

"The wicked, *wicked* man." How dare he presume to make my decision for me? "I'll make him. You'll see." I turned on my heel, but Charlie grasped my elbow.

"Jane... No–"

"Go home, Charlie. And tomorrow, visit the rector." Not caring who saw, I kissed him on the lips, closed the door and went in search of Father.

I found him in his study, bent over a stamp album, as if nothing unusual had occurred.

"There's no more to be said, Jane."

I swallowed hard, determined not to falter or show my fear. "There's a lot more to be said." I pulled back my shoulders and thrust out my chin. "You are an evil man, Father. You think I'm a silly girl, don't you? That I don't know what you do to frighten those poor boys witless. Or what you do to Ginia. You think you've silenced her with your bullying and threats. Well, I've got eyes, Father." My voice escalated. "I can see through keyholes and look into the window of the shed. You are a disgusting, depraved man and if you don't allow Charlie and me to wed, I'll– I'll–" I stopped. What would I do? Tell the police? Tell Mother? Would it make a difference? My word against the authority of my father, the respected schoolteacher?

There was a long silence. Father fingered his belt and my heart pounded, fit to burst through my ribcage. He wouldn't dare attack me, would he?

"You must have misunderstood, Jane." His voice was calm, and his eyes remained fixed on his stamps. "I'm delighted you and Charlie wish to marry." He looked up. "It will be my privilege to give you away."

I held firm. "And my job on the trams?"

He waved his hand at me. "If they'll take you, which I doubt. Just as long as you still do your household duties." He cleared his throat. "I meant to mention it earlier, but news of your forthcoming nuptials intervened. The fact is, I shan't be here much longer. I received my papers today. I'm joining Kitchener's Army. The battalion leaves in a week."

Kitchener's Army? "Does Mother know?"

"Yes."

She'd kept that quiet, doubtless leaving Father to tell us himself. But why the sudden decision, when he'd always insisted teaching took precedence and he'd wait to be conscripted? I thought I knew; he was leaving before any scandal surfaced. "It's because of that man who came here the other day, isn't it?" He'd been a common-looking fellow with a bulbous nose, yelling at Father, calling him names. "The one who said you were a disgrace to education and shouldn't be allowed in a position of authority."

Father's expression – just the merest twitch of his eyebrow – signified my wild guess had hit its mark. "Eavesdropping again, Jane? As I told you at the time, the man's known for drunken outbursts and wild accusations." He blocked me by returning his attention to the stamp album. "His sort are only interested in having enough money for the next pint of beer."

"And a few pounds dropped into his palm would keep him sweet? How generous of you." Sickened, I turned to go, then faced him again. "I shan't require you to give me away, Father, or attend my wedding. I think you've forfeited that right, don't you?"

5

ESME

GUERNSEY, JULY 1958

*E*sme found it hard to understand how Junction Cottage got its name, as it was nowhere near a crossroads. Perhaps once, long ago before the neighbouring homes were built, it had acted as a travellers' landmark. Whatever the reason, she didn't ponder its origins for long, too captivated by the whitewashed stonework, dormer windows and hanging baskets tumbling with red, pink and orange geraniums. She was barely able to believe her good fortune: not only did she have her very own home, but it came rent-free, saving her almost ten guineas a week in hotel tariffs.

She clutched the oversized key, left under the mat by the next-door neighbour, Mr Travis. She'd only spoken to him once, when she telephoned in response to the advertisement she'd spotted in a newsagent's window the day after her arrival: *Caretaker required for three months. Live in.* He'd told her the owners had temporarily moved to Geneva – the husband was organising a United Nations trade delegation – and sought someone to maintain the garden, clean the house and feed Jasper, their cat. Esme had jumped at the chance, and when she asked if he could wait a few days for references, he'd dismissed the notion. "You sound perfectly respectable," he'd said and gave her the address, just off Le Foulon.

"Aren't you going to open up?" She swung around at the sound of a man's voice behind her. Tall, in baggy corduroy trousers and a fisherman's jumper, he sported a beard and a weathered face.

"You must be Mr Travis," she said.

He nodded. "Just Travis." He picked up her suitcase and the smaller one containing her precious typewriter. "Allow me."

Esme turned the clunky key and pushed the door inwards. In truth, she wanted time alone to savour her first moments at Junction Cottage, but manners prevailed and she invited him in.

Travis dropped her belongings onto black and white flagstones. "I won't stay," he said. "You'll want to settle in."

At the door, he turned back. "Could you use the loan of a bicycle?"

"Would I ever." Esme was thrilled. It would make getting around the island so much easier, although cycling up the hilly roads would be a challenge. She'd never known a place quite so steep. But if she wanted to explore further afield than the town, anything would be better than grappling with the complicated bus timetables, which her *Ward Lock* guidebook rightly described as 'devious'.

"It's a little rusty, but the brakes are in good condition and it's got a wicker basket attached to the handlebars. I'll get the rear light fixed and pump up the tyres."

"You're very kind."

"Not at all." Travis puffed his cheeks. "It was my wife's. Be nice to see it put to good use."

After she closed the door, Esme was struck by the silence. In her London building, there was always noise: people on the stairs or conversations seeping through the walls, traffic on the road outside, screeching brakes. She took her time to absorb her new surrounds. The hallway was small, with a coat rack of anoraks and windcheaters, an umbrella stand, and a corner table adorned with a crystal fluted vase and an empty wooden bowl. No telephone, but aside from her father, who would she call? And after their last conversation, she doubted there'd be much point. When she'd phoned, alerting him to her plans to spend time in Guernsey tracking down Arcadia's family, he'd done his best to dissuade her. "No good will come of it," he'd said. When pressed to explain, he'd clammed up. Since their divorce more than a decade ago, the mere mention of Arcadia's name sent him into an apoplectic rage, causing his face to redden before he stormed out of whatever room they occupied. More than once he'd railed at Esme, "I've told you never to mention that woman's name in my presence."

Before her, a narrow staircase soared. A heavy, maroon velvet curtain, serving as a door, blocked the entry to the room on her left. Esme pulled the drape across its brass runner to reveal a cosy living room. Weathered armchairs and a sofa clustered around the fireplace. Shelves crammed with books covered two walls.

To her right was a dining room-cum-kitchen. A square table, large enough to seat four and set with lace doilies, nudged close to a dresser. A rocking chair covered in a tartan rug graced the bay window alcove that overlooked the front garden. Carved out from under the stairwell was a kitchen. She ducked her head and found a sink, gas cooker, small cabinet with a few tins of food and – glory of glories – a refrigerator.

As she hooked back the window shutters, she felt a swish of silky fur graze her leg. She flinched in surprise and saw her housemate, Jasper. She stroked his sleek black coat. He purred at her touch, flicked his tail into the air and jumped onto the rocking chair.

Thrilled with her luck, she carried her case up the steep stairway. Her bedroom had a tiny window tucked into the eave, rosebud wallpaper and a non-working fireplace, but the mantel offered a shelf with a mirror above it. Next door, a bathroom, with matching pink bathtub, basin and toilet. She looked at her reflection in the shaving mirror, still getting used to her shorter hairstyle, a farewell treat at Selfridges' salon. A new hairdo for a new start. Yes, it made her scar more visible but it made her feel younger – even a touch elegant – and she liked how easy it was to take care of.

In the morning, Esme opened her front door to be greeted by the sight of a bicycle propped to one side of the garden wall. Putting aside all thoughts of catching the bus, she quickly went back inside, re-dressed in more practical slacks and set off. Enjoying the freedom of whizzing along quiet roads, she cycled past hedgerows peppered with honour-payment boxes of fruit and vegetables, and made a detour through Candie Gardens with its exquisite pathways and well-kept floral beds. The magnificent statue of Victor Hugo, striding, pensive, caused her to pause. If Victor Hugo could find inspiration for his books when exiled here, then surely so could Esme Fanstone?

She took the path towards the town centre, soaking up the diverse French and English influences, carefully steering her bike along the cobbled lanes. She tried to imagine her mother as a young girl, standing at the old quay, watching the fishing boats come in, or trussed up in an Edwardian frock playing sticks with boys. It was hard to conjure: the Arcadia she'd known was smart, funny and brittle, given to witty turns of phrase and drawing-room banter, not romping around a shoreline getting all mussed up.

After parking her bicycle just beyond the Town Church, Esme walked at a brisk pace across Market Square, through the arch of a tall, granite building, and into the Guille-Allès Library. For a fee of 2s 6d she became a member for a month, but instead of entering the main borrowing area to seek out a few novels, she headed to the spacious reading room where Guernsey newspapers were archived.

The letter from M to Arcadia had been dated 6 October 1945, but its contents implied that C's trouble may have occurred a few days earlier. Esme planned to peruse the local papers to see if any attempted murder had been reported at that time, and she'd start by searching headlines from the last week in September onwards.

She settled at a weathered oak table with the relevant leather-bound volume of back issues. In the October 1 edition of the *Guernsey Evening Press* she found a story about the sporadic resumption of boat services to England, making it likely Arcadia had to wait a few days to secure a crossing. Two days later, another headline, *Airport Back Under Civil Control* caught her attention. Was it possible her mother had flown to the mainland? Either way, there appeared no barrier to her reaching Guernsey, as encouraged by M.

Esme skimmed page after page, trying not to be distracted by stories about war heroes, reform plans, help for deportees and evacuees, and the hardships besetting locals struggling to piece together their lives.

In the October 4 issue, she found a small story sandwiched between an advertisement for Bucktrouts cigarettes and a notice advising the reopening of Guernsey Groceteria:

Naked man charged

Arnold Carson, 82, has been detained and charged with indecent exposure after being discovered bereft of clothing, wandering the cliff path at Corbière Point. The magistrate has held his case over for seven days whilst further evidence is gathered. Anyone with information is advised to attend Guernsey Police Headquarters.

Next to it, ran another short story:

Man breaks arm

In an unfortunate incident, Jonathan Elve, 57, broke his arm after falling downstairs in the dark, claiming he missed his footing...

Esme paused and reread it. The reporter described it as 'an unfortunate incident', but could the man have been pushed? Or got into a fight? Might this be the attempted murder referred to in M's letter? With Arnold Carson the perpetrator?

She reread the articles. If Arnold was some sort of elderly relation of Arcadia's, it might explain why M contacted her to come over and sort it out. Aged eighty-two, at a stretch he could have been her grandfather, a great uncle, or even a close family friend. But why call him C? Esme could think of no reason for calling an ancient relative or friend by their surname's initial, unless it was some sort of pet name.

Setting aside Arnold Carson, Esme kept reading. Little piqued her interest, the most harrowing event being a man who walked into a stationer's and had a seizure. By the time she finished checking the crime news and court reports, she'd found nothing else. Nevertheless, she flipped through another week's worth of papers. In the October 8 edition, the leading story caught her attention:

Exclusive report: sensational murder attempt

Esme pulled the newspaper closer and speed-read the article, but it only contained hazy details about a woman called Francine Mellon being rushed to hospital with suspected poisoning.

She kept turning the pages and was soon rewarded. In the

October 12 issue, a large-print heading was emblazoned above the main story of the day:

Housemaid charged with gruesome murder

Esme made a small 'whoopee' under her breath: Clara Denier, twenty, was under arrest awaiting trial. Esme, fascinated, read on, devouring every article about the crime. When she'd finished, she sat back and reviewed the facts.

Francine Mellon had raised the alarm after suffering severe gastric pains. She accused the housemaid, Clara Denier, of trying to poison her. She gave no motive for this, other than to say Clara 'wasn't right in the head'. In Esme's view, Clara was charged with attempted murder on the thinnest of evidence: a jar of rat poison found in the kitchen pantry, hidden between similar jars containing flour, sugar and tea. The most damning testimony came from M. Mellon who claimed to have seen Clara stirring white powder into Francine's night-time cup of Ovaltine. The doctor was called to the house, but he was a young locum, not the Mellons' usual GP. His diagnosis was torn to shreds by the prosecution for his lack of experience in such matters. The locum insisted Francine had only suffered a bad bout of food poisoning, probably from the shrimp she'd eaten at dinner. He then told her husband to allow her nothing other than water to drink. But the next morning, Francine was found dead in her bed. It was unclear whether she'd experienced another seizure in the night; M. Mellon said he'd slept in his dressing room and was a heavy sleeper. The Mellons' habitual GP, also called to the stand, claimed Francine's symptoms were more likely to have been caused by arsenic, the active ingredient of rat poison.

Following a short trial lasting three days, Clara had been declared guilty of murder and the judge had sentenced her to the death penalty. The newspaper reporter described her as:

A poor, frail looking creature, whose wicked crime hung heavily on her shoulders.

After poring over the reports of Clara's trial, Esme wasn't sure who interested her most: Clara, or her mistress, Francine Mellon. As for Francine's husband – only ever referred to as M. Mellon – suspicion clung to him like a mouldy carpet. She turned over in her mind whether Clara could possibly be the C of Arcadia's letter. Everything fitted, even M might have been M. Mellon. But what was their connection to Arcadia?

Setting aside the newspapers, Esme went to the front desk and asked the librarian where she could locate World War I military records. They would be another avenue for finding mention of any family members – perhaps her grandfather had fought, although by her reckoning, he would have been over forty at the start of the war so he may have missed front-line action.

The librarian, an elderly woman with lipstick applied in a wonky line, looked flustered by the question. "I'm only a volunteer here, but for my money, I'd go to the Priaulx Library. It's where they keep everything there ever was about the island."

Esme remembered passing the Georgian town house which housed the Priaulx Library in Candie Gardens. She could go there tomorrow. "And how would I go about locating people who were residents at the turn of the century?"

"Oh dear... I'm not sure..." Her face brightened. "Let me introduce you to Anthony Fellowes. He's an archivist, cataloguing the war and our time under the Occupation, though goodness knows we all want to put it behind us."

Esme wasn't sure how this Anthony could help. Her mother had left Guernsey before the start of World War I; archives from World War II would be of little relevance. "If you think–"

"Not often." The librarian tittered at her joke. "But he's sitting over there, and it can't do any harm, can it?"

Esme made her way over, introduced herself and apologised for interrupting. A rather serious man with soft brown eyes, a smattering of freckles across his nose and ink stains on his right index finger, looked up. "How can I help?"

"A good question. I'm not sure you can."

Anthony smiled and his entire face transformed from humourless to brimming with curiosity. "Now you've issued an irresistible challenge. Of course I can. I must." He placed his elbows on the table and rested his chin on his hands, peering at her from behind horn-rimmed glasses.

His change of demeanour relaxed Esme; she took the seat opposite and plunged into her story. "I'm looking for my mother's family. She left here as a child after her parents died, but we never spoke about Guernsey because she had no brothers or sisters. And now my mother has died and something's happened..." Esme trailed off. It wasn't this young man's business.

"Go on. I'm intrigued. What's happened? A deep, dark, family secret? Oh, please, say it is."

"I found a letter from a stranger, which doesn't make much sense."

Anthony clapped his hands together. "I knew it."

His enthusiasm was infectious. "Would you like to see it?"

"Would I ever. Have you got it with you?"

Esme took it from her bag, examined the envelope, and held it to her chest. "On one condition."

"Yes?"

"You respect the contents."

"Of course I will. Why wouldn't I?"

Esme grimaced. "I'm not sure. There's something... oh... troubling. I'm afraid of where it might lead me, if you must know. On the one hand, I want to know what it means but on the other, I'm scared I'll find something out I'll wish I hadn't." Her father's words wouldn't go away: *No good will come of it.*

Anthony crossed his arms and sat back in his chair. "Then don't give it to me. I didn't mean to trivialise your mother in any way, but I do love family histories. It's my work. Unearthing the past."

"I thought you were documenting the war."

"Right now, I'm archiving everything I can lay my hands on. Largely, records of who remained on the island, evacuees, people who were deported. It's interesting stuff but what I'm really keen to lay my hands on are personal records and diaries." His eyes shone. "That's where the real stories are. The untold bravery and courage. Small acts of resistance. And those accused of collaboration. Were they traitors or survivors?"

Arcadia was momentarily forgotten. How wonderful if Anthony fell upon an enigma, maybe even something Esme could base her next novel on.

"What have you found so far?" she asked.

"After the Germans confiscated wireless sets, one fellow began printing a clandestine newspaper. I've a few copies. He was caught and imprisoned, caged like an animal, he claimed. I've also been given anecdotal accounts about deportees sent on forced marches or chained in cellars under appalling, cruel conditions. And there's plenty of chatter about acts of defiance and protests, especially from teenage boys. For some, the memories are still too raw at the moment. But as the years go on, more will come to light as people die and their families hand over letters, memoirs, bits and pieces tucked away in drawers."

"I'm afraid my little mystery won't add much. My mother left before the First World War... although this letter is dated 1945, so I suppose it must be linked to the Second World War in some way."

"You funny girl, of course it will be. It has to. History is history, after all." He cocked his head. "So, am I to be trusted?"

Esme passed the letter across to him. Anthony adjusted his spectacles and pored over the envelope. Then he extracted the letter and read the contents. Once. Twice. Three times. "Do you have any idea who A or C or M might be?"

"I'm certain A is my mother. The letter is addressed to her. A Fanstone. Née Robin." She thought of Clara but decided against mentioning her; there might be other explanations and she was interested in Anthony's train of thought.

"You said her mother had died so M can't be Mother or Mummy." Anthony tapped his fingers on the tabletop. "Well, of course it's possible that the letter's author, M, was merely visiting Guernsey and just happened to post the letter from here. But that's unlikely given the date. In October 1945, Guernsey had only recently been liberated. It certainly wasn't a tourist destination in those days. The only boats arriving came with supplies, not visitors. More likely to be someone who lived here, or was posted here during the war, don't you think?"

Esme gave a doubtful nod.

"Your mother's maiden name is a start. I'll see what I can find out." He put the letter back in the envelope and handed it to her.

"That's marvellous." With Anthony's help, she might now get somewhere.

"I'll need to update you." His eyes twinkled. "Shall we meet for tea next week?"

6

ESME

GUERNSEY, JULY 1958

*E*sme pushed open the door to Café Central on Smith Street, and the bell tinkled overhead. As she stepped over the threshold, the aroma of toasted teacakes and the clatter of cups gave her a funny feeling of déjà vu: sitting at the window table as a child, legs dangling halfway to the floor, her bottom lip protruded in a pout. Yet as quickly as it had come, the impression disappeared, replaced by the busy café.

A girl in a black frock with a white apron and frilly cap asked: "Do you mind sharing a table?"

At this time of day, all the tables bar one were taken by women – mothers with small children, friends meeting for a natter and a group of pensioners cackling like a gaggle of geese. The only man, Anthony, had his nose in a newspaper and a Dalmatian at his feet.

"I'm meeting the gentleman over there," said Esme and weaved past the tables to him, carefully stepping over his large spotted dog.

Anthony jumped up when he saw her, scattering pages to the floor and causing his dog to yelp.

Esme smiled at his confusion. "He's a lovely boy." She sat and bent to pat the dog's rump.

"He's a girl. Judy. I don't hold with giving dogs silly names. She deserves a name like anyone else, don't you think?" He squinted through his spectacles. To Esme, he had the look of an owl, bent on dispensing wisdom. "Tea?"

Esme nodded and waited while Anthony poured from the teapot, passed her a cup and offered milk and sugar, both of which she declined. "I hope you're here with some news?" she said.

He picked up his cup. "I have good news and bad news. The bad is that I can't find anyone in the records called Arcadia Robin."

Esme frowned. "What? No birth certificate, even?"

"No. But don't go all conspiratorial on me. Remember, two wars have come and gone, and many records have been lost or destroyed along the way. The good news, however, is that I found one family of Robins – sounds like a nest of birds, doesn't it? – still alive."

"Oh, Anthony, that's marvellous. What do you know?"

"Not much. There's an old woman of eighty-four, Elizabeth Robin, and it seems she had three daughters." He pulled a notebook from his inside jacket pocket and flicked through the pages. "Virginia, Mavis and Jane. They'd all be in their mid to late sixties now, so possibly cousins of your mother?"

"Were you able to find out where they live?"

"The mother, Elizabeth, yes. She's in the telephone directory. The daughters, no, which seems odd."

"Why?" It didn't seem strange to Esme. "They probably all married and changed their names."

"Therein lies the rub. Back in the day, women here often didn't change their names when they married."

"How about marriage records?" That would soon reveal who

the Robin girls had wed, possibly even their addresses, although in all likelihood they would all have long moved elsewhere.

Anthony pulled a face. "Any chance your lot are Catholic? Church of England marriages weren't registered until after the war."

Esme shook her head; her family were Church of England through and through, right back to the days of Henry the VIII. "Sorry, no Catholics amongst my ancestors as far as I know." But then the way things were progressing, there seemed to be many things Esme didn't know, perhaps including what religions her forebears had married into. "How frustrating. Still, we've got Elizabeth. That's a start. Do you think she'd be happy to meet me?"

"One can but ask." Anthony took a pipe from his breast pocket and tapped it on the palm of his hand.

It unnerved Esme, the idea of meeting an old lady who might be a relative, especially given Arcadia's insistence that she had no family. "A visit might be an unwelcome – possibly, confusing – intrusion," she said.

"How about I contact her on your behalf? Ease the way, so to speak. If it makes you feel more comfortable, I'll come with you."

"And if she's not a relation?"

Anthony wedged the pipe between his teeth and struck a match. The flame curled up and down as he sucked in air to light the tobacco. "We apologise profusely and be on our way. No harm done."

"I'm not sure–"

"Oh, come along, Esme. What are you here for, if not an adventure? It's an opportunity to solve a mystery. We'll be like Tommy and Tuppence."

Esme laughed at his reference to Agatha Christie's sleuthing couple. "All right then." She paused. "I'd be glad of your company, thank you."

"Try keeping me away. I'll telephone her in the next day or so and arrange a time when I can get away from work." He snapped shut his notebook. "That's enough of that. Tell me about you. What do you do? Where do you live when not chasing down elusive letter-writers?"

"London." She thought of Hugh, and the newspaper offices. "I resigned from my job as a deputy editor to visit here."

She didn't like to talk about herself but with jobs hard to come by, Anthony might conclude she was spoiled or unreliable, so she ploughed on. "As well as tracking down my family, I hope to write a book. If only I can come up with a plot."

"A novelist. I'm impressed. The idea of putting all those words down, one after the other, confounds me. Have you had anything published?"

"I have, but it wasn't terribly successful. It's called *The View From Here*."

"In my eyes, anyone who can write a whole book deserves every accolade imaginable."

Esme squirmed in her chair. If he knew the extent of her book sales, he might not be so generous. "And you? Have you always lived here?"

He shook his head. "I'm an outlaw from Cambridge. I came here a couple of years ago."

"For work reasons?"

Anthony laughed. "Quite the reverse. After the war, at my father's insistence, I qualified as an accountant and joined the family firm. Hated it."

"How was your war?"

He narrowed his eyes. "Lucky, you'd say. I'm good with numbers so I got co-opted onto secret code-breaking stuff. I never saw real action."

Lucky, indeed. "Hence becoming an accountant."

"On my thirty-second birthday, I threw in the towel. I wanted to get away from–" He paused, as if unsure how to proceed. "From dull routine, from my parents' expectations. I packed a bag and jumped onto a ferry, with little in my head other than *not* being in England. I became enthralled by the Occupation and never left. History had been made here and I wanted – *needed* – to capture it. Does that make sense?"

Esme thought of Arcadia and nodded. "Yes," she said. "Perfectly."

He blew smoke rings into the air and then drained his teacup. "Judy needs a walk. Will you join us?"

Her spirits lifted. "I'd love to." A walk with Anthony, to her surprise, was exactly what she'd like to do.

JANE

GUERNSEY, SEPTEMBER 1917

*T*he telegram delivery boy cycled past me, head down, not even a nod of acknowledgement. My heart went cold, and my thoughts flew to Charlie. The last I'd heard from him he'd been sent to the front line near Ypres. Funny to think he was now stationed closer by than when he was training in Kent but he feels farther away than ever. In his letters he says the chaps are getting bored waiting for some action. As far as I'm concerned, they can wait until the war is over. I'd rather he be cooling his heels than wounded – or worse.

I walked slowly along the road towards home, my legs tired from standing all day. I still haven't got used to it, but working on the trams is such fun, even if it is hard on the feet. The run between Town and The Bridge is certainly a study in human nature at its best and worst. Today, a woman left her cat in a basket on a seat, and a young lad jumped off the tram with it and ran after her. She'd done it deliberately! At the next stop he got back on and said he'd adopt the puss. Everyone cheered.

I'm so glad to be doing something. It keeps me from fretting about Charlie, even though I tell myself he's invincible and he'll be home soon. There are days when I have to force my mind away from terrible imaginings, but seeing the telegram boy makes all of us clench with fear that this time, it's our turn. And that awful double-edged relief when he delivers it to a neighbour.

I have to believe that Charlie will fulfil his promise to come back to me, no matter what. In the meantime, all I have is his photograph, and the memories of our wedding and honeymoon. Charlie never took his eyes off me as I joined him at the altar, wearing a white dress with a drop waist cobbled together from scraps in Mother's glory box, and we took our vows. Afterwards, albeit we were under the same roof as Mother and po-faced Mavis, we had ten wonderful days and nights filled with loving tenderness; a journey of discovery that brought us closer each hour. All too soon, Mavis and I were huddled with Mother and Aunty Susan at the edge of Belvedere Field watching the rows of soldiers on parade before they were despatched to England for training. Seeing Charlie in his uniform, which he complained scratched, had made me burst with pride and choke with sorrow. Ramrod straight, rifle and bayonet poised on his shoulder, he'd shown no sign of fear at what was to come. My heart splintered into little pieces at losing the warmth of his arms so soon. Nevertheless, I'd put on a brave face and waved with the crowd whilst inside I felt terror.

I squared my shoulders, set a perky smile, and turned into our driveway. I was learning to keep a hard veneer on the outside; feeling sorry for oneself was unfair on everyone else who had loved ones at the front. As I approached, it seemed there was something ominous about the set of the front door, closed and shuttered to the rest of the world. I shivered and then resolutely turned the handle. A murmuring came from the kitchen at the end of the flagstoned hall and after hanging my conductorette's bag over the bannisters, I made my way to the source of the noise.

A tableau greeted me. Mother, ashen-faced, was sitting at the kitchen table with a telegram in her hand. Mavis wept in the corner. Ginia leaned against the tub, her expression hard and unreadable. I raced to Mother's side and tried to take the piece of frightful paper, but she crumpled it into a ball.

"What's happened? Who–?" I looked from Mother to my sisters. Mavis bawled louder. Ginia sucked in her cheeks and slowly shook her head from side to side.

"It's your father," said Mother.

My mouth went dry. Not Charlie. Thank God, not Charlie. "Is he–" I paused. "Still alive?"

Mother turned glazed, confused eyes to me. "I haven't... I'm not sure..." She glanced wildly around the kitchen and then fixed her sight on Mavis. "Yes, he's alive."

Again, I went to take the telegram from Mother, but she tightened her hand around the scrunched-up missive and refused to yield it. "Captured. Taken prisoner." With that, she abruptly pushed back her chair and left the room. I supposed she wanted to be alone to cry.

Mavis made to go after her.

"Don't," said Ginia. "Leave her."

But within seconds, we heard Mother coming down the stairs and along the hallway. She'd put on her coat and hat. "I'm going to Susan's." Before anyone could stop her, or ask why she was abandoning us in favour of Aunty Susan, with a slam of the back door, she was gone. Through the window, I watched as she pushed her bike towards the gate. With one hand on her head to steady her hat, she pedalled off.

Handkerchief to mouth, Mavis fled upstairs. Ginia sighed and said, "I'll take care of her," before following.

I wondered if I should feel sad like Mavis, but all I could conjure was a numbness, and curiosity at Mother's reaction. Since the day Father left to join Kitchener's Army, he'd hardly been mentioned except by neighbours and friends who'd asked about his welfare. If anything, Mother had been lighter in spirit and Ginia had ceased barricading herself in her room.

I remembered the day I'd gone to St Peter Port harbour to farewell him with Mavis, Ginia, Mother, and Aunty Susan. I only went because my absence would have meant awkward questions. Mavis was the only one who cried. Mother and Aunty Susan held each other's arms and I swear I heard Aunty Susan say "good riddance" under her breath as his ship left port. Despite my anger at Father's behaviour, I was shocked and yet felt a new-found respect for Aunty Susan who must have had a sharp eye.

The house creaked around me. Mother would be gone for a while yet. I took off my shoes and in stockinged feet, made my silent way upstairs to her room. The bed was neatly made, with perfect hospital corners. Her dressing table was exactly as always – hairbrushes to the left, a porcelain bowl with hair grips to the right. I tiptoed to the bedside table, opened the drawer, and there it was, the crumpled telegram. I smoothed it out:

```
Captain   Frank   Arthur   Robin:   Court-
martialled  and  tried  for  the  offence  of
gross   indecency.   Sentenced   to   be
imprisoned  with  hard  labour  for  two
years. Confirmed and signed...
```

The words jumped around before my eyes... *court-martialled... gross indecency... hard labour*. A hard ball of anger brewed inside me; fury at Father being unable to repress his urges, and bringing shame on his family. I thought of the postmistress, taking it all down; the looks and whispers we'd endure if she couldn't keep her mouth shut.

I screwed the paper up and replaced it in the drawer. The only way to get through this was to hold one's head high. I'd say nothing to anyone; Mother could keep her secret for the time being, and her pretence of Father's 'capture'. But when he came home, my knowledge would be a weapon. I wasn't sure how I'd wield it, but if I got a sniff of him returning to his old ways, he'd find me a tough adversary.

~

GUERNSEY, DECEMBER 1917

The log fire crackled, and by half past three I'd drawn the curtains, shutting out the wintry cold and gloom. Another Christmas beckoned but it would be hard to celebrate with almost half our men who'd been sent to France reportedly killed or wounded. Today's *Guernsey Evening Press* lay unopened beside me; the more this war lingered on, the harder it became to turn the pages and read the names of those dead or missing. Even Charlie, who usually made an effort to sound cheerful, made little pretence in his last letter about the waste of it all, and he wrote of too many friends gone, too many good men's lives cut short.

I picked up the pile of Christmas cards which Mavis had made, decorated with pressed flowers as a reminder of Guernsey. We'd agreed to send one to all the lads we knew at the front. And of course, to our own: William, Charlie – and Ginia, in Belgium with the Red Cross, brave girl. As for the card to Father, I merely signed my name and left it to Mavis and Mother to write some fancy message.

I unscrewed my pen and selected a card for Charlie, one with his favourite purple orchid – albeit faded to a paler facsimile – and began to inscribe the love poem that expressed everything I felt:

How do I love thee? Let me count the ways.
I love thee to the depth and breadth and height–

The doorbell jangled, interrupting my concentration. Everyone was out so I carefully put aside the card, not wanting to smudge the ink, and went to answer it.

My blood ran cold when I saw the lad in his peaked hat, his bicycle in front of him like a protective barrier. I swallowed hard and forced myself not to shut the door in his face. Without a word, he handed me the telegram, touched the tip of his hat and scurried off, pedalling as though he feared for his life.

Very slowly, I closed the door, not game to look at the envelope. I wanted a few more minutes of hope. Yet almost immediately, Mavis arrived home via the back door and came stomping down the hall, yabbering about how there was snow in the air. She stopped short when she saw me standing there, stunned and mute, telegram in hand.

"Here, I'll open it." She took it from me and flipped the envelope over. "It's addressed to me." Her voice was matter-of-fact, devoid of emotion. My legs began to shake in uncontrollable judders, the relief unbearable.

"Oh, Mavis–" I put my arm around her and held her close as she withdrew the telegram. I read the first few words, *I regret to inform you*... and knew that William had fallen.

"It says he was killed in the Battle of Cambrai," she said. "Poor William." And then she turned away. "I think I'll go to my room."

I watched her retreat up the stairs, struck by her calm demeanour. I knew I should follow, but I didn't know how I'd comfort her. William and Charlie had vowed always to fight side by side – if William had copped it, what of Charlie?

Days later, after finishing my shift on the trams, I went straight to Charlie's house. Another telegram had followed swiftly – Charlie was missing in action – and since then my days had followed a regular pattern. His mother would make us tea and we'd sit and hold each other's hands, saying little.

A small woman with jet-black hair lightly peppered with grey, she stared, unblinking, at a bleak table set with a candle and a photograph of Charlie. "We must believe in the power of prayer," she said, "and our prayers will be answered. Charlie will come home to us."

I wanted to scream. For more than three years, God hadn't been listening. Why would He start now? But I held back the words that threatened to burst from me. Charlie was her only child; without him, her belief in a bright future would be shattered. So I squeezed her hands, in what I trusted was female solidarity, and then topped up our cups of tea before being enveloped in another silence.

It was hard to know which was worse: being cloistered with my mother-in-law, or being at home listening to Mavis telling me we must have hope. Since the delivery of the second telegram, Mavis seemed to have taken the news of Charlie being missing in action harder than William's death. She'd shown no grief at the loss of her husband, no sadness or regret at no baby, no legacy of William, and yet she was forever weeping about Charlie. I snapped at her and told her that he was my husband, not hers. She told me it was obvious I didn't care, as I never cried. I nearly hit her. Didn't she realise if I cried, I'd be giving in? Charlie must be alive. He must. I held on to that every single day. I hoped when I cried, it would be tears of joy. The alternative couldn't be countenanced.

"When will we know?" moaned Charlie's mother. "When?"

I repeated what I'd told her every day. "No news is good news." If he'd been taken prisoner of war, the Germans would provide paperwork, but I'd also been told there was no guarantee of this. Better that his mother cling to the best outcome, that of hearing nothing, than watching for the telegram boy who might not come.

She picked up her rosary beads and twisted them through her fingers, reciting a psalm under her breath. "We must stick together, dear. For Charlie's sake."

But for how long? How many more days, weeks, years could I

sustain her neediness without drowning under the weight of her prayers? It was clear that Charlie must either be hospitalised, or taken prisoner. If he'd died alongside William, we'd have been informed by now. Besides, he had nine lives, as well as the strength of my love willing him to come home in one piece.

The clock in the hallway chimed the hour and I made a decision. "I can't come tomorrow," I said. "I'm working a double shift, and I've promised Mavis I'll help on the food control committee. With Christmas coming, there's a lot to do." It wasn't exactly a lie; Mavis had said volunteers were needed to help ensure everyone received a fair share of the dwindling food supplies. Away from the cloying atmosphere of Charlie's home, I'd be able to keep myself busy and avoid brooding or allowing my mind to run amok.

Charlie's mother dabbed at tear-filled eyes. "I will send up prayers from both of us."

8

JANE

GUERNSEY, 18 NOVEMBER 1918

There was a rap on my bedroom door, and Mother poked her head around. "I've more bad news, I'm afraid. Can I come in?" She was wringing her hands in a nervous fashion and still wore her apron; she never ventured upstairs in it, but always left it on the hook behind the kitchen door. Somewhere in the back of my brain, I registered this puzzling fact but couldn't work out what it might signify, too wrapped up in my own world.

I nodded and she sat on the end of my bed as I pulled the bedclothes up around my chin. I'd not left my room for days, not since the letter had come from the War Office advising they were in possession of Charlie's identity discs, and as his name appeared on no prisoner of war or hospital lists, he was now presumed dead.

"What's happened?" I asked, more out of politeness than any real interest.

"I've had notice that your father has died. Spanish flu, the letter said."

I frowned. Could I believe her? Spanish flu sounded too convenient, given it was wiping out people by the thousands.

Another lie of Mother's to cover up a harsher death? Did I care? However much I'd once wanted to punish him, without Charlie, it all seemed pointless.

I heard Mother say Father's body had been buried in England, but my mind was in a vague fog and the details drifted past me. I still couldn't believe I'd never see Charlie's beautiful face again, hear his laugh, watch his freckles dance when he smiled, listen to him play the cello, his fingers pressing down the strings, the same fingers that stroked me and made me tremble with love for him.

Mother rested her hand on my leg. "Jane?"

"All our plans and hopes. All gone. For what?"

She knew I meant Charlie. "For freedom. For the greater good. For a better future."

"I don't have a future. My husband's..." I choked on the word 'dead', unable to say it. "Gone. My job is gone too." It had been given back to a returning serviceman, which was only right and proper, but I'd had a taste of independence, and now all that loomed for me was a lonely spinsterhood without the man I loved. At best, I'd live out my days with my mother, perhaps teaching children how to read and write, while Ginia stayed away – a missionary life, she said in her last letter – and Mavis did 'good works'.

"Buck up," Mother said. Her tone was sharp and penetrated my shroud of grief. "Men didn't fight this war and give up their lives for young women to live in mourning. Charlie wouldn't want it, and he certainly wouldn't expect it from you. He'd want you to choose your path. The world is changing and you must start afresh. Look at Ginia, fighting for women's rights – *your* rights, Jane. Broaden your horizon. Follow your dreams. Don't bury yourself here."

I couldn't have been more surprised. The idea of leaving St Peter Port, and all the badness and sadness, was alluring. It wasn't just the thought of not seeing Charlie in my shadow wherever I went; it meant I could leave behind the demanding burden of

Charlie's parents' grief, the endless prayer evenings, their lack of understanding at my heartache because they were too wrapped in their own.

Staying on the island also meant constant reminders of Father's disgusting behaviour, and trying to ignore the gossip behind my back. I knew they talked, the good people of St Peter Port. My mother was no better. If Ginia and I had known what Father did, then so did she, and yet she'd done nothing to stop him – and she'd lied about the nature of his imprisonment. I clenched my fists; I wouldn't let it drop. One day, when the time was right, I'd have it out with her.

I turned my head to the wall, already keen to pack my bags and go. "I'll think about it."

Mother patted my leg and eased off the bed. "Good girl. We'll talk more. Maybe you could find a position as a children's nanny, or even a housekeeper. There are some wealthy families in St Helier, but I doubt you'd want to stray that far, miles from your family."

St Helier? Surely Mother joked. I might as well remain here as move across the water to Jersey. I dreamed of France, where Charlie and I had talked of living, and the excesses of Paris. Or across the Channel to England. London! When I sneaked a look at the women's journals in Carr's Store, I was captivated by glamorous fashions, stories of high society balls, the latest theatrical sell-out. That was what I wanted – a life filled with excitement, not one stuck at someone else's home teaching brats their times tables.

Alone, I rolled onto my back. I needed a plan and once I'd figured out what that was, I'd spring it on Mother and be gone before she could stop me. The main thing would be to save enough money for the fare and to survive for, say, two or three months while I got settled. And when I arrived at my destination, how would I earn money and where would I live? I wasn't qualified to do anything, except work as a conductorette. My mind raced through my possible skills. I could teach English – spelling and grammar; I was a reasonable seamstress and knitter; a good dancer... and I was very good at talking my way into things. If I put my best foot forward, pretended to skills I didn't really have but could easily learn, surely I could bluster into a position.

~

JANUARY 1920

Mother served me a plate of stew and passed the bread basket. I looked around the dining room where I'd eaten all my meals since I could remember and wondered where I'd dine the next day. I'd booked a room at a women's hostel. Although cheap, it was a long way out from Central London. I didn't think I'd stay there long.

"What are your plans for tomorrow?" Mother asked.

I'd hoped Mavis would be here tonight, but she was at the needlework guild, so my announcement would be made to an audience of one. I took a deep breath. "I'm taking the ferry to Southampton."

"I beg your pardon?"

"I'm leaving, just as you advised me."

"But–" Mother spluttered. "Why so suddenly? You've said nothing. I mean... England?"

"It's not sudden. It's been more than a year since Charlie died and it's time for me to throw off these black clothes before I become like Queen Victoria, forever dressed in widow's weeds. His parents will manage without me. They'll have to. Like you said, I have to get on with my life. I want to make Charlie proud of me, even if he won't be there by my side, sharing our adventures together."

Mother twiddled with her serviette ring, thumbing its worn

silver edge. "I see," she said, slowly. "Have you considered how you'll manage?"

"I've taken a typing course." I'd figured that office work would be far more interesting than domestic service. At least I'd meet people and be in the thick of it. "I'd like to be a novelist." It sounded pompous, but I wanted Mother to know I had ambition.

She took a mouthful of stew and swallowed it down. "How long will you be gone?"

"I haven't booked a return ticket. At least two months." Although I had no intention of racing back for a visit.

Mother nodded. "Is that long enough to write a book?"

I laughed. "I doubt it. I'll have to get a job too. A secretary, perhaps." I had little notion of what secretaries did and whether I was qualified. But then, neither would Mother. "Anyway, I haven't even come up with an idea for a novel yet."

"Write what you know about – your life growing up here, the people and places. Your childhood."

My brain snapped and before I could check the words they blasted from me, bitter and unexpected. "Should I write about what I saw Father doing with a small boy? And in the shed with the under-gardener? Or what he did to Ginia, which she won't talk about? Maybe I should describe the time he stood at my bedroom door, naked?"

Mother gawped and her hand flew to cover her mouth. "What on earth do you mean?"

"Don't be so naive, Mother, and don't imagine I'm stupid either. I've seen what went on in this house. I know all about that man's depravity. He wasn't taken prisoner of war and God knows if he really died of Spanish flu. Perhaps he did things to other young men in jail and faced a firing squad. I don't know and I don't care. But you–" I pointed an accusatory finger at her. "You should have known better. You're our mother and you did noth-ing, *nothing*, to protect us. You can't have been blind to what Father did to Ginia."

Mother burst into tears. "I knew Frank could be cruel, but you must understand, I was powerless–"

"No you weren't. That's utter nonsense. You're a weak woman who let awful things happen in this house and rather than report him to the police, you let it go on. You disgust me." Bottled up for years, the torrent of words wouldn't stop, and I paused to steady myself.

"You must believe me. I tried to stand up to him, but he threatened me. I let him beat me and sometimes–" her voice faltered, "–he did worse than that and I didn't fight him, so he'd not molest any of you, or those poor boys." Tears coursed down her face.

"You could have done more. You should have." I wouldn't be mollified.

"Please... let me explain... He told me he'd have me prosecuted and sent to jail. I couldn't have that. You girls would then be left totally at his mercy."

"What tosh. What on earth could send you to jail?"

Mother looked wildly around the room. "He said Susan and I committed carnal sin. It wasn't true, it wasn't true at all, but he said if word got out I'd be done for and never see any of my family again." She covered her face with her hands.

I stared at her, appalled by her gullibility. I was amazed she had done nothing, but merely allowed herself to be pinioned under Father's thumb and blackmailed by his bullying. I scraped back my chair. "I'm going to finish my packing." My voice was cold and hard. "Nothing you can say will wipe out the past. You're a despicable excuse for a mother and I never want to set eyes on you again."

The sound of her weeping echoed behind me as I ran up the stairs, but I felt no remorse, only a sense of triumph that at last I'd lifted the lid on this shameful chapter.

9

ESME

GUERNSEY, JULY 1958

*E*sme dressed with care in her best, and only, pencil skirt, crisp white blouse, and low-heeled court shoes. Anthony was taking her to meet Elizabeth and in the expectation that she'd prove to be a relative, Esme wanted to make a good impression. Or that's what she told herself, pushing away an annoying little voice in her head asking if Anthony would like her outfit. His approval was immaterial because he probably had a girlfriend, and anyway, after Hugh she couldn't face another rejection.

A tooting horn broke her reverie and she dashed out of the cottage as Anthony pulled up in a cream, open-top MG.

Without opening the door, he hurdled over the side. "Change of plan." He gestured to Esme. "Hop in. We're getting the ferry to Herm." He held open the passenger door.

Esme could hardly believe it. She'd assumed they'd be walking or taking a bus. "Oh my! A car. No one has a car here."

"I stole it from a junkyard."

Esme's eyes widened. "You did not."

"Quite right. It came with me on the ferry from England. I couldn't bear to part with the old girl."

She eyed the roofless car. Even with her shorter haircut, the sea breeze would render the tangles unmanageable. "Do I have time to get a headscarf?"

"If you're quick. The boat leaves in ten minutes."

She dashed back inside and up the stairs to her room, grabbing the first scarf she saw and ran back to the car, wishing she'd thought to change out of her heels.

"That was quick." Anthony started up the engine.

"Why are we going to Herm?" She knew from her guidebook that the island was part of the Channel Islands. "Isn't it pretty well uninhabited?"

"It was abandoned during the war, but it's getting going as a bit of a tourist place. It's a favourite spot for beach lovers. Seems Elizabeth lives there."

"Oh?"

"When I rang her number, a man answered. Said she'd moved to Herm years back when her sight started to go. He didn't have an address."

"So she doesn't know we're coming?"

"Nope. But there's only a couple of dozen people living there, so she won't be hard to find."

With seconds to spare, they jumped on the already packed ferry and headed out of the old stone harbour. Crammed between Anthony and a young girl wrapped in a bathing towel, Esme watched the outline of Herm gradually come into focus. Nestled behind trees and foliage, only a few buildings peppered its shoreline. If Elizabeth had moved to such a remote spot, was it possible she wouldn't welcome visitors? And why had she chosen it, an old lady, going blind? Unless, of course, her daughters lived there.

In less than half an hour, the boat pulled up alongside a short jetty. They disembarked and made their way up a flight of whitewashed stone steps. Ahead, Esme could see scattered rooftops poking above the treeline.

Anthony took off his glasses and used the end of his tie to polish the lenses. He pointed to the right, along a rocky path. "Let's try our luck this way." He folded Esme's hand around his elbow. "Here, hold tight."

His clasp was firm and authoritative. Given Esme had no time to dress more appropriately and change into lace-up walking shoes, she was glad of his steadying arm as she picked her way over the bumpy track, and the nearness of his body next to hers held a reassuring warmth.

They rounded the corner and a large manor house with a sign, White House Hotel, came into view – and with it, a smooth gravel path. Reluctantly, Esme released Anthony, who was already charging on ahead. "I'll ask at reception," he said.

She sat on a wooden bench on the lawn outside the entrance and gazed out beyond a tennis court to the sea. A deep peace settled on her. No matter what happened, whether or not she solved the conundrum of Arcadia's letter, coming here was lifting her out of a fog. As each day passed, she saw more clearly how she'd been beguiled by Hugh's charm, his flattery and constant reminders of how 'he couldn't manage without her'. She'd allowed her love for him – or was it merely infatuation? – to prevent her from pursuing her own dreams. Here in the Channel Islands, she was certain she'd find the story she wanted to write. It was waiting for her. She just had to unearth it.

A hand ruffled her hair and, startled, she looked up.

Anthony had a broad grin. "C'mon, daydreamer." He grabbed her hand and pulled her to her feet. "Turns out Elizabeth's home is a bit further down this track. I met the hotel's owner – nice chap, actually he owns the whole of Herm – who said she lives with his former housekeeper. How's that for a piece of easy investigative research?"

"I'm impressed. What else did you find out?"

"The housekeeper, Susan somebody or other, came here after the war to help get the hotel up and running." Anthony strode along the lawn to a side gate, with Esme trotting to keep up. "Elizabeth is her oldest friend and, what with her poor sight and them both being widows, they decided to come together, look after each other."

"Makes sense, I suppose."

"You don't sound convinced?"

"Well, it wouldn't be for me – leaving my daughters, and perhaps grandchildren too, to live on an island with only a handful of people."

Anthony stopped suddenly and swung around, coming nose to nose with Esme. "Have you got children?"

"No." Esme blushed. "I'm not married."

"That's a relief." He renewed his fast pace. "I never thought to ask."

Esme said nothing, unsure how to respond. If only she were one of those women who could make a bright, flirtatious comment.

"We're here." Anthony pushed open a rickety gate and Esme followed him up a neat, shrub-lined path to a pink stone cottage with a red front door. He lifted the brass knocker and banged three times.

After a couple of minutes, they heard a shuffling and a tap-tap. The door slowly opened and an elderly woman with glazed eyes appeared, leaning on a stick. "Yes?"

"Elizabeth Robin?" Anthony asked.

She nodded. "The same. Who wants to know?"

Anthony introduced Esme and himself. "Esme believes you may be a distant relative."

"Fancy that," said Elizabeth. "I've never heard about an Esme, but come in."

They followed the old lady down a hallway devoid of decoration to a spartan front parlour. It had a musty, unlived-in air, furnished with only four shabby armchairs equally spaced around the fireplace, each with a side table to the left. Watching

Elizabeth manoeuvre her way around, it became clear the lack of clutter was deliberate. She didn't offer tea, and there were no obvious noises to signal Susan was at home. No one spoke until they were seated.

"Well?" said Elizabeth.

Anthony nodded to Esme.

"I'm looking for my mother's family," she said. "Her name was Arcadia Robin. I'm afraid I don't know my grandparents' names. Just before the Great War, my grandmother contracted tuberculosis and my grandfather went to fight. I don't believe either survived, so Arcadia was sent away to England when she was about fourteen. I hoped you might remember?" She left the question hanging in the air. It was reasonable to think the tragedy of an orphaned child would have been talked about amongst the Robin family.

Elizabeth perched on the edge of her chair, steadying both hands on top of her stick. "Arcadia. Odd name. Never heard of her. I recall an Angelina. But she wasn't a Robin. Didn't she fall off a swing? There was a little girl once. Had an accident. Broke her back?"

A shard of memory, an instant she couldn't quite grasp, shot through Esme. She ignored it, keen to keep up with Elizabeth.

"Or did she die? I can't recall. Your grandparents... *Titanic*, did you say? Drowned. No, no, TB. That's right. Oh dear."

Esme exchanged looks with Anthony. This wasn't going to be easy. "Perhaps my mother was at school with your daughters?" she ventured. It was worth a shot. Anthony grinned and gave her a surreptitious thumbs up.

"Oh, those girls." Elizabeth smiled. "Virginia, whatever happened to Virginia? My Mavis, she's a good girl." She sighed. "As for Jane, her corporal came home with no leg."

Before Esme could express her sympathy, Anthony cut in. "Do they live here still? Guernsey, I mean?"

"Do they? I don't know. Yes, they must. The war's over now."

Elizabeth turned watery eyes in Esme's direction. "Go and see them. I'm sure they'd remember Arcadia. Arcadia Robin you say? Never heard of her."

Anthony cocked his head towards the door. "*Let's go,*" he mouthed.

But Esme had one more question. "Before we go... Did your husband fight in the Great War?"

Elizabeth froze. "We don't talk about those times."

"I'm sorry, I didn't mean to bring back bad memories." Esme could have kicked herself for bringing up the war so abruptly. It was obviously still upsetting, even four decades later.

"Too many young boys hurt. What a disgrace." She turned her face away, but not before Esme saw the tears forming.

Anthony caught Esme's attention, shook his head and tugged on her sleeve. "Thank you, Mrs Robin," he said. "We'll see ourselves out."

With the tide in, the afternoon ferry would depart from Herm harbour, rather than the steps where they'd disembarked. There was half an hour to wait so they sat on the low stone wall in the warm sunshine; a relief after the dark chill of Elizabeth's spartan home. Esme fell quiet, replaying Elizabeth's ramblings, and Anthony didn't interrupt. In the distance, the ferry came into view, chugging its way from St Peter Port.

The afternoon wind whipped up and Esme reached into her jacket pocket for her headscarf, but there was nothing other than a handkerchief. "My scarf–"

"In your bag?"

She was already checking its contents. "No. I must have dropped it or left it at Elizabeth's house."

Anthony jumped up. "We've still got about twenty minutes.

Come on. Run." He strode back along the harbour wall, Esme hurrying behind, her toes twinging in her unsuitable court shoes.

"Oh gosh, I hope I don't twist an ankle on these rocks," she said.

He called over his shoulder, "If you do, I'll give you a piggyback."

When they reached the fork, he said, "You take the coastal path and I'll go back via the hotel. We'll meet at Elizabeth's house."

Esme jogged and hobbled over the rocky track as fast as she could. On the sleepy island of Herm, she made a strange sight and a couple of passers-by stopped, incredulous, as she sped by. She heard the man say, "Whatever could be so important?"

Esme ignored him, focussed on checking the trees, hedges and path for any sign of her yellow scarf. Nothing.

Back at the pink cottage, this time Elizabeth's front door opened within seconds, but a stranger – a fat woman in a navy-blue apron – blocked the entry.

"Are you Susan?" asked Esme.

Susan frowned. "I am. And you be?"

"Esme. I was just here, talking to Elizabeth – Mrs Robin. I left my headscarf–"

"I thought so. Stay there. It's in the parlour."

While Esme waited, Anthony appeared at the gate. She signalled him to stay out of sight. A long shot, but maybe Susan would yield the information Elizabeth had been reluctant to give and she didn't want Anthony whisking her away before she had the opportunity.

Susan reappeared. "You dropped it on the floor," she said in an accusatory tone.

"Thank you so much." Esme flipped it over her head and made a quick tie. "I wonder... I don't wish to seem presumptuous but there's something I forgot to ask Mrs Robin."

"Not now. She's having her nap. You tired her out with your questions."

"Maybe you could help me?"

Susan appeared torn between loyalty and curiosity. "Maybe I could."

Esme sensed Susan's desire to insert herself into this rare moment of domestic intrigue, and took her chance. "It's about her late husband."

Susan's face scrunched into a hard knot. "That bad lot. None of your business." She made to close the door.

"Oh please," Esme begged. "My mother's maiden name was Robin and I'm trying to track down my grandfather. When I went through military records at the library, I came across a man called George Duclos Robin, who died in France in May 1917."

"You're barking up the wrong tree there. Sounds like one of the Jersey Robins. Nothing to do with us." Susan lifted her chin. "And if you must know, Elizabeth's Frank died in the Somme. But that's all I'm telling you."

Esme's heart lifted. If there were two different Robin families, it meant the war record for George Duclos Robin could belong to Arcadia's father. "Thank you. One more thing—"

"Enough. We're not interested in talking about Frank. And don't come back asking more questions. I won't be having you upsetting Elizabeth anymore."

She closed the door leaving Esme no option but to retreat, only a little wiser. So Frank had been a bad egg. But why? How? And did it matter?

Ignoring her sore feet, she joined Anthony. "What's a Jersey Robin?"

He roared with laughter. "There's a deal of rivalry between Guernsey and Jersey. I'd say a Jersey Robin is someone deemed unrelated to anyone born and bred on Guernsey. Why do you ask?"

"I meant to tell you... I searched the war records in the library and found one for a George Duclos Robin who was with the Royal Jersey Militia. All the other Robins listed were with British regiments. As Jersey is just across the water and part of the Channel Islands, I thought he could have been Arcadia's father. My grandfather. He might have gone to Jersey and signed up there. Perhaps he was rejected by the Guernsey Army... for flat feet or bad eyesight... and so tried his luck across the water. You never know."

Anthony pulled a face. "Doubtful. The Royal Jersey Militia didn't have any soldiers from Guernsey."

That was a blow, but only a minor one. It was still a *possibility*. She wouldn't give up yet.

"Quickstep, now. Our boat awaits." He increased his pace, and shepherded Esme to the waiting ferry. The wind billowed and they took seats inside. Esme shivered and Anthony took off his jacket, insisting he drape it around her shoulders.

"I tell you what," Anthony said. "I'll contact a fellow I know in St Helier, another archivist, and ask him to check out this George Robin. But even if he was your grandfather, it doesn't help us solve the mystery of the letter from M. Your mother was being urged to come to Guernsey, remember? Where she grew up. So it's far more likely you're related to Elizabeth's lot." He rubbed his hands together. "I must say, your family gets more interesting at every turn. This is terrific fun, isn't it?"

Esme grinned at his infectious enthusiasm. "It is rather," she agreed. "But we mustn't get too carried away. We don't know yet that they're part of my family. It could simply be another family called Robin, and no relation at all."

"Don't be daft. In a place this small, anyone with the same surname has to be related."

Esme knew he was right. They must be cousins of some sort. It was just perplexing that Elizabeth had no recollection of a young girl called Arcadia. It crossed her mind that maybe she'd been known by another name, a nickname or a shortened form of Arcadia – though nothing obvious occurred to her. As far as she was aware, her mother had no middle name either. When she'd cleared her flat she'd found divorce papers and under *Full Name* it clearly stated: Arcadia Fanstone, née Robin.

Perhaps it was too soon to be despondent. "I'm expecting too much, aren't I? Elizabeth's got an unreliable memory and I want her to remember people from fifty years ago. I mean, she doesn't even know what happened to her daughter, Virginia."

"Aha. Another mystery to solve."

Esme groaned. "You're incorrigible."

"So my mother always says." Anthony blew on his hands and narrowed his eyes. "For my money, we need to find the other sister, Mavis."

"How do you figure that out?"

"Think, Esme. The letter. Signed by M. Mavis?"

"You're right." She pulled his jacket more tightly around her chest. "So what next?"

"Mavis, or any of the daughters offer our best hope. I'll do some more digging, see if I can locate their whereabouts. One of them has to remember Arcadia. Wouldn't teenage girls think it impossibly sad to have a mother dying of TB and being sent away, all alone, to another country?"

Esme demurred. "I don't want you wasting your time. Surely you should be working on your archive, not chasing after wild geese?"

"There's plenty of hours in the day to do both. Besides, it's one thing to document the facts of war, it's another to unearth real-life experiences."

"But–"

"My nose is twitching. I have a feeling, an instinct. And while I'm at it, I'll see if I can get into the police records and find anyone with the initial C who was in jail in October 1945."

"I'm ahead of you there. I looked through the newspapers and found a possible match."

Anthony gave her a sideways look. "You sly dog, you've been holding back on me. Tell me more."

After she'd explained about Clara and M. Mellon, Anthony's expression went from interested to downcast. "Great start, except for one big problem. It can't be Clara. The letter said 'he.'"

"No, it didn't. I remember being struck by the fact. You assumed it referred to a man, because murder usually does. "

Anthony raised one eyebrow. "True. Very astute of you."

"It may be a blind alley," she said. "But I'm going to see what else I can find out about Clara."

"Shall we reconvene next week to pool our findings? How about dinner?"

A sharp memory came over her of that last, fateful evening with Hugh. Her breathless, stupid anticipation and the devastating let-down. "I don't–"

"My treat. I insist. How else can I repay you for this sleuthing adventure?"

Esme laughed at his cheek. Anthony wasn't Hugh, about to lead her up a path of hope. He was a decent fellow, asking her on a date, not for her hand in marriage, for goodness' sake. She could shut him down now, or see how the friendship progressed. "Thanks, Tommy, that would lovely."

"My pleasure, Tuppence."

10

ESME

GUERNSEY, JULY 1958

*D*inner with Anthony wasn't quite as Esme had imagined. She'd assumed he'd take her to one of the fish shops by the harbour, or possibly a hotel restaurant. But once settled into the passenger seat of his open-top car with a rug tucked around her legs, he passed her a small basket fastened with leather straps.

"Hold this," he said. "We're headed to The Plough, one of the island's oldest pubs. Only for a drink, mind you. The food doesn't run to more than a pickled onion or a bag of Smith's crisps, so I packed us a picnic. Afterwards, as it's such a fine night, we'll drive over to the west coast, lay out the rug, and with any luck, be there a good hour before the sun goes down." He wound a scarf around his neck and revved the engine. "Off we go."

Esme, prepared this time, had tied her hair back with a wide bandeau. Grinning to herself, she tamped down the ungracious thought that Hugh would never dream of eating a meal sitting on the ground.

In less than ten minutes, they drew up outside a large white-washed eighteenth-century house, with a pretty garden bursting with pink and purple sweet peas. As they walked along the footpath, he pointed across the road. "I live a bit further down there. Allez Street. I've got a very cramped one-bedroom flat. Nothing like as swanky as your cottage, but it suits me." He pushed open the door to the pub and took a step back to let Esme through. "As you might guess, the landlord here knows me well."

Before Esme could reply, a hearty red-faced man behind the bar called out, "Evening, Mister History Man."

"Evening, Mister Publican." Anthony ushered Esme forwards. "Let me introduce my friend, Esme Fanstone."

"And about time, if you don't mind my saying so." The barman winked at Esme and she felt her cheeks go red.

To cover her embarrassment, she looked around the cosy room at the groups of working men crammed around misshapen tables and sitting on stools at the bar. Not a woman to be seen. The conversation was earnest, with occasional bursts of guttural laughter. Pictures of St Peter Port and various football teams jostled with horse brasses and European flags on the wall. In one corner, two men took turns to throw darts at the board whilst a third chalked up the score.

Anthony, holding two half pints of beer, nudged her. "Let's sit outside. Less noise."

They sat on a small wooden bench in the courtyard and sipped their drinks. Esme stretched out her legs and tipped her head up to the warm rays of the evening sun.

"You first," Anthony said.

Esme kept her eyes closed and tried to withhold an air of triumph from her voice. "No need to find Mavis, she found me. I'm meeting her in a couple of days."

"Wow. How come?"

"She left a note for me at the post office and the postman delivered it. I suppose there can't be too many strangers here by the name of Esme Fanstone."

"And?"

Esme shrugged. "She wrote she understood I'd visited her

mother and would I like to meet for tea at La Collinette Hotel. Of course, I replied in the affirmative."

Anthony tapped the toes of his shoes together. "There's definitely some dark hidden secret. I can feel it. I can sniff it."

"You sound like a police dog." Esme giggled and sat up.

"I've definitely got a knack. Seriously, I'm lost as an archivist. I should've been a detective. I've got the nose for it." He took a long draught of beer. "Perhaps that's a slight exaggeration. Put it this way, with a little persuasion in the form of a pouch of baccy, my friend in the force handed me the criminal register for October 1945."

"What did you discover?"

Anthony pulled a small notebook from his breast pocket and flipped back the cover. "I jotted down everyone who had the initial C for their first name. Pretty disappointing as it turned out. Most were arrested for petty crimes... stealing a packet of cigarettes, being drunk and disorderly, fare evasion on the bus. Nothing that would warrant someone writing that letter, urging the need for help. Except for your Clara, of course."

Esme sat up straighter. "And?"

"The ledger only noted the crime. Murder by poisoning. There was one baffling thing though, the entry was dated October 7, the day *after* that letter was sent to your mother, which rather rules out Clara, especially given she wasn't arrested until a couple of days later. It may mean nothing more than a clerical error though."

How had Esme missed that? "Hmm. I'll recheck the newspaper articles."

"Good idea. After drawing a blank, I decided to check anyone with a middle initial C." Anthony gave a triumphant look. "And I came up trumps. In early October, Bernard C Vautier was arrested for assaulting a military officer. However, the officer later dropped the charges."

Esme sighed. "Doesn't sound like a possibility, does it? What would be the point of causing Arcadia to panic if it came to nothing?"

"Because the letter was sent before the charges were dropped, of course." Anthony closed his notebook.

"Is that all?"

He grinned. "The police made a note on Bernard C Vautier's file. He'd had his leg amputated. What do you think of that?"

"What should I think? It was war. Lots of men lost limbs."

"Yes. But not all of them had the middle initial C. Which stood for Charleston, by the way."

"You think–"

"Well, it's a major coincidence, isn't it? Your mother gets a letter about someone called C who has got into big trouble. We find out a man called Bernard Vautier – who for all we know could have answered to Charleston – assaulted a British officer. And what's more, Elizabeth talked about Jane's corporal who came home from the war with no leg."

"She never said 'from the war'. Just that he came back. They were probably sweethearts or friends."

Anthony appeared unperturbed. "You can ask Mavis. If it's the same man, she'd know wouldn't she? And we might be a little closer to finding out why Arcadia was pressed upon to come here, the place she'd not visited since leaving as a young teenager. It would be a less tenuous link than Clara at any rate. Gosh, it's exciting." Without waiting for her response, he patted her knee. "Drink up. Time to enjoy the sunset at Cobo Bay."

On the way, Anthony espoused theories about C, Charleston, Elizabeth and Mavis. He shouted his suppositions, competing to be heard above the noise of the engine, a stiff breeze, and the tyres grinding over the gravel road. Esme could only catch every third word, but it didn't matter. Anthony's ebullience about solving the mystery surrounding her mother was contagious. But to her mind, no matter what Anthony thought, Clara was the most likely candidate to be C, and she was determined to dig further.

He drew the car up alongside a long, white-sand beach. A group of young people loitered on the sea wall, eating fish and chips, their transistor radio blaring Elvis Presley's 'Jailhouse Rock'. Anthony swung the picnic basket in one hand and took Esme's hand in the other. "Let's find a quieter spot."

She tingled at his touch and allowed him to guide her away from the crowd, past a large pub towards steps leading down to the beach. The tide had retreated, so they took off their shoes and made their way barefoot to the water's edge. Anthony laid out the picnic rug, and Esme unpacked the basket: cheese, bread, ham, tomatoes, a jar of pickles and a thermos of tea. He broke slices off the baguette, and she poured them each a cuppa.

After being hunched over her typewriter all day, the balmy evening was an unexpected salve. The food was delicious, and being in Anthony's company, peaceful. Esme watched the setting sun, rich in orange and red hues, glittering on the water above what had once been a sea fort and yet another reminder of Nazi dominance. She found it impossible to conjure this beauty and serenity being so utterly threatened by the presence of Hitler's troops, instilling terror and destroying the islanders' way of life.

Anthony tucked a strand of her hair behind her ear. "You look miles away."

"Just enjoying the evening. Thinking how lucky we are not to be speaking German."

He traced his finger down the scar on her cheek. "How did you get this?"

Her hand flew to where the ugly, jagged line marred her complexion. No one ever asked. No one was that bold. "I had an accident as a child. It's a horrible reminder."

"It's beautiful. It gives your face character."

Esme blinked back an involuntary tear. "That's... You're very kind... I mean, I hate it. People look at it."

"I bet they don't. It hardly shows. You just think they do."

"I fell from a swing. I don't really remember it. I was very small, three or four."

"Like the little girl Elizabeth mentioned."

"Angelina, wasn't it? Funny, it gave me a jolt when she said it. I had a flash of memory, tumbling off a little wooden seat onto a patch of grass, and cutting my face on a sharp rock or stone. I wonder what happened to Angelina."

"Who knows? Elizabeth's ramblings were rather, well, rambly. She might have mixed things up."

A thought struck Esme. "You don't suppose she confused Angelina with Arcadia, do you? The names are quite similar."

He gave a look of scepticism. "Except Elizabeth said Angelina broke her back, which means she wouldn't have walked again."

"True." Esme gave a rueful smile.

"That's better." Anthony lifted her chin, leaned in and gently pressed his lips against hers.

Esme stayed quite still. Seagulls squawked and waves lapped the shoreline. But the only noise she heard was the beat of Anthony's heart against hers. When he moved away, she felt *wobbly* inside. There was no other word for it.

Anthony stared out to sea. Esme snuck a look at him, but his eyes remained fixed on the horizon. Then he seemed to make up his mind about something, drained his teacup and pulled her to her feet. "Let's walk along the seafront before the sun goes down. Come on." He tucked her arm though his and they strolled along the promenade. Her momentary worry that he'd regretted his impulse passed and she relaxed into the warmth of his body, enjoying what was left of the evening.

He folded his hand over hers. "Lots to look forward to, eh?"

Esme couldn't contain the smile that lit her face. "Indeed there is."

∼

Anthony waved and with a rev of the engine, sped off. Esme watched his MG retreat down the hill, trying to figure out what just happened. She'd been in love with Hugh for so long, she couldn't remember ever having fantasies about any other man kissing her. Yes, there had been boyfriends here and there but they'd never lasted long. Compared to Hugh, she found them dull, pompous or lacking in chemistry. Anthony, with his bookish enthusiasm, was quite different. His quick intelligence and easy manner made him excellent company. And that kiss had quite shaken her.

She pushed open the garden gate. Junction Cottage was swathed in darkness and she started at the sound of Travis's voice cutting through the night air.

"Good evening." He tossed a paper bag into his dustbin and replaced the lid.

Esme dragged her mind from Anthony and focussed on Travis, who looked as glum as ever. "Can I ask... have you ever heard of Clara Denier?"

"The poisoner?" Travis's scowl deepened. "Everyone knows about Clara. A right mystery, if you ask me."

"What do you think really happened?"

"Lord knows. For my money, the whole thing never smelled right. Something fishy went on in that house, I'd say."

"How awful if she was hanged for a crime she didn't commit," she said.

"She's still in jail, claiming her innocence."

"I thought she was sentenced to death?"

Travis gave a derisory snort. "No one's been hanged here since 1854."

Esme's pulse quickened. "Do you know which prison she's in?" If Clara was C, the best way to find out would be to visit her. Then Esme could ask her face to face, and look into her eyes when she asked if she'd known Arcadia.

"Not here. She's on the mainland at Her Majesty's pleasure in Holloway."

That was a blow. "Why not here?"

"All the worst criminals are exported. And before you ask, it was the High Court in London that commuted her sentence to life, so perhaps they had doubts too."

His words mirrored Esme's opinion about how the circumstances of Clara's conviction didn't add up. Could Arcadia have had similar misgivings? Had she intervened in some way, petitioned the British courts? "Travis, forgive me, I must go. I've got... I left a pot... I mean, I need to put-" She fumbled with the key, anxious now to get into the cottage, and plot her strategy – but she needn't have worried about offending him, Travis had already stomped back to his house.

Seated at her dining table, Esme considered the options. She knew little about Holloway, England's all-female prison, except that prominent suffragettes had been detained there. During the war, she recalled a stink when Winston Churchill had allowed hated fascists Diana Mitford and her husband Oswald Mosley to live in the grounds. And hadn't Ruth Ellis been hanged there a few years back? Esme shuddered at the thought of Clara living with the worst offenders in appalling conditions, probably struggling to get enough food and warmth.

To gain access to Clara, would she have to go through the prison authorities? Or could she simply write to her? If, however, Clara had never learned to read or write, in all probability Esme wouldn't receive a reply. The best way, she realised with a sigh, would be to wait until she returned to London in a few months' time and see if she could pay her a visit.

No, no, no. The intriguing identity of C needed to be solved now, not sometime in the future. She had to find a way to enter into correspondence and gain Clara's trust, see if Clara was forthcoming about knowing Arcadia. What would capture Clara's attention? Money? A gift of some sort?

She gave a small fist pump. That was it – she'd say she wanted to discuss Clara's case, give it some publicity. Better still, she'd say she was a journalist for *The Monitor*, Hugh's newspaper. There was no way Clara would turn down the chance to pin the crime on someone else, or seek sympathy for wrongful arrest, in order to potentially secure her freedom. And who knew, maybe Esme really would unearth another version of the truth.

ESME

GUERNSEY, JULY 1958

Thursday dawned wet and cloudy. The rain pelted down in a continuous sheet all day, compounded by northerly gusts of wind. Not a day to ride her bike, Esme donned her mackintosh, sou'wester and waterproof boots, and for added protection took her brolly. By the time the bus deposited her on the corner, a brisk breeze whipping in from the west had blown the rain away.

La Collinette Hotel, a finely proportioned Georgian residence with a half-moon driveway, dominated its neighbouring walled houses. Window boxes decorated its exterior, overflowing with cascading red, orange and purple blooms. As she was half an hour early, Esme explored outside. More flowers – fuchsias, sweet peas, orchids – graced the beds where vegetables had flourished during the war. The grounds at the back of the hotel, overgrown and neglected, still held reminders of German occupation and were peppered with fortified stone bunkers linked by a tunnel, including one which had acted as Signals Headquarters. She shuddered at the thought of armed men parading along the narrow streets which led to the hotel and trampling what had once surely been a charming garden.

Pushing her way through plants strangled by weeds, she fell upon a derelict outdoor bowling alley, and experienced another unexpected moment of déjà vu. She saw herself bending over, a large brown wooden ball in her hand, wearing a three-quarter length white frock and laughing over her shoulder at someone behind her.

The moment passed, fleeting but unsettling, before she was driven inside by a fresh downpour of rain. Drenched, Esme hurried to the hotel's cloakroom, divested her wet outerwear and ran a comb through her hair.

At the entryway to the lounge, an elderly lady in a smart maroon velvet coat with neat black buttons hovered. A black leather handbag was hanging over her forearm, and she had a wary expression on her face. For a moment, Esme felt quite giddy. The woman... the way she held her bag... she'd seen it before. She tried to grasp the memory, but it slipped away.

"Miss Fanstone?" the woman asked. "I'm Mavis Lucas. Mavis Robin what was."

Esme, conscious of her bedraggled appearance, joined her. "Please call me Esme." Close up, Esme could see the woman's likeness to Elizabeth. No wonder she looked familiar. The same dimpled chin and puffed cheeks.

Mavis led the way to a table laid with a silver teapot and all the trimmings, flanked by two floral armchairs. "I took the liberty of ordering tea."

Esme smoothed her skirt and sat opposite Mavis, who handed her a cup and saucer. She took a sip of the welcome hot tea, and got straight to the point. "I was very glad to get your note. I imagine you know why I'm here in St Peter Port?"

Mavis frowned. "Not really. Susan telephoned to say a young woman had visited and upset my mother, Elizabeth. Apparently she – that is, you – had asked questions about Father. I thought I should find you and see if there's something I should know. Or can help with. As you have no doubt guessed, Mother has a rather fragile state of mind."

Maybe that explained the hesitant look on Mavis's face. Susan had referred to Elizabeth's husband as a 'bad egg'. Perhaps Mavis had concerns about Esme's motives, afraid she might be muck-raking.

"I'm here to try and find my mother's family who had the name 'Robin'. The same name as yours. I thought Elizabeth might be a relative, but she seems to have no recollection of my mother. Her name was Arcadia. As for my grandfather, I can't recall his name. I'm not sure I ever knew it."

Mavis sat a little straighter. "Was?"

"What do you mean?"

"You said her name *was* Arcadia. Is she... dead?"

"Yes, she died a few months ago."

Mavis stared at a spot over Esme's head. "I'm sorry to hear that," she said slowly. "But I'm afraid I can't help you either. I never knew anyone called Arcadia."

Mavis's tone brooked no argument, yet Esme wasn't sure she believed her. "You have two sisters, don't you? Do you think either of them might be able to help?"

"Unlikely. It was such a long time ago. Jane left here after the war. The Great War, that is... and died shortly thereafter..."

"And the other?"

"Virginia? She's a hard one to pin down. Always fighting for some cause. Votes for women. Workers' unions. Tricks to outwit Germans during the Occupation."

"Does she still live here?"

"Yes and no. Right now, she's off in Africa somewhere. Helping to civilise tribespeople or some such nonsense. With Ginia, you never know how long she'll be away."

No wonder Elizabeth had been so vague about her daughter's whereabouts.

"How long are you planning to be here?" Mavis asked.

"A few weeks, perhaps."

Mavis looked taken aback. "Oh? Why? Do you have friends to visit?"

"No. I–"

Mavis smiled. "What of your folks in England?"

"Just my father and grandmother."

"I expect they miss you. Don't stay away too long."

Was Mavis hinting she should leave Guernsey, and stop asking questions? Fat chance. Esme leaned back in her chair. "Do you have any relatives in Jersey?"

That suspicious glance fell across Mavis's face again. "Distant cousins. Why do you ask?"

"I've been checking war records to see if I can find my grandfather. I've no idea whether or not he fought, and the problem is I don't know his name, so I can only do it by process of eliminating anyone called Robin of about the right age. There was a man, George Duclos Robin, who fought with the Royal Jersey Militia."

"Sad story. Both he and his two sons died in the same battle. Battle of Arras, I think. I remember reading about it."

That rather put the kibosh on George Robin being her grandfather. Maybe one Guernseyman could have signed up in Jersey, unaccounted for, but not a man and two sons. And Arcadia had been an only child, she'd never mentioned any brothers killed in the war.

But it did raise another question. Why hadn't Esme found a war record for Frank Robin, Mavis's father, who had died in the Somme? "Can I clarify something Susan told me?"

Mavis narrowed her eyes. "About Father? No... no, I really don't think this is a good idea." She made a deliberate pantomime of looking at her watch. "I know you hope to find these relatives of yours, but what with the war, so many refugees, people moving here and there, paperwork gone, I question whether you'll have much luck." She sighed. "Please promise me you won't bother Mother again. She's easily confused and upset. Her age, you know."

"I wouldn't dream of bothering her. Not without your permission." Esme kept her voice light. "There is just one more thing you might be able to help me with though."

"I'll try." Mavis didn't sound encouraging.

Esme stirred her tea. "A man called Bernard Vautier. It's an awfully long shot, but I think my mother may have known him." That is, if Anthony's theory about C's identity was correct. "The thing is, he had his leg amputated and when I met Elizabeth – your mother – she mentioned a man with no leg. She referred to him as your sister Jane's corporal. A friend, or boyfriend even?"

The expression on Mavis's face – unreadable, blank of emotion – didn't waver. "There was a local boy called Bernard Vautier." She spoke slowly, as if picking her words. "I suppose if I knew him, Jane may have too, but I don't recall our families being particular friends." She cleared her throat. "A sad story. Bernard indeed lost his leg in the Great War and ended up in a prisoner-of-war camp. He came back a few years after the war ended, a wreck. Badly shell-shocked with memory loss and dreadful facial wounds. He became a recluse. I heard he kept to himself, growing vegetables for a local grocer in exchange for food staples. I'd occasionally see him when he ventured out to the shops, but he was a broken man. Children ran away, screaming at the sight of him." She splayed her hands. "That's all I know. He's probably dead by now."

"Did you hear that he got into trouble with the law? Assaulted another soldier? An officer?"

Mavis frowned and pushed aside her tea. "Rubbish. Charlie was an invalid. Impossible." She picked up her gloves and stood. "You must excuse me. I have to catch my bus."

"I'm sorry... I didn't mean–" Esme's apology was left hanging. Mavis had bolted from the lounge.

Esme sipped her tea and pondered some of the odder aspects

of their conversation. Despite her controlled manner, Mavis had seemed watchful, on the alert. And yet her last remark: *Charlie was an invalid.* Not Bernard but Charlie. Charleston. C. A slip of the tongue, but had Mavis just confirmed that Bernard was C? Not Clara, after all.

Had she imagined Mavis's flicker of recognition, her interest, when Esme mentioned Arcadia's name? If C was Bernard Vautier, did that mean the person who wrote to Arcadia – *M* – could have been Mavis? If that were the case, why lie? For a fleeting second, Esme flirted with the idea that Arcadia had been born out of wedlock. It might explain why everyone denied knowing an Arcadia Robin; they were too ashamed of the slur on the family name. She shook her head at her own stupidity. Back in 1899, when Arcadia was born, an illegitimate baby would have been quickly hidden away or adopted out, not brought up in full view of disapproving neighbours. No, that explanation smacked more of a plot from one of Arcadia's lurid historical romances. A Victorian conspiracy, with the whole of Guernsey still keeping it hush-hush sixty years later? Hardly.

Their conversation certainly didn't have the effect Mavis desired. Clearly, she wanted to warn Esme off but had only succeeded in arousing her curiosity. What was Mavis hiding?

JANE

LONDON, AUGUST 1922

*S*ix nights ago I decided to cut up my wedding dress. When I first had the idea, rather than filling me with sadness, I felt elated. Unless I did something radical, I'd have to go back to St Peter Port, which simply isn't an option. I've made the break and that's all there is to it.

By the same token, I'm not going to live out my days in this spartan attic room, catching the number twenty-four bus to the bureau in Bloomsbury and typing out dreary transcripts. I shouldn't mind half so much if I were given the works of D.H. Lawrence, Somerset Maugham or even Richmal Crompton – at least I might pick up some ideas. But all I get are stories not even worthy of penny dreadfuls. To top it off, I'm paid a pittance.

So when I heard about a nightclub in the West End where the best-dressed lady – as judged by the famous couturier, Paul Poiret – wins a twenty-five-guinea clothes voucher, I saw my chance. Imagine the wardrobe I could buy!

The club's called the Trocadero and it's where the rich set go. That was the catch of course. Well, two catches actually. I'd no money to buy a dress which might win me the prize, and I didn't know any bright young thing who'd invite me to the Trocadero as their guest. But I was determined to find a way around these obstacles, otherwise I'd never get a foothold, meet people who matter, and have some fun.

I found a pattern in *Woman's Life* for a gorgeous dance frock – low V-neck, drop waist, hip-hugging bandeau and layered skirt with loose pleats that rise and dip to expose the knees. If that didn't get me noticed, nothing would. The final effect, however – even with a few added touches of my own – would be utterly dependent on the quality of the fabric.

Silk or satin were beyond my means, and there was nothing in my wardrobe that I could magically repurpose – except for my wedding dress. Everyone said I'd looked beautiful that day, and I told myself Charlie would love to see me – from his seat on high – reprising the dress in a more modern reincarnation.

It took six evenings of unpicking the voile and lace, dying the material a deep rose, cutting the pieces and hand-sewing them in place. The result, to my eyes, was stunning, even viewed through the grimy, silvered mirror on the wardrobe door. I shingled my hair, rouged my cheeks and crossed my fingers that my wedding shoes, which I also dyed rose, were still fashionable enough to survive the scrutiny of London's chic and famous.

Attacked by a few nervous butterflies, I took a bus to Shaftesbury Avenue and stepped out amidst crowds of people, dressed in their finery, spilling from the theatres and restaurants. I hoped to somehow blend in with the revellers – rowdy young people shouting to each other, men linking arms and singing songs, on their way from one party to another. I attached myself to a group of drunken lads and tipsy girls, who didn't seem to realise I wasn't one of them, but when we reached the Trocadero, one yelled out, "Let's eat at Kettner's first," and they kept going.

Undecided what to do, I stood to one side and tried to look nonchalant, as if I were waiting for someone. I couldn't enter the club alone because I might be refused entry. My best bet would be to wait for another group and try to surreptitiously latch onto them.

After a few minutes, the doorman approached. "Yes, ma'am?" He looked me up and down in such a way that implied I had no business being there.

"I seem to have mislaid my friend," I said, with the air of one who casually lost people as a regular occurrence.

At that moment, a man in full evening dress swept up beside me and took my arm. "Here I am. Let's go in, shall we?"

The doorman bowed and opened the heavy door. "Good evening, Mr Fanstone."

Things were going swimmingly. I couldn't have wished for better. I allowed myself to be led by this young man up the magnificent, rococo stairway to the restaurant where hectic chatter rose above the strains of saxophone, piano and trombone. Tables encircled the dance floor where couples shimmied to American jazz. A gushing, glorious wave of utter excitement welled up in me and I prayed I'd get my chance to be on that dance floor.

My saviour snapped his fingers at a waiter. "Champagne. Krug." He turned to me. "You will join me, won't you? While you wait for your friend?" His voice was lazy and seductive.

How could I refuse? "That's very kind, Mr Fanstone. Thank you." In a blink, I was in the heart of London's nightlife and I was going to enjoy every blessed second. And – if my luck held – leave with a cheque for twenty-five guineas.

"Call me Lewis," he said and without waiting for my reply, escorted me past several tables, nodding at various patrons and ignoring their entreaties to join them. "Boring, boring, boring," he declared and pulled out a gilt-edged chair for me at a table for two.

Seated, he leaned back, flipped the lid of a silver cigarette case, and passed it across. I took a cigarette and while he held his lighter to the tip, I took the chance to inspect him. Mid-twenties.

Chiselled cheekbones, mousey-brown wavy hair and hooded eyes. Despite the way he slouched in his seat, he owned an elegant posture.

"Do you approve?" he asked.

I smiled. "I haven't seen you dance yet." More to the point, for my dress to win, it had to be out on display.

He raised his eyebrows lazily, but with interest. "And to whom do I owe the pleasure?"

Oh dear. Plain Jane would never do. "Arcadia," I said. That would make Charlie smile – choosing a name synonymous with a promise we'd made that our home would always be our Arcadian paradise. And I couldn't bring myself to use Charlie's name – a bitter reminder I'd never again be his wife. "Arcadia Robin."

"How delightful. Where do you hail from, Arcadia Robin?"

I hesitated. "Up north. I lived with my aunt until she died." I imagined a stern, downtrodden woman who resented having her young niece foisted on her. "A village in the Yorkshire Dales." Wasn't that where the Brontës lived?

"Your aunt?"

"I was sent to her during the war," I said, warming to my story. "We lived in Guernsey, but my father died and my mother caught TB." I pulled a sad face. A little truth couldn't hurt. Not too much though.

"It's an island, isn't it? In the English Channel?"

"That's it. Very isolated and windy."

He frowned, his interest evidently waning at the idea of such a bleak, unwelcoming place. "What brought you to London?"

I could see no glamour in admitting I typed manuscripts. "I'm an aspiring writer."

"Living in a garret, I bet."

"Of course." That much was true. My attic indeed was draughty, cramped and lacking in charisma.

He gave a small snort of disbelief – whether at my ambition

or my clichéd habitat wasn't clear. "And you?" I asked before he demanded to know the plot of my latest non-existent book.

"Oh, this and that. Dabble in the markets, follow the safe bets. Stocks and shares, you know. Play a bit of cricket and tennis. Lunch at the club." A man of means then.

"Did you fight?"

"Yes." He took a deep drag of his cigarette and gestured to the youngsters slapping each other around at the bar. "Unlike this lot. Spoilt brats who don't know what they missed. Half their luck." His tone held a bitter twang. "I copped a blighty though, in 1916, and sat the rest of it out behind a desk."

I wanted to ask more. Army, Flying Corps, Navy? Which battle? How was he wounded? But he stood, buttoned his jacket and held out his hand. "May I?"

I could sense eyes watching me as we made our way to the dance floor, and the hiss of gossip behind my back. I'd need to make a jolly good show of this, or the whole shebang would have been for nothing. A line of flappers performed that new craze, the Charleston (the irony!), legs and arms flying akimbo while their beaus clapped in rhythm and egged them on. Lily and I had tried it out one afternoon when we were alone in the bureau. Oh my, what fun. What freedom. I couldn't wait to join in, but just then the music ended, and the band switched to a waltz.

Disappointed such a staid melody meant I couldn't swirl and show off my dress, I allowed Lewis to take the lead. He held me firm and danced with an assured confidence. As we got the measure of each other, my brain let go and my legs took over. He twirled me, caught me. I spun around him, arms outstretched. Our bodies curled together and swayed, like two trees in a summer breeze. Gradually, others on the dance floor moved away and we took centre stage. The band upped its tempo and we matched them, beat for beat. I heard cheers from the crowd. Lewis took my hand, and my back arched, falling away, my head almost to the ground. He lifted me and in a seamless move we circled each other, coming breast to chest. His hand caressed the back of my head and all too soon the music stopped.

We barely acknowledged the applause but made our way to our table, smiling. The waiter poured two glasses of champagne.

Lewis lifted his glass. "I think I've met my match," he said, locking his eyes on mine.

My breath tightened, and I could barely sip the cool frothy liquid, but I accepted the challenge and didn't look away. I sensed my world on the precipice of change if I just played my hand with skill and daring; not too eager, not too aloof. "Tell me about the most exciting thing you've ever done."

He raised his eyebrows in surprise, cocked his head for a moment and went to speak, but I shushed him.

"The most exciting thing you've done," I said, "which you never told anyone about. Not even your mother."

His roar of laughter caught the attention of the neighbouring tables, but he ignored their curious stares and leaned across the table. "You're a wicked girl," he whispered. "And I think I'm about to be a very lucky man."

13

ARCADIA

BRIGHTON, ENGLAND, NOVEMBER 1922

*T*he summer whirled by and soon it was autumn. When Lewis went down on one knee at the end of Brighton pier, I should have been expecting it, but I wasn't. Until then, it had all been fun and parties, nothing serious.

"Get up, you oaf," I said. Passers-by looked at us enquiringly, and I couldn't stop laughing.

"Not until you say yes." He opened a small square box to reveal an exquisite square-cut diamond. "It's from Cartier."

A gang of lads sloped past, hands thrust deep into their pockets, joshing each other. "Go on," yelled one of them. "Put the bugger out of his misery."

"All right. Yes." I held out my hand and Lewis slipped the ring on my finger. Such a fabulous jewel, twinkling with grandeur, was beyond any of my expectations and I couldn't stop smiling.

Lewis leapt to his feet and swept me into an embrace. The boys cheered and whooped. Soon there was quite a crowd, wondering what all the kerfuffle was about.

"Come on, everyone." Lewis pointed over the road. "To the Star Inn. Drinks are on me!"

I nestled into him. "You're crazy."

"Crazy about you," he said, taking my arm to steer me across the road. Ahead, a phalanx of strangers led the way into the pub. At the bar, Lewis slapped down several one-pound notes and ordered us two beers.

When everyone had a glass in their hand, riotous toasts were made to the happy couple and then we slipped into a corner booth.

"Start as we mean to go on, eh?" he said.

I lifted my beer glass. "Not unless you want me to get fat."

He laughed. "Champagne must wait for the wedding. A big society affair, I think, don't you? It's what my parents will want. I know your parents have died, so we'll foot the bill. And you must invite whatever family and friends you want."

A sudden chill raised goosebumps on my arms. "There's something I must tell you." I stumbled over the words. "Arcadia is my middle name. My other name is Jane. Terrible, I know." I tried to make an unconcerned laugh, but it came out as a cackle.

"Your point being?"

"I thought you should know." If he ever found my papers, he'd see everything said Jane Robin. Best to clear up any misunderstanding now. "As for the wedding," I gabbled on, giving him no time for comment, "don't you think we're too modern for all the pomp and circumstance of hundreds of guests when so many are still starving after the Great War?" I thought of Charlie's parents, and how upset they'd be to learn I'd remarried. In their eyes, I'd remain Charlie's bride forever. A large society wedding would be splashed across the papers and was bound to be reported in Guernsey.

Lewis hugged me. "Oh, you darling. What would you do? Race off to a registry office?"

That's exactly what I'd prefer – anything to avoid causing more pain to Charlie's family. They never needed to know. "How romantic, Lewis. Let's do it. Forget the fanfare, just you and me."

For a split second he frowned, and I thought he might back

out. I flashed my diamond ring, tilted it to the light, and gave him my most alluring smile.

"My mother will have a fit."

"Let's give a large donation to war veterans. Would that make her happy?"

He grunted. "I doubt it. She can be a cranky dear when the mood takes her." He grabbed my hand and pulled me to my feet. "If we hurry, we'll be in time for the 5.50 to Victoria, and I shall take you for oysters, quail's eggs and cocktails at Rules. Tomorrow I'll get the licence while you shop for a trousseau. What do you say?"

It sounded marvellous, but... "I'm due at work tomorrow." Early on, I'd had to admit that I supported my publishing aspirations by working alongside other authors. True, I made it sound grander than the reality, implying I was more an editor than typist, but Lewis was none the wiser.

He popped a kiss on my forehead. "My darling, forget about that dusty old place. You've got me to look after now. Perfect isn't it? And you can get stuck into writing that book of yours." He drew an imaginary banner in the air. "I can see it now. My wife, Arcadia Fanstone, famous authoress. As for me, I shall be your book carrier and keep the hoards at bay while they queue at your signings."

We pushed through the crowd to a chorus of back-slapping and congratulations. Lewis handed the publican another wad of cash, and to a roar of approval, we hurried off to the railway station.

~

LONDON, JANUARY 1924

A couple of stiff martinis the worse for wear, Lewis crashed down the narrow hallway of our Cheyne Walk mews and into the sitting room, waving a sheaf of papers. "I've found the answer for you." He plonked a kiss on my forehead and flopped, sprawling, onto the sofa, one leg hanging over the armrest.

Somewhat preoccupied with a rather large problem, I had little time for Lewis's latest enthusiasm but nevertheless, it acted as a distraction. "And what was the question?" I asked.

"How to get you published, of course." He stretched an arm to the wall and tugged the bell-pull.

After twelve rejections from twelve publishers, I'd all but given up hope of seeing *The Party Dress* in bookshops. My hastily written rags-to-riches story about a young woman who designs a ball gown which wins a competition, and leads to her success as one of London's leading couturiers, had not captured anyone's imagination. "Have you come across another publisher?"

"Better." Lewis tapped the papers in his hand. "I met a chap at the club who knows a chap who has some sort of printing press. For a fee, he'll print your book. And he knows a chap who, for a percentage, will take your novel to the bookshops. What do you make of that?" He gave a smug smile.

Well, it was better than nothing. "How much is the fee?"

"Oh, never you mind about that. I'll take care of it."

Dear Lewis. He so loves to surprise and pamper me.

"Virginia Woolf published her own books, you know." Lewis also loved to show off snippets of trivia. "If it's good enough for her and all that. All you have to do is sign here." He flipped through the papers and passed them across. "Ah, Benson." Lewis's manservant hovered in the door. "A whisky and some walnuts. Anything for you, darling?"

A wave of nausea caught at my throat. "Just water."

I have to tell him, but maybe not tonight. One baby at a time. My book first, and then... a boy? A girl? Oh please, not a girl. Girls tended to be needy and faced so much opposition in life. Boys took care of themselves. And a boy, silly as it may seem, in some crazy way would make up for the loss of Charlie. It would also make it easier to tell his parents – and my family – that I'd remarried.

Lewis broke my train of thought. "Damned exciting, eh?"

I twiddled my wedding ring. With any luck, we could get *The Party Dress* released before I began to show. I tore myself back to the matter I *could* control. "We'll need a book launch. Something flashy and memorable."

"I'll rent a reception room at Claridges."

How stuffy. "I'd far rather take over one of the jazz clubs. The Kit Kat, perhaps? Have a themed event in keeping with the book. We'll have a competition for the best dress design. I'll ask Paul Poiret to be the judge." He owed me a favour. I'd never quite forgiven him for not awarding me that twenty-five guinea cheque. And, given he was all the rage in Paris, I'd ask him to design my gown. My mind raced ahead. Everyone important must be there. "We must invite the Mitfords. Cecil. And Edith of course. Do you think the Prince will come?"

"You betcha, if he's not off chasing heiresses in America." Benson returned, laid out our drinks and discreetly backed out of the room. "You make a list, darling. Whatever you want." Lewis took a slug of whisky and peered at me. "You look a little peaky. The shock of finally getting your book out, I dare say."

I smoothed my hands over my stomach. "I dare say."

LONDON, SEPTEMBER 1924

The baby is a dear, sweet thing, but my goodness she is noisy. Lewis dotes on her. In his eyes she can do no possible wrong. His little possum, he calls her, and he constantly pops into the nursery 'for a peek'. Nanny, fortunately, is strict about routine and makes sure I'm not bothered except to breastfeed the wee mite – and soon that horror will be over, as we are weaning her onto a bottle.

Smelling of baby powder, she steals the show when Nanny brings her in at cocktail hour, and any guest who's dropped in coos over her. Eventually I'm allowed a goodnight cuddle – all the time crossing my fingers she won't spoil my dress – before it's off to her cot.

Tonight, only Teddy Aysgarth and Boy Millscroft popped in on their way to the opening night of Gershwin's new musical, *Primrose*. Lovely couple. So glad they've got people like us to visit where they can relax and be themselves. They had Lewis and me in fits of giggles singing their camped-up version of 'Boy Wanted'.

After they'd left for the theatre, dancing down the mews in high spirits, the living room felt bleak and lifeless. "Put some music on," I suggested. "I'm in the mood for more Gershwin."

Lewis cranked up the gramophone and settled the needle over 'Rhapsody in Blue'. It's the latest rage and we can't stop playing it.

"Marvellous," I murmured and leaned my head against the back of my chair, listening to the lilting strains of clarinet.

Benson, who has a terrific knack for good timing, came in bearing a letter on a silver plate. "G and Ts, Benson, please." I picked up the paper knife and checked the postmark. Guernsey. The handwriting belonged to Mavis. How unusual, we never corresponded except for an obligatory Christmas card. Something must have happened to Mother.

I waited for the violins to reach a crescendo, then slit open the envelope. Benson sidled over and I took the crystal glass he proffered before unfolding the single sheet of airmail paper.

Dearest–

I write with the most wonderful news. A true blessing. Charlie has returned...

The piano in the background played in time to the quickening of my heartbeat. I couldn't comprehend what I was reading. What Mavis had written made no sense. It was my worst nightmare and my ultimate fantasy: Charlie returning, unharmed, from the battlefields of France. I'd dreamed of it for so long, praying for an impossible miracle, but now it had happened I felt ill, worse than I had ever felt during my pregnancy. A dull thud of sickness pounded in my stomach and my head. *Oh God.*

I looked across at Lewis. He caught my eye and frowned. "What is it, darling? You've gone sheet white."

What should I tell him? I'd never spoken of Charlie. Oh, I had my reasons. What little I'd had of Charlie's life, I wanted to keep to myself and never share with anyone. I could hardly blurt out that my husband had reappeared. *Oh God.* My husband, Charlie. My husband, Lewis. *Oh God.*

"Darling?" Lewis prompted. "You're worrying me. What's in the letter? Bad news?"

I tried to remember what I'd told Lewis about my family but my brain refused to function. No brothers or sisters. An aunt in Yorkshire. My father, dead. My mother– Had I told him my mother was dead? Or merely ill?

Caught in a horrible tangled web, I said the first thing which came to me. "A schoolfriend. My best friend. Luella." I'd never known a Luella. "She's been in a terrible accident." I scrunched up the piece of paper and shoved it in my pocket. "I have to go north for the funeral. Tomorrow."

Lewis relaxed. "Sorry to hear that. Will you be gone long?"

"A few days." I tried to calculate. A day's ferry journey to Guernsey and then what would greet me? What would I say? Where had Charlie been? Did he know where I was? Why had Mavis written, not he? I desperately wanted to smooth out her letter and read on, find clues, learn more. "I better check the train times and pack my things. Black, I suppose." I stood, amazed my legs held me up. "Excuse me."

The music accelerated its pace, a frenzy of orchestration. Lewis sipped on his gin and shut his eyes. "Take your time. I'm not going anywhere. And don't worry about arranging anything for me while you're away, I'll take my meals at the club."

I slipped from the room, knowing with sick certainty that something had changed tonight that could never be righted. I'd long ago locked Charlie away in a corner of my heart only I could reach, and I'd tug out a memory to comfort me during dark hours when the raw loss of him smashed me again. No one was hurt by my moments of self-indulgence, but now it was as if my terrible grief had conjured him from his grave.

14

ARCADIA

GUERNSEY, SEPTEMBER 1924

*M*y heart sank when I stepped onto the quay at St Peter Port and as I feared, Mavis was waiting for me. Despite not having seen her for a few years, I really didn't want to be bothered with her. She'd want to take charge, and claim priority over the situation. I took in her prim coat with its neat buttons. Shiny shoes. Tightly clasped black handbag at her waist. Pursed lips and eager expression.

I walked towards her, momentarily struck by the oddness of being back amongst the oh-so-familiar surroundings that seemed conversely alien and remote, and kissed her smartly on the cheek. "What a turn-up." I tried to sound brisk and surprised.

In truth, my head hurt from lack of sleep and churning thoughts. Charlie's return meant I'd have to divorce Lewis. If we were even legally married. Where did that leave my daughter? How on earth could I explain this muddle to Charlie and my family when no one knew about Lewis or the baby. As for my family – Father's behaviour had forfeited all desire to ever see them again. Yet here I was, back in St Peter Port to be reunited with my husband.

Mavis spilled over with sombre excitement. "You can't

imagine the past few days. Charlie appeared at his mother's funeral, looking like... like–"

That caught my attention. "How did she die?"

"Cancer, they said. Anyway, you'll see for yourself, but he's not in a good way."

"Where is he?"

Mavis took my arm and pulled me to her. She spoke in a hushed whisper. "There's more. Two nights ago, he found his father hanging from a hook nailed into the rafters of the old stables."

"What?" I couldn't take it in. Both parents dead?

"People said he only kept going for his wife's sake. He'd come back from the war badly shell-shocked and in a miserable way. Without her, I imagine he saw no point carrying on. We'll never know, as he left no note."

Poor Charlie. What a homecoming; it beggared belief. "Where is he?" I asked again.

"In the shed at the bottom of the garden. He won't come out. I've tried and tried. All he says is, 'Where's my darling Jane?'. I've tried to find out where he's been all this time but he won't answer. Thank goodness you're here at last." She didn't sound relieved but put out. "We'll go right there if you like."

"No, we won't."

"Oh... yes... of course... you'd like to freshen up... have breakfast–"

"I'll go on my own, thank you, Mavis." It was bad enough that I hadn't been here to greet him, and comfort him through the past few days. I didn't need my sanctimonious sister watching our reunion. I hastened my step in the direction of the bus stop. "We can talk later."

Mavis dropped my arm. "I told him you were away on holiday and we weren't sure when you'd be back. I didn't know what else to say."

I hadn't given any thought to how I'd explain my absence.

How irritating and typical of Mavis that she'd had the fore-thought to provide my excuses, which I'd now be stuck with, whether I approved or not.

"I shan't contradict you," I said. "Don't worry." I handed her my case and said I'd see her later.

The exterior of Charlie's old home looked as neat and tidy as ever, the only sign of a lack of maintenance being the slightly overgrown hedge. In trepidation, I opened the squeaky back gate and made my way past the greenhouse to the end of the garden. I looked across at the old stables – in disrepair, the horses sold off many years before – and swallowed hard, trying not to imagine the scene that had confronted Charlie.

The shed was closed up and silent. Aside from some scratching in the undergrowth – a bird perhaps, or a hedgehog – there was nothing to suggest Charlie's presence. I looked up to the sky for, oh I don't know what – strength? Inspiration? I wanted to turn away, pelt back to the harbour, and jump on the first boat no matter where it was headed. Pretend this wasn't happening. But how could I when a few feet away, closeted in the outhouse, Charlie suffered far more than I did at this moment. And by Mavis's account, he needed me.

I knocked gently on the door and knelt with my ear to the wood paling. "Charlie, it's Jane."

There was a scuffling and then a muffled voice, which was hard to understand. "A-are you on y-your own?"

It didn't sound like Charlie, but I knew there had been no mistake, this wasn't some dream scenario I'd soon wake from. "Yes. Just me. Can I come in?"

"Y-yes," he growled.

I pushed open the door and took a second to acclimatise to the gloom. In the corner, behind a stack of planter boxes, a figure was curled over, rocking. It took all my self-control not to react to this shell of a man, hideously deformed, scarred almost beyond recognition, his clothes tattered and dirt-encrusted.

I pressed my hand to my mouth to stop from gasping out loud, and went to his side. I knelt, and gently placed my arm around him. His shoulder felt bony and he shook. "Charlie?" I glanced down, and saw he had only one leg. The other had been cut off at the knee.

The face which stared up at me was unrecognisable, but the eyes hadn't altered – except for a deep pain, which shrouded what once had been youthful optimism.

When he spoke, he stuttered, catching his breath in pain. "You c-came." His eyes filled with tears which spilled down his mangled cheeks. "You w-waited for me."

That's when my heart disintegrated. What a fraud I was, what a faithless wife I'd been. I'd lost belief in his survival and far from waiting, I'd run away and into the arms of another husband. I squeezed him even tighter and he reached up to stroke my face. "Our love k-kept me alive."

At the touch of his hand on my skin my resolve fell away. Charlie, my Charlie, had come home to me. I held him close until the shaking subsided.

"Let's get you inside," I said. "Clean you up, and then we can talk."

Leaning heavily on me and using a garden hoe for balance, we managed to get to the house. I filled a tub with warm water and persuaded him to let me peel away his clothes and wash his wounds. His arms and part of his back were badly scarred. As for his amputated leg, he told me he suffered dreadful phantom pains. I soaped the stump and when I glanced at him to be sure I hadn't caused more suffering, his head was thrown back and more tears coursed down.

"Am I hurting you?" I asked. "We need to get you to a doctor."

"No, no." He became quite agitated. "M-mustn't."

I kept my voice gentle, feeling out of my depth and terrified that I'd do or say something to cause Charlie to clam up. "What happened?"

"I c-can't tell you." He took the towel I offered and wrapped it around his shrunken body. "I'm too ash-ashamed."

"I'm your wife. You must. No secrets between us." I turned away, appalled by my hypocrisy, but seeing no alternative – not just yet, anyway. Later, perhaps, when he could cope.

I went in search of clean clothes and found some pyjamas of his father's. With difficulty, I got him into them and then, with my shoulder for support, led him down the hallway to the first bedroom.

Once in bed, he seemed to relax a little. "You c-can't tell. Ever."

I took both his hands and promised that whatever had happened would remain strictly between the two of us. I'd never tell anyone, nor ever write it down. I listened while he very slowly told his dreadful story. The strain was enormous, and he had to stop every now and then to recover his breath. Day turned to dusk and I could tell the effort had worn him out.

"I'm going to pop back to see Mavis and get my bag, but I'll return later," I said.

He gripped my arm. "W-what will you say?"

"What would you like me to say?"

In halting words he gave me his well-rehearsed cover story for his long absence, and I assured him it was what I'd repeat; he need have no fears of being found out. Only one aspect of it held a truth: he'd returned to Guernsey because he had to see his darling Jane one more time, knowing he didn't have long to live; his injuries were too far beyond reparation to hope for many more months, let alone years.

∾

I found Mavis busy in her kitchen, bursting with curiosity. While she filled the teapot from the kettle and swirled the tea leaves with a long spoon, I worked to get my thoughts in order.

"Please sit. Help yourself." She poured tea and lifted the covers off the serving plates: paste sandwiches and a bowl of fruit salad. I filled a plate and murmured polite appreciation. I had no appetite but peeled an orange, picked away the pith, and separated the segments. Through the open window came the tuneless strains of a man whistling 'Swanee' as he walked past.

Mavis removed her apron and sat opposite at the kitchen table. "Tell me everything. How is he?"

I burst into a great torrent of tears. My sobs came out of nowhere, overwhelming me like a tsunami, and I struggled for coherent thought. The shock of the last twenty-four hours swamped me, and I couldn't make sense of my muddled feelings. I ached for Charlie: broken in so many ways and dealing with such horrendous wounds. What a burden he'd carried, and now he was asking me to help shoulder some of his shame. I couldn't refuse him and yet, had I known he'd survived, how different these last years would have been. I tried to staunch my distress but then new realisations piled on one another – it wasn't just Charlie who had suffered and was now in a bind. Choices had to be made. What on earth was I to do?

Mavis, to be fair, let me cry my eyes out while the tears I'd never wept for Charlie – not even after I heard he'd died – poured from me. She found me a handkerchief when mine was too sodden to be of use and waited until I could speak.

"Sorry, Mavis, it's all been such a shock." I dabbed at my eyes. "He's in such a terrible way. Not just physically, but his mental state." I bit down on my lip and repeated what he'd told me to say – some truth, some lies. "He was taken prisoner of war but wasn't properly operated on. As a result, he lost a leg and never received an artificial limb, and his face, which caught a shell blast, got infected causing even more scarring and damage."

Mavis sharply inhaled. "How dreadful. But why did we never know?"

I stayed faithful to Charlie's reimagined version of events. "When he was captured, he was unconscious. After he came round, he had no memory. And according to the Germans, he had no ID. One moment he was in the trenches, he said, and after that, he only has blurred memories of camps and hospitals. When the war ended, he found his way to Scotland – I'm not sure how – and survived by helping a laird, who let him live in one of his shepherds' huts. Gradually he regained his memory and, well, you know the rest." Tears threatened again, but this was not the time. I had to think, to plan, decide how far I could trust Mavis. "It doesn't matter how deformed he is, underneath, inside, he's still Charlie, the boy I loved. Still love. But I'm in an awful predicament."

"I can imagine... you've made your life in London and coming back here will be a huge upheaval. And looking after an invalid–"

I cut her off. "Stop it, Mavis." I couldn't bear to hear her carrying on, knowing what was best, making assumptions about things she knew nothing about. "Stop presuming you have all the answers. Stop presuming you understand everything that's at stake."

"I'm only trying to help."

Oh dear. I hadn't meant to sound so harsh. In truth, I needed Mavis on my side. We may never have been very close as sisters, but now – for the first time ever – on finding myself in desperate straits I wanted her advice. Or at the very least, her sympathy for my situation.

On the bus journey here after seeing Charlie, I'd turned everything over this way and that. I could see a possible fix, but it was daring and risky, and my only chance of success was by throwing myself on Mavis's mercy. It was a long shot, but if my sister could be persuaded to see things from my point of view and set aside her own set of long-held scruples, perhaps we could find a workable solution.

But first, I had to fill her in on a few gaps. I took a deep breath and just blurted it out, with no embellishment or excuses. "I'm married, Mavis. What's more, I have a baby. A daughter." There, I'd said it.

Mavis's face was a picture of shock. She said nothing, just stared at me with her mouth open, looking like a fish waiting to catch feed. Finally, she composed herself. "Poor Charlie."

"He doesn't know. I dare not tell him. He's been through enough and learning this would destroy him. Oh Mavis, what am I to do?"

Mavis squared her shoulders. "Return to London. I'll take care of Charlie. Cut the cord, go back to your, er, new husband and bring up your child."

I furrowed my brow and shook my head. "I love Charlie, Mavis. I've always loved him. I can't leave him now. Not when he needs me more than ever."

"Then you must divorce this other chap." She picked at a minute piece of fluff on her immaculate skirt.

Her peremptory advice annoyed me. "His name is Lewis," I said, "and I can't. I love him too, it's as simple as that."

Mavis's eyebrows shot up.

"Besides, think of the consequences. I've no way of knowing how Lewis might react, how hurt and angry he'd be. His mother hates me, thinks I'm not good enough for him, and I've no doubt she'd insist he demand sole custody of our daughter, who he adores. He'd get it too, once the courts got wind I'd lied about my marriage to Charlie. Even if, and it's a big *if*, Lewis allowed me to keep the baby, he might refuse to help support us financially. Imagine the intolerable pressure it would put me under, bringing up a child on my own."

"See sense, Jane. It's clear Charlie will never recover, and meanwhile you've got your whole life ahead. There's no logic to throwing away your future for a broken man. As for me, William's died, I've no children, I can easily look after Charlie."

Overlooked by Charlie, I'd always suspected Mavis only married William to ensure I wouldn't pip her to the altar. And now she saw her opportunity to get her own back, but I wouldn't be swayed. Ignoring her suggestions, I ploughed on. "I have a plan, but I need your help and absolute secrecy because what I'm about to suggest is illegal and could land us all in jail."

"No—"

"Hear me out. I've told Charlie that I run a publishing company. School books. I didn't tell him I write novels because he'd want to read them, and then he'd learn I publish under a different name which would be hurtful. Tomorrow, I'm going to tell him that in order to pay his medical bills, it's best I return to London and keep working, but I'll come back to Guernsey often. Every summer, say, and whenever else I can manage."

"It would never work."

"You've said it yourself – he's not got long to live. At most, it might be a year, maybe two. But at least he'll know happiness and that I never abandoned him. And Mavis, you've already said you'll look after him so we can make it work. Truly, we can."

Mavis stood and brushed down her skirt. The sandwiches were curling at the edges, and she covered the plate before taking it to the pantry. I watched her without saying a word; I knew she was thinking it over... her chance to play let's pretend with Charlie.

"He'll write to you. Telephone. How can you avoid being found out?"

I was ready for her. "I'll get a post office box. You can write to me there too, if ever there's an emergency. He won't telephone, I'm certain, his speech is too badly impaired. And there's no phone in his house."

Mavis still needed convincing. "What if he needs treatment only available on the mainland?"

For a second, I hesitated, knowing I must choose my words with care. "Charlie mustn't be found. If he stays on the island, it should be all right though."

"What do you mean?"

"Trust me."

"Oh, you mean he's worried how people will treat him because of his frightening appearance. He'd rather be left alone."

I didn't deny it.

"You've got guts, Jane, I'll give you that." Mavis narrowed her eyes and took her time. "Charlie deserves kindness, and eternal thanks for his wartime sacrifice."

I held my breath. Agreeing to nurse Charlie was a big undertaking. Agreeing to protect me from discovery was even bigger.

"I'll be honest," she said. "I always thought one day Charlie and I... well, it didn't happen that way, he fell for you instead. But we all grew up together and that counts for a lot. So God help me, I'll do this."

"Oh, Mavis..." A torrent of relief flooded through me, and I feared I'd faint. Despite my entreaties, I hadn't really expected her acquiescence and I could only manage a weak smile of gratitude.

She squeezed my hand and gave a brief nod of understanding. "It's decided."

It was a dangerous game we were embarking on. One that would need all my skills of deception. If Lewis ever got a sniff of Charlie's existence, all hell would break loose, he'd divorce me, and without doubt I'd lose my dear darling daughter, Esme.

15

ESME

GUERNSEY, AUGUST 1958

The grandfather clock struck five, and Esme shuffled her papers together. Tonight, Anthony was taking her out, and her first priority was to have a bath and wash her hair. Although it was silly, she couldn't help the tremor of pleasure she felt every time she thought of seeing him again.

"Don't get your hopes up, Esme Fanstone," she murmured and turned her mind to what she could wear that Anthony hadn't already seen. All her clothes were more serviceable than fashionable or frivolous. She peered out the window. The clouds had disappeared, and the sun beamed down. She'd dress up her black jersey shirtwaister with a red belt and red neck scarf. It would have to do.

About to run up the stairs, she saw the day's mail lying on the hall mat and pulled out an airmail envelope – a letter from London, addressed to the local post office and efficiently rerouted to Junction Cottage. She went cold when she saw Hugh's handwriting. What could he possibly have to say?

She slowly climbed the stairs and went into the bathroom. After turning on the taps, she put aside the letter on the bath rack, dreading its contents.

Once undressed, gasping at the sting of hot water, she eased into the tub and shampooed her hair. After rinsing it, she lay back against the stone rim, trying to ignore Hugh's familiar, hasty italic scribble staring out at her, until she could bear it no longer. In one movement, she swung out of the bath, wrapped a pink towel around her body and another around her head in a turban. Clutching Hugh's letter, she padded barefoot back to the bedroom and perched on the side of the bed.

The envelope contained a single sheet of watermarked Basildon Bond paper, covered in Hugh's quirky green ink from his trusty Osmiroid fountain pen.

Dear Esme–

Where to begin, my dear? I feel such a fool. It took what should have been an amiable Sunday stroll in Hyde Park to make me realise, frankly I had made a big mistake. Can you forgive me, I wonder? I am mortified when I recall introducing you to 'the future Mrs Tate'. How crass of me. How could I have been so blind not to see what was clearly in front of my nose?

Miranda, despite her protestations otherwise, kept stalling about leaving for America. Finally, I confronted her (see the walk in Hyde Park, above). She freely admitted that she never thought marriage to me would mean leaving all her friends and family behind. I ask you! We had discussed it on many occasions. She seemed to think going to America was like going on a shopping trip to Harrods, and she'd be home by teatime. The girl is frankly, a simpleton. We had a row and I took myself off around the duck pond, which was when I had my epiphany.

It's you, darling Esme, it always has been. All those years crammed together in the same office, working cheek by jowl, and I never saw it. Please, please forgive me and reconsider. Come back to London and let's plan our future together. I know we will make a great team. Frankly, the office has fallen apart since you left. No one knows anything, not even how to find a paperclip. I plan to keep the London paper going but God knows how they'll cope without our joint guidance. And I am miserable, not seeing your sunny smile each day and the way you frown while you chew the top of your pencil.

America will be the biggest adventure imaginable. A new frontier with opportunities galore. Please, please pack your bags and get off that island and come home so that I can propose to you properly. On one knee, if you like. Say YES.

Hugh

A tight knot twisted in her stomach and a sour taste filled her mouth. She screwed the piece of paper into a ball and placed it on the bedside table. It was the letter she'd waited years to receive and yet, now she had it, what did it contain? Words, empty words. Nothing about love. No concern about her welfare. No interest in her progress with her novel. So why did she feel a flutter of hope? How could she even consider granting a molecule of clemency for his boorish behaviour?

She smoothed out the sheet of paper and reread the contents. Wasn't this what she'd always dreamed of, prayed for? Was it shallow of her to want a declaration of love and be hurt at its lack, when surely that was what Hugh meant? She mustn't be too harsh on him. After all, he admitted he'd been a fool, asked her forgiveness, hoped it wasn't too late. Of course he wasn't perfect, and understandably he'd miss her efficient management of the office. As an Englishman, perhaps writing down his feelings didn't come naturally. She could tell by his almost illegible scrawl he'd written hastily, presumably eager to get his thoughts down and into the post. Unlike a woman, he wouldn't consider each word, each sentence, to ensure every aspect of intent was clearly enunciated. Maybe he wanted to hear her response first, and then tell her of his love, his passion, to her face.

A reluctant worm crept into her heart. Did she even want this? She'd spent the last few weeks getting over her disappointment and had even started to enjoy Anthony's company. Could her feelings alter so quickly? She didn't believe it possible. Hugh had been a fixture in her heart for too long to be so easily dismissed.

She shivered, suddenly aware of her wet hair and the damp towel clinging to her body. The bright prospect of dinner with Anthony and sharing their findings had dimmed. It wasn't that she'd prefer to sit at home and brood over Hugh. Quite the contrary. She was cross with Hugh for spoiling her evening, because now she wouldn't be able to shake his letter from her mind until she'd decided how to respond.

As for Anthony, she didn't want to lose his friendship, nor did she want to lead him on. She'd clear the air between them and tell him about Hugh. Soon. Tonight. Before things got sticky.

Anthony was waiting outside the Prince of Wales, and his face lit with joy when he spotted her coming down the street. Unbuttoned jacket flapping, tie bobbing over his shoulder, he strode towards her. "Aren't you a welcome sight," he said, leaning in to peck her on the cheek.

She dodged his embrace by straightening his tie. "You need a tiepin."

"I don't. I've got plenty. My mother gives me one every Christmas in the hope I'll remember to wear it." He took Esme's hand and pulled her in the direction of the pub, but she shook him off. "Something wrong?"

"I need to speak to you."

"Ah." He plunged his hands deep into his trouser pockets and rocked on his heels. "It's about that kiss, isn't it?"

For a moment, she hesitated. "Let's go inside. We can't talk standing out in the street."

In the cramped, low-beamed lounge bar, Anthony motioned Esme to a corner table while he bought drinks. She watched him lean against the bar, foot on the brass guardrail, passing pleasantries with the landlord. A man comfortable in his own skin, and yet she knew so little about him, and vice versa. Their conversations had mostly revolved around unearthing the meaning of the letter to Arcadia. He'd not asked about previous boyfriends, neither had he mentioned any love interest in his life.

He slid onto the bench seat beside her and emptied a small bottle of tomato juice into her glass.

She chinked her drink against his mug of beer. "Cheers."

Anthony pushed his spectacles up the bridge of his nose. "Talk to me."

Esme took a deep breath. "There was... is–"

"A man." He sounded resigned.

"His name is Hugh. I thought it was over between us. To be honest, it never really started. And now... I don't know... I'm in a muddle." She ran her hands through her hair.

"Because I kissed you?"

"Yes and no."

"Go on."

"I like you. You've been marvellous ever since I arrived. But I need to know where I stand with Hugh, and it wouldn't be fair to lead you on. It wouldn't be honest." She scanned his earnest face, trying to read his expression.

Frowning a little, he tipped his head to one side. "Yes, you must. There's nothing worse than loose ends, or forever wondering 'what if'."

"You sound as if you've been there."

"I had a girlfriend for six years. Belinda. Our parents introduced us. In the beginning she was great fun. She loved parties, dressing up, dancing till dawn, that sort of thing. I'd fall in with her plans, but in truth, the constant socialising wore me down. I expect I was a bit of a bore, studying hard for my final exams. Everyone started to sort of assume we'd get married as soon as I qualified and could afford a down payment on a house. Yet while everyone around me was getting engaged, I couldn't quite bring myself to propose. It got to be a bit of a joke. Last man standing and all that."

"What stopped you? Were you afraid of such a big commitment?"

"Not at all. I loved Belinda, but over time, more like a sister. We got on well and were great chums, but I wasn't too sure what we really had in common. My head told me we'd make a good team, as well as making our parents happy. But in my heart I couldn't help thinking, is this all there is? I agonised for over a year, convinced if I ended it, I'd have regrets."

"And did you?"

"End it? Yes. Have regrets? No." He looked up at the overhead beams. "Not quite true. I regretted wasting her young years when she could have been meeting a far better man. But, selfishly, I was also glad I'd taken the time to make the right decision for me. In fact, it was another reason for coming here. To make it easier on her, be out of her way, nowhere in sight." He squeezed Esme's hand where it lay in her lap. "So, whilst I'm disappointed to know there's someone else in the queue – because I'm in danger of becoming quite smitten with you – I applaud your frankness. I promise I shan't get in the way and I'll continue to help you solve the puzzle of your mother."

Esme took a long sip of juice. He was so horribly nice, she almost wanted to cry. "Thank you," she said at last. "I'd hate not to be friends."

"Oh, me too. And by the way, don't take my little speech to mean I've given up. All I'm saying is that I'll be on best behaviour."

Esme smiled and, with a pang of reluctance, slipped her hand from the warmth of his grasp.

~

Esme lay in bed, her mind churning, fearful she'd made a fatal error by telling Anthony about Hugh. It hit her with unexpected force that she'd developed strong feelings for Anthony. His insistence that they remain friends might just have been kind words, and the idea that she might never see him again panicked her. She loved his enthusiasm for finding her family, his spontaneity, and his thoughtfulness. She loved the little creases that furrowed his forehead when he considered a question. And the way he'd spoken of Belinda showed him to be honourable and true to himself.

And yet... nothing would shift her long-held image of pausing at the church lychgate on her father's arm, before heading up the aisle to where Hugh waited to love and cherish her, for better or worse. She'd been so sure of their future: building the business together, returning home each evening to a smart London town house, sharing every decision, ambition, private longing. For years, she'd dreamed of long nights in Hugh's arms. Of babies. Of growing old.

He'd ripped all that from under her, destroyed her hopes and made a fool of her misplaced affections. Yet she still wasn't sure she wanted to cut all ties with him. His letter had stirred up all sorts of confused feelings – anger, relief, longing – and surely she owed it to herself to unravel them and come to a conclusion she could live with. How terrible if in a fit of jealousy over the short-lived Miranda, she'd thrown away her chance of true happiness with him.

Dawn filtered its dusky light through the bedroom, and Esme lay on her back staring at the shadows dancing on the ceiling. Anthony. Hugh. Was it possible she loved two men at the same time? She closed her eyes, shocked; to be capable of such a thing was unthinkable. Love was a steadfast emotion; love meant being true to one man; love wasn't a game of cards to be shuffled and gambled with. Love signified till death do us part. Anything less was unnatural; it certainly wasn't love. Infatuation, perhaps. Not love.

Anthony was right, she had to sort out her heart.

Maybe she'd set Hugh a test. In his letter he'd asked her to come back to London. What if she asked him to come here? Whatever happened, she intended to spend a few more weeks in St Peter Port. It struck her as monumentally important that Hugh understand why Guernsey captured her imagination, how coming here had fuelled her desire to find a connection to her roots. If he really cared about her, he'd come. And they could get to know each other – properly, as a prospective couple, not as work colleagues – but this time on her territory.

And if he said no? Did she just run into Anthony's arms? How crass of her, to be overthrown by one man and then pick up with another waiting in the wings. Although wasn't that exactly what Hugh was doing?

16

ARCADIA

GUERNSEY, JUNE 1927

*B*y the time we docked at St Peter Port, I was a wreck. If it hadn't been for a charming woman who also travelled with a child, and offered the services of her nanny to help with Esme, I'm not sure what I would have done. Flung myself overboard, most likely. How on earth do people cope? I'd planned to have a quiet dinner, read my book and settle in for the night. But no, Esme jumped up and down, ran around the cabins or out on the deck, and when I did get her to sit still, she kept up a stream of chatter and refused to eat the meal I ordered. Apparently Nanny never gives her steak. That was when Audrey Carstairs intervened and Esme trotted off with her little boy and their nanny for playtime. For an hour peace reigned, accompanied by a welcome whisky sour with Audrey. Two, actually. But all the excitement exhausted Esme and by the time I tucked the little poppet into her bunk and kissed her forehead, her eyes were folding over into sleep. Mine, too.

At the harbour, I had to manage Esme's feverish curiosity, farewells to my travel companion, and two suitcases, without being spotted and recognised. Fortunately, it was too early in the morning for many folk to be out, and despite Esme frolicking with excitement, exclaiming her fascination with the boats, cobbled streets and a vociferous newspaper seller, I bundled her into a cab without mishap.

When I dropped her off with her case in St Martin, I warned Mavis. I felt I had to. "She's a very busy little girl." I looked around Mavis's stern living room with its clean lines and lack of ornamentation. What on earth would the child do to keep occupied?

Mavis knelt down and gave Esme a hug. "We'll be fine together, won't we, Esme?" She looked at me. "What should she call me?"

"Mrs Lucas," I said firmly.

Mavis's face fell.

"Oh, don't be silly, Mavis. She can't possibly call you Aunt." I took Esme by the hand and walked her to the French windows. "Mrs Lucas has rabbits. Would you like to see them?"

"Flopsy and Mopsy?" Esme asked.

I wasn't at all sure what she meant, but I nodded and opened the door. "Kiss Mummy goodbye. I'll be back in a few days." Esme pecked my cheek, far more interested in rabbits, and skipped into the garden.

"I thought you were here for six weeks." Standing by the window, Mavis kept an eye on her young charge.

"I am, but Esme won't understand the difference. Time holds no meaning for children."

"Will you visit?"

"Better not. It would be upsetting for her. And what if she called me Mummy and someone heard? Rather hard to explain." Even bringing her was a risk, but I'd had no choice, what with Nanny abruptly handing in her notice, for which I blame Lewis. He can be so indiscreet. It's one thing to squire someone in our set, but chasing after a domestic's skirt is plain daft. Beneath him. He said it was a momentary slip and blamed it on all this talk of a looming stock market catastrophe. Told me I should take my head out of the sand and face reality. We'd had quite a blue.

I'd considered leaving Esme with Granny Fanstone but the mere idea of picking up the telephone and asking for a favour stuck in my gullet. Besides, she always takes the waters in Harrogate at this time of year. All I could do was pray Mavis would stick to our story and not slip up.

"I still don't see why she shouldn't call me Auntie Mavis," she said.

Auntie? I shuddered.

"After all, if Esme's supposed to be the daughter of an old friend of mine, sent here for a holiday, it's natural she'd call me Auntie."

I ignored her. Her logic made sense but was too close to the truth. And could cause problems when we returned to England if Esme began jabbering about staying with her Aunt Mavis. "If anyone asks, you have a friend in St Thomas' Hospital having back surgery and you're looking after her little girl until she's recuperated."

"I shall enjoy having her here. You mustn't worry. I shall find lots for us to do. Exploring, walks, a treasure hunt. I'll go to Mother's attic and see what's in the dress-up chest. I think our doll's house might still be up there." Poor Mavis. Were these the things she'd hoped one day to do with her own children?

I hadn't visited the island for seven months. Lewis, bless him, decided we should go on a book tour now that I'd had half a dozen romances published. We went to seaside towns in the south of England where I did readings, signings and book soirées: Ilfracombe, Bournemouth, Torquay. It was quite a lark. We followed the smart set to be sure of interesting company and plentiful audiences. Lewis sent out racy invitations to journalists who, after enjoying outrageous company together with free food and booze, gave marvellous reviews. "You're developing a certain notoriety, darling," he said, pleased to be travelling on my coat-tails. But it meant longer gaps between trips to Guernsey.

"How's Charlie been?" I asked.

"His leg gives him pain. He never says, but I see it in his face. He's started a vegetable patch."

"Really? How wonderful. Does he manage all right?" I so wanted Charlie to find a hobby to distract him whilst I was away, something that gave him enjoyment and purpose.

"He's an inspiration. I've tried to talk him into getting a false leg, but he insists he's better without." Mavis spoke with her back to me, her eyes never leaving Esme, who darted between flower beds, squealing with excitement. "He's got big plans to supply the local grocers. But I'll let him tell you himself. Anyway, he's much brighter."

I should feel grateful to Mavis, but her proprietorial air where Charlie was concerned, and the fact that she saw him every day, on both good days and bad days, irritated me. It made me jealous, if I were honest. Not that I had any business being so childish. Mavis didn't have much in her life. Being Charlie's nursemaid must have filled the void left by William and the lack of a child of her own. Surely I could be gracious?

"I better go before Esme comes in." I looked over Mavis's shoulder. My little girl, almost three now, had discovered the birdbath. She sploshed her fingers in the water bowl, flicking the droplets into the air and watching the sparkles of water catch in the sunlight. Dear child. No wonder Lewis was so besotted with her. She might be a little intense, but her inquisitive nature was endearing.

"Will you explain to Charlie?" Mavis urged. "That I shan't be visiting for a while because I'm babysitting?"

A flicker of relief ran through me. For once, I'd have Charlie all to myself, without constant interruptions from Mavis offering to shop or cook or do the laundry. Of course, she couldn't take Esme with her to his house. Charlie had a horror of children, of hearing their screams of terror when they saw his ravaged face. And there was always the fear Esme would let slip she was my daughter.

"He'll understand," I said. "Besides, you need a break too."

Mavis's back stiffened. Mean of me, I admit, but she needed reminding Charlie was *my* husband.

I paused outside Charlie's house, delighted he'd started to take an interest in doing it up. On my last visit, we'd talked at length about getting rid of his parents' dreary, mahogany furniture, and giving the whole place a facelift. Already, he'd whitewashed the exterior, and new plantings along the path sprouted green shoots, which I took as a sign that Charlie had started to care, and find meaning in his existence. He'd spent too many years brooding and hiding. "You can't keep licking your wounds forever, my love," I'd told him. "You must find a purpose, a reason to get out of bed. If not for you, then do it for me."

I breathed in the fresh, breezy air. No matter that London offered wild parties and social standing, the scent of Guernsey always gripped me with nostalgia. A flutter of nerves caught me as I pushed open the door. Since the day we met, seeing Charlie never failed to arouse a thrill of anticipation. How would he surprise me this time?

Paint-spattered sheets lined the hallway. I edged around a stepladder with a pot of paint balanced on top. However did he clamber up it? No longer a darkened corridor, the entryway gleamed white and welcoming. Light streamed from the back of the house and I hurried to explore its origin. The old farmhouse kitchen, once a clutter of heavy furnishings, had been stripped bare. Only a shabby wooden table laden with tools, and two stools remained. He'd knocked out the back wall and installed large-frame windows, transforming the depressing, dark room into a bright, airy studio overlooking the garden.

Through the open window I heard Charlie humming – a Chopin violin sonata – and the swoosh of his trowel turning earth. Listening to his pitch-perfect rendition gave me an idea; while I was here, I'd buy him a piano. Surely he'd be able to tinker on it with his good hand. Playing might even be good therapy for his damaged fingers. And I'd look in the attic, see if his cello had been stored away. There might be sheet music too. He'd be rusty, but music had been his first love, and with practice I felt certain he'd be able to manage the bow and pluck the strings, giving him back his hobby.

I spied him crouching at a flower bed. He wore loose, baggy trousers and a chequered shirt with the sleeves rolled up, revealing a ripple of muscle amidst the scars, as he gently ploughed. I watched for a few moments, glad to note a frown no longer deepened his forehead. His recovery had been a miracle none of us expected, but the regular setbacks all too soon reminded me that I couldn't bank on his longevity.

I removed my shoes and tiptoed out. He only noticed me when I knelt beside him.

"You," he said. "At last." He brushed the soil from his hands, calloused from hard labour, but I longed to stroke every knuckle, feel the strength of him. "I've been trying to keep occupied." He spoke slowly, as one unaccustomed to lengthy conversation.

"The ferry was late." If only I could tell him about Esme... but I pushed the thought quickly aside. Time with Charlie was precious, too precious to waste on regrets, or to spend any other way than in the moment.

"I've made up today's rules." He grinned. His eyes sparkled with mischief and his mouth drooped where the bullet had shattered bone.

Was it his words, or his smile, or his nearness? In an instant, desire took over all my senses – warmth flooded my thighs, my breasts swelled, and I yearned to rip off every shred of clothing. But that wasn't the game. Not the way Charlie liked to play, anyway. His body might have lost the capability to make love, but that didn't stop him from inventing ways for our mutual pleasure.

I moistened my lips. "Where is it?"

"Beside the bed."

I stood. "Will you come too?"

He grinned again, cracking my heart. "Read it first."

I ran inside, not pausing to put on my shoes, and along the hallway to the bedroom. Here too, Charlie had made changes. The nightmarish green-and-yellow wallpaper had been peeled away, and the rugs discarded in favour of floorboards which he'd painted very pale blue. But I wasn't interested. My eyes went to the bed – clean sheets, hospital corners – and a fluted vase on the bedside table with a rolled-up piece of paper jutting from its rim.

Wait for me. Don't speak. Not a word.

I heard the thump of his foot and the tap of his crutch. I sat on the edge of the bed, hands clasped in my lap, every nerve end tingling. He appeared in the doorway and oh, how I yearned to throw myself into him and feel his arms around me, but Charlie insisted on having the first touch, deciding where to begin and where to end.

He pulled the curtains so only a soft glow of light permeated the room, propped his crutch against the wardrobe and sat in the corner, on a newly upholstered chair. "Come here. In front of me."

He never took his eyes from me as I moved around the bed. "Undo your buttons. Slowly."

The agony of it, when I wanted to cast off my cardigan along with every other item of clothing as fast as I could. But I took my time and with every button I felt Charlie's love for me; with every button my longing increased.

"Slide out of your skirt." His voice thickened and I felt my power then and turned so he could watch the outline of my backside as I slithered free. "Your slip."

I faced him, suffering the delicious agony of throbbing between my legs, pulled my petticoat over my head and shook my hair free. Charlie took his time to study my blue brassiere edged with brown lace and matching satin culottes, chosen for him. For this.

"Come here."

At last, at last he'd touch me. But no – Charlie undid one stocking suspender, two. "Turn around." And he undid the third and fourth suspenders. "Take them off."

I lifted my foot and placed it on the front of the chair, between Charlie's thighs. He gasped and I smiled at him, not allowing his gaze to leave mine, as I rolled down my stocking and tugged it free of my foot. He raised his hand, and for a second his finger hovered at the rim of my knickers. I held my breath, waiting for him to stroke beneath the lace. "The other one," he said and I meekly obeyed, praying my reward would be his finger, his touch.

I lay my stockings over the end of the bed.

"Turn around."

His hands pressed the edges of my suspender belt together, unhooked it and pulled it from my panties.

"Undress me."

Had I heard him right? Surely not.

"Undress me," he repeated.

I knelt in front of him and undid his shirt buttons. His chest hair, golden brown and silky, tantalised me, waiting to be kissed but forbidden. I pushed the cotton over his shoulders and leaned my body close to his as I eased him free. I pulled his boots and socks from his feet and then placed my hands on the waist of his trousers. Did he mean for me to go this far? I looked at him and he closed his eyes in silent acquiescence. For a moment I hesitated – Charlie never showed me his nakedness. He preferred darkness. But even in the black of night I could feel his scars, sense his weakness, hear his profound dismay at his body's failures.

He sat, tensed, until he wore only his underpants. "Let me see your breasts."

My nipples hardened and I watched him while I removed my brassiere. I saw his desire, his torment. I cupped my breasts, stroking their roundness. His breath came fast, and I glanced between his legs, astonished to see a stirring of passion.

"Take them off." He nodded at my knickers. I eased them over my buttocks, and stood naked before him. "You're beautiful," he said. "Lie on the bed."

I went closer and took his head in my hands, pressing his mouth to my breast. While he sucked, gently at first and then with mounting ferocity, I reached down and felt his groin, now hard with longing. He trembled at my touch and I whispered in his ear, "Make love to me."

He pulled back, a cloud of anxiety across his face. "I can't... what if I–"

I backed to the bed and lay, propped against the pillows, waiting. The air between us became still, expectant. A flash, a memory came to me of Charlie on our wedding night. I'd reached to turn out the light and he'd stopped me. "When I love you, I want to see you," he'd said.

I repeated his words. "When you make love to me, I want you to see me," I said. "And I want to see you."

He raised himself out of the chair and stumbled to the bed. I pushed away his underpants and in an instant we found each other again. We moved in unison, slowly, skin on skin. I'd forgotten the sensation of him, how he teased, held back, then thrust forwards. We found our rhythm and my body overtook my mind, blocking everything out except the moment. Too soon, Charlie shuddered and I arched my back, crying out with joy, amazement, ecstasy.

I lay back in a contented fug. Charlie laughed and laughed as he held me tight. "I never believed it possible, Mrs Vautier, that we would be truly married again."

At his words, I tensed. I stared at the newly-painted ceiling, joy leeching from me.

For a while, lost in finding Charlie again, I'd forgotten Lewis and Esme. Now, Charlie's hand on my rump felt heavy with ownership. I shifted under the weight, for I couldn't keep living this double life. Somehow I had to resolve my dilemma, but whichever way I looked at it, there was only one person who would be the loser. Me.

17

ARCADIA

LONDON, OCTOBER 1927

J paced the living room, impatient for Lewis to get home so I could get my plan underway. At last the door opened, but it was Benson, asking if I cared for a drink. I'd have killed for a gin and tonic but sense prevailed and I waved him away.

He backed out with a bemused expression on his usually inscrutable face. "Yes, ma'am."

Standing by the fireplace, I tapped the mantelpiece, lost in thought. The door opened again, but it wasn't Lewis. Dear Esme skipped across the room, giggling with naughtiness, and flung her arms around my knees. Her hair was wet from her bath and she wore only her flannelette nightie.

"Mum-mee, mum-mee," she chortled. "I escaped from Nanny!"

The new nanny followed, a heavy unattractive woman, a little breathless with her hair out of place. "Sorry, ma'am, the wee devilish mite ran off before I could stop her."

I knelt. "Esme, darling, dressing gown and slippers. Remember?"

Esme pouted.

"And do as Nanny tells you." I gave her a quick hug. "Now off you go. Daddy will be home soon, and I need a private chat." I gave Nanny a meaningful look.

"I'll put Esme to bed, ma'am."

I kissed Esme's cheek; she smelt of soap and talcum powder. She clung to me, but Nanny took her hand and pulled her towards the door, much to Esme's dismay. "You take me, Mummy." Oh dear, this wasn't going to be easy; Esme evidently hadn't taken to the woman.

"Not tonight, darling," I said firmly. "And Nanny, I'll be going away for some weeks so please don't plan any days off unless Mr Fanstone agrees. Do you understand?"

Nanny tucked a wisp of stray hair behind her ear and I swear I saw her pinch her lips together. "Yes ma'am."

Another ten minutes went by. The clock struck six. Finally, at ten past, I heard noises in the hallway and Lewis threw open the door. I could see at once he'd been at his club all afternoon and when he advanced to kiss my cheek, his breath stank of whisky.

"Dearest heart," he said and sank into the sofa, "ring for Benson and ask for a Scotch and soda, would you?"

I closed the door and leaned against it. Taking a deep breath, I plunged in. "I've had enough, Lewis. This cannot go on one moment longer."

He started to lever his body up. "Oh, okay, I'll ring for Benson then."

"No, you will not."

He took notice then. "Whatever's up with you?"

Oh God, I wasn't sure I could do this and make it stick. "You. You're making a fool of us and it has to stop."

He scratched his head. "Am I missing something?"

"Our marriage, that's what you're forgetting. You're so damned busy flirting with everyone's wife and mistress, or out partying with God knows who, you've become a joke. I'm not taking it one moment longer. It's time you behaved like a grown-up and did something more than hang out with your cronies playing cards or betting on horses and running through our money."

"I say... be fair. I had a huge win just yesterday. Enough to keep you in a few dresses this side of Christmas." He flopped back onto the cushions. "And you're usually with me at the parties."

"And the women? I've seen the way they look at you. As for that Diana Hummings, she's constantly hanging off your arm like she owns you. Does she?"

He pulled his little-boy face. "Oh well, you know..."

"You're a father, Lewis. Little Esme deserves better."

He perked up. "I better go and say goodnight–"

"I've not finished yet." I circled the sofa, dragging my courage together. "I want you to clean up your act, prove you're worthy of Esme and me–"

"Yes, yes–"

"Don't interrupt." I gathered momentum. "I'm sick to death of your womanising and complete failure to stick at anything, so I'm going away and I shan't return until I can see that you're taking things seriously."

"That's a bit harsh." He grinned. "You don't mean it. Come here, darling, give me a hug."

God, he was impossible. "I mean it, Lewis. I'm heading to Cornwall tomorrow. I've research to do for *Smuggler's Cove* and this time I shall stay on and rent somewhere while I write the book."

He spluttered. "But that could be months."

"Yes, it certainly could. Plenty of time for you to miss me terribly and realise that life without me is deadly dull."

"Will you be back by Christmas?"

I did a quick calculation. "Probably not, but I'm sure Granny will be delighted not to have to put up with my presence." She'd never forgiven me for denying her that large society wedding, and my relationship with her – if it could be called that – had never recovered from the perceived slight.

"You're serious, aren't you?" All of a sudden, he seemed to sober up, and it took all my inner strength not to cave in.

"Yes, I am." Before I could no longer keep up the pretence, I swung on my heel. "I'm going to read Esme a story. And then I'll be busy for the rest of the evening packing my bags. I suggest you sleep in your dressing room tonight." And I walked out of the room before I could hear his reply.

18

ARCADIA

GUERNSEY, OCTOBER 1927

*W*ith Lewis believing my reasons for leaving him, I now had to pray I wouldn't lose my nerve and that I could also bluff Charlie. But to successfully pull off my deception, galling as it was, yet again I had little option but to confide in Mavis.

After the ferry docked at St Peter Port, I went straight to her house. I'd given no prior warning of my arrival, and the way her face fell at the sight of me left me in no doubt that my visit wasn't especially welcome. But she quickly recovered her equilibrium.

"I have to talk to you. Let's go for a walk," I said, not stepping over the threshold. "I need to clear my head after the journey."

It was a gorgeous blue-sky day, with no sign of rainclouds gathering and once Mavis had put on her coat, we turned in the direction of the headland. I breathed in the fresh air, conscious of Mavis being in a slight huff, as I considered how best to get her onside. At any rate, I wasn't eager to get to the heart of matters – as ever, I first wanted an update on Charlie's health.

"Since you were here in summer, he's had a bit of a setback," she said. "He caught the flu and it's been a long recovery."

My heart thumped to hear about it, and I was hit by a feeling of helplessness. Mavis obviously didn't consider flu an emergency, else she'd have written; and Charlie never wrote, his right arm too weakened to hold a pen properly. "Is he all right?" I asked.

"He's put on a little weight now, but he's still very frail." Mavis spoke with authority. "He's most content in his greenhouse. I stop by every day with the newspaper and any shopping, change his library books, pay his bills at the post office and what have you. When I'm there, he takes a break from his plants to have a cup of tea, but even that distresses him. As you know, he doesn't like eating or drinking in front of people."

"Has he seen a doctor?"

"He keeps saying there's little point."

I had to disagree. "Surely there's something which could be done to make him more comfortable?"

"It's a funny thing. Whenever I raise it, he says there's plenty of soldiers in a worse state than him. It's almost as if he doesn't want to be more comfortable. As if he's... well... punishing himself in some way."

I thought of what he'd told me. Perhaps that's exactly what Charlie was doing. "Thank you for all you're doing for him."

Mavis tried to sound modest. "It's nothing." But of course, it wasn't nothing and we both knew it.

We reached a small park, and I led the way to a bench seat under a spreading oak, which sheltered us from the breeze.

"Why didn't you let me know you were coming?" Mavis asked.

"Because I might have lost my nerve." I turned to face her. "I'm five months' pregnant."

"Five months?" I could see her doing the arithmetic. "That means–?"

"It's Charlie's, yes."

The look on Mavis's face would have been comical if the situation wasn't so dire. She obviously hadn't realised Charlie's injuries didn't extend to his entire body. Pink spots tinged her cheeks. "What on earth are you going to do?"

"Have it, of course. What else?"

"Oh, I see." Mavis frowned. "You'll pass it off as Lewis's..."

So easy for Mavis to move the pieces around the chessboard. "No, I shan't."

Her face fell. "You've left him? You're going to set up house with Charlie? But I thought we agreed–"

I shook my head, dismayed at the tangle and all it meant. "Even if it were an option, Charlie's in no state to have a baby in the house."

"Will you tell him?"

I picked at my skirt. "No."

"Doesn't he deserve to know?"

The agony of it. "Why would I add to his pain? He may not have long to live but at least he now has some peace, and he's coping with his limits." I stroked my hands across the bulge of my stomach. "But he couldn't possibly manage a baby, and then a toddler."

"Why can't you tell Lewis it's his? Then you could look after the child in England, and bring it with you on your visits. Charlie wouldn't be any the wiser and he'd have the joy of being a father."

"Lewis isn't stupid. Given I was away this summer for almost two months, he'd soon work out it isn't his. And if Lewis didn't have suspicions, his mother – Granny Fanstone – would. That woman has a nose for the smallest indiscretions and things that don't add up." I'd given this so much thought, agonised too long really, although an abortion – even if I dared risk the services of a disgraced doctor – was never an option. I couldn't end that small life, not a child made by Charlie and me. "And if I did keep the baby, how would it work? At home we have a nanny. That time I brought Esme here was because I had no option. What possible reason could I have for taking one child – and not Esme – on my so-called location-scouting trips?"

"What will you do?"

"I'm going to stay out of sight – Jersey, perhaps, or Alderney – have the baby and give it up for adoption."

Mavis looked horrified. "You can't, you just can't. Let me have the child, I'll bring it up."

Another thing of mine that Mavis wanted. "Hardly practical. You're an unmarried woman." I realised how harsh I sounded. "And you've helped enough. No, I'm afraid this is something I have to shoulder alone. Although–"

"Yes?" She looked at me eagerly.

"Would you be with me when I have the baby? I'll make all the arrangements, speak to an adoption society, but when the time comes, I might not have the strength–" I choked, and my chest constricted. How would I be able to give up Charlie's child? Hand over a tiny swaddled bundle and say goodbye quickly, before my heart wouldn't let go?

Mavis sat bolt upright. "Of course I will. And I won't have you with strangers either. I've friends on Jethou with a large house. I'll cook up some story, and I'm certain they'll be happy for you to go there. It's only a ferry ride away so I'll visit when I can, bring you news of Charlie."

Jethou. The neighbouring island to Herm, with few inhabitants, where I'd be safe from curious eyes. I'd write *Smuggler's Cove* and enjoy the next weeks – my last weeks – with our unborn child. "Thank you. For everything." I got up and turned away from the water. "Let's walk back. I must get to Charlie. It will be several months before I can see him again and I want to spend as much time with him as I can."

"What will you tell him?"

I'd thought of that too. "That I have to go into hospital for an operation to have my spleen out. It will explain my distended stomach too, if he notices. I'm not sure if such swelling is a feasible side effect, but I doubt he'd know one way or the other.

What I do know is that the operation takes weeks of recovery." I hesitated for a moment. "Can I ask one more favour?"

Mavis nodded.

"When the child is born, don't let them tell me whether it's a boy or girl. The less I know, the better." *What you don't know can't hurt you.* Or so it was said.

19

ARCADIA

JETHOU, FEBRUARY 1928

$\mathcal{I}$t was peaceful on Jethou. The first time I'd ever been truly on my own for any length of time. The couple who Mavis knew turned out to be the caretakers of the house; the owners lived in Brittany. It was a rambling old place in need of some renovation, but it suited me. Monsieur and Madame Aubert hardly bothered me, treating me more as a house guest, and aside from Mme Aubert cooking my meals and tidying my room, they left me to my own devices. I think Mme Aubert was rather in awe of me – *an authoress* – and she tiptoed about, not wanting to disturb me while I wrote my book and grew larger by the day. Mavis told them my husband was with the diplomatic corps, on a posting to Africa where hospital services were minimal and I'd be putting myself and the baby at risk if I joined him. The Auberts never questioned it, but I suspect they knew it was a trumped-up story as I never received any mail or had any photographs of my beloved out on display or beside my bed.

The house had a library, with a desk facing a bay window which overlooked the garden. I'd wake early, breakfast, and set myself the task of writing for four hours. When sleep overtook me, which it did without fail each day at two o'clock, I moved to the large brown velvet armchair, which was threadbare and needed reupholstering, but big enough to curl in comfortably for a nap. When I woke, I'd often chat aloud, telling stories about Charlie and me. I'd reminisce, stroking my stomach and when the baby stretched inside me, I'd rub its tiny toes or knuckles.

I should have missed everyone – Charlie, Esme, Lewis – but I didn't. This was a special time I'd never be able to repeat, and I wanted to cram a lifetime into the few short months. I vowed once the child was born, I'd never look back, never regret, never feel sorry for myself or let this decision define me. The child's unknown legacy from its real mother would be *Smuggler's Cove*, the story of a woman whose fiancé, a sailor, was lost at sea. On discovering she carried his baby and not wanting to heap shame on a bastard child, she gave up the baby to a childless couple desperate for their own family, and the boy grew up to be a hero amongst Cornish smugglers.

I finished the manuscript just two days before I gave birth. I wrote the inscription: *For every parent of every child*, parcelled it up and asked Mme Aubert to mail the package to my publisher.

And then I waited.

20

ESME

GUERNSEY, AUGUST 1958

*I*f Esme were honest, she'd held little hope of receiving a reply from Clara. So when the letter came, addressed all in capitals, in a brown envelope stamped HMS Holloway, she couldn't have been more surprised or thrilled. She swept Jasper off the rocking chair, and against the backdrop of rain falling in a solid, unrelenting downpour, she withdrew the contents.

Pinned to the letter, was a note:

Dear Miss Fanstone,

Clara dictated this letter to me, so it is written in my hand, as she has no education. She also said should you wish to visit her, she'd be most pleased to see you. However, I want to caution you against getting up her hopes of release. Her crime was of the worst kind, and she has come to terms with her sentence of life imprisonment. She is known for befriending new prisoners and is a keen gardener.

Lady Charity Taylor

Governor

Esme folded Lady Taylor's note behind Clara's letter, which was equally short.

Dear Miss Fanstone,

Thank you for writing to me. I don't ever get letters. All I can say is that I swear on my Bible I didn't kill my mistress. I never would have. I know I am here in this place for God's own reason but if you can do anything to set me free or find the truth of the matter I promise I will live a good and true life. You ask the date of the crime. It is a day I shall not forget. October 7, 1945. You ask, if not me, then who tried to do her in. I have my private ideas is all I can say.

Please help me.

Yours,

Clara Denier

Esme sat back in the rocking chair and stared at Lady Taylor's writing, whilst Clara's words rang in her head. Several things struck her, most notably that Clara could not be C. Not only had she confirmed that the crime was committed a day after the letter that was sent to Arcadia asking for help, but she showed no recognition of the name of Fanstone.

But Esme didn't think she could drop the matter. Clara's story fascinated her, with its many unanswered questions. *I have my private ideas*, she'd written, and then specifically asked Lady Taylor to let it be known she could visit her. To Esme, that seemed to infer Clara didn't want to commit her theory to paper, fearful perhaps of reprisals? But if Esme were going to pursue this further, under her guise as a newspaper reporter, she owed it to Clara to be genuine in her investigations.

Although her heart wanted to believe Clara innocent, her head told her not to judge but to review the facts. When the weather cleared, she'd visit relevant locations: the scene of the crime, the Mellons' house; the courthouse where Clara was tried; and the jail where she would have been held. The same jail where Bernard Charleston Vautier may have been incarcerated.

A clap of thunder interrupted her musings. Jasper jumped onto her lap and she clutched him to her chest. As she stroked his fur to calm him, inspiration hit. At last, she knew what her next book would be about: Clara and the Mellons. If Clara was guilty, what was her motive? If innocent, was she set up and by whom? She'd use whatever facts she could unearth to fictionalise Clara's life, with as many elements of truth as possible. And if along the way she found out something that exonerated Clara, well, that would be an added bonus.

Still cuddling Jasper, she set up her typewriter on the dining table. To the gentle ticking of the grandfather clock and the rain beating against the windows, she plotted an outline and began character sketches of her three main protagonists: Francine, M. Mellon and Clara. Words flooded her brain and she needed to write them down before she lost her opening thread, those first few paragraphs which would set the scene for what would come next. They'd be rewritten, of course they would, but she needed an anchor, a starting point.

Seated at the dining table, her hands shook. She hadn't felt this frisson of anticipation since she'd embarked on *The View From Here*. She checked the typewriter ribbon, aligned a sheet of paper, and began typing:

The Trial of Clara Denier
Chapter One

```
The  poison  of  choice  was  arsenic.  The
year,  1945.  In  the  dock,  a  poor,  frail
young  woman.  Victim  or  villain?  What  had
brought  her  here,  to  be  judged  and
condemned?  This  is  a  story  that  begins
many  years  before...
```

∼

148

After propping her bicycle against the wall of the Royal Court Building, Esme ran up the steps, passed beneath the Guernsey coat of arms, and through the main doors of the impressive granite building. An elderly gentleman in smart livery hovered in the lobby, and advised she was welcome to sit in the courtroom's public gallery.

"There's no sitting today, though you can look around." He crooked his finger. "Follow me."

He showed her into the imposing wood-panelled court. "This is where the bailiff presides over criminal cases," he said.

"Who are they?" Esme pointed to portrait paintings in extravagant gilt frames either side of the bailiff's chair.

"The one on the right is Saumarez, the famous admiral. The other is former Governor Sir John Doyle. A great man. Responsible for many public works. We've a lot to thank him for."

"Was this where Clara Denier's trial took place?" said Esme.

He nodded. "I followed all the proceedings. A travesty of justice, to my mind."

"What happened?"

"Bedlam. Sheer bedlam. St Peter Port had never seen anything like it." The usher spoke with relish. "Of course, she was tried in French. Wouldn't have understood a word."

How barbaric, thought Esme. "Did she have a defence? Or someone to translate?"

"No, nothing like that. She was tried by the bailiff and twelve Jurats. Judges, to you. There's no trial by jury here," he said. "The Jurats' decision is final."

Esme shuddered to imagine Clara – that vulnerable, frightened woman – cowering before thirteen men who decided her fate. She envisaged the large crowd baying in the gallery, greedy for salacious titbits about the housemaid's murderous intentions.

"Did you think she was guilty?"

"At the time it seemed cut and dried. But then things took a curious turn."

"How so?"

"That M. Mellon, he married again not long afterwards. Some surmised the pair had been having an affair and perhaps Mellon wanted his wife out of the way and did her in. Others preferred to believe he'd found happiness after the fiendish devilment of Clara. Then two years later, his new wife died in mysterious circumstances, a drowning."

"Heavens. Was M. Mellon charged?"

The usher stroked his chin. "No evidence that it was anything but an accident. Public sympathy went with the grieving widower, and there were plenty of women keen to comfort him, though he never married a third time."

"But you weren't convinced."

The usher looked around, then spoke in a low voice. "Follow the money." He tapped the side of his nose. "Twice M. Mellon inherited from his wives, but these days he lives in social housing, barely scraping along from all I hear."

"What do you think happened to the money?"

"Who knows? But ask yourself this, if a man is desperate for money to save his own skin, what lengths would he go to?" With that, he shuffled off.

Deep in thought, Esme followed, giving him a small tip before exiting to Court Row. The daylight was a welcome relief after the cold austerity of the court. She crossed the road and leaned against the wall of St James-the-Less Church, thinking of Clara in her dank cell, alone and friendless, and considered what no one had ever raised: what had been her motive for killing Francine Mellon? In love with her master, perhaps Clara decided to clear the way by getting rid of her mistress. Or, cruelly treated by her mistress, she exacted the ultimate revenge. Possibly, M. Mellon lured Clara with promises of marriage, and incited her to murder his wife.

Whatever the answer, Esme had begun to intensely dislike M.

Mellon and his careless management of two legacies. Something stank, and she intended to dig deeper.

~

A long row of dull, neat houses fronted onto a large car park, each with the same cream-painted exterior, mean windows and no garden. Esme located number eleven, which unlike its neighbours had no flowering pots outside, giving it an uncared-for air. There was no bell or knocker, so she rapped her knuckles on the door and stepped back.

A man, shorter than she expected, unshaven and bleary-eyed, opened the door with a wary expression on his face. He wore filthy trousers which looked as if they'd never been laundered, and a chequered shirt frayed at the neck with two missing buttons. Grey chest hair poked through. Esme tried not to show her revulsion by maintaining a bright, friendly demeanour.

"M. Mellon?" It hadn't been hard to locate him; a visit to the post office had soon yielded his address, no questions asked, although the postmaster had said, "Be careful."

He folded his arms across his chest and tilted his chin. "What do you want?"

"My name is Esme Fanstone. I'm a reporter with *The Monitor* and I was hoping you could spare me a few minutes of your time."

"Is it about that burglary?"

"No... I'm writing an article about people who have lost a loved one to violent death. I'm sure it's still very upsetting for you, but I know your wife was murdered and then you sadly lost your second wife, and I think our readers would benefit from hearing how you've coped with such double tragedy."

He narrowed his eyes and Esme moistened her lips, sure he could see through her deceit.

"What's it worth?" he asked in a belligerent tone.

"I beg your pardon?"

"What will you pay me?"

"Pay you? Oh, I see. That would be up to my editor. First, I'd need to know what you're prepared to talk about on record." Her misgivings had been spot on about M. Mellon, whose first thought was how he could profiteer from his wives' deaths. She toyed with asking if she could come inside, but her instinct and the postmaster's warning told her to remain on the doorstep.

"What do you want to know?"

She chose her words with care. "How you dealt with the grieving process and living with the memories." Taking a breath to calm herself, she pressed on. "For example, was this the house you lived in, or did you move here later?"

"After that murder, I couldn't bear to be in that place. Sold up straightaway."

"And you bought this house?"

"No. After Stella – that was my wife who drowned – I sold that house too. Nice place, near L'Ancresse Common."

"And then you came here?"

Mellon shifted his weight. "Yes, had a bit of bad luck."

"Oh?" Esme left her question hanging in the air.

His face shut down. "Let me know how much you're paying, and I'll decide how much I'll tell you."

It seemed Esme wouldn't find out today what his 'bit of bad luck' had been – blackmail? Poor investments? Or just a spend-thrift? But it didn't really matter. He'd confirmed her suspicions. Follow the money, the usher had said, and it appeared he was right. She thanked Mellon, said she'd be in touch, and hurried back to the bus stop, relieved to escape the man's grasping ways.

21

ARCADIA

THE COTSWOLDS, ENGLAND, FEBRUARY 1937

*S*eated at the dressing table, I gazed out across the fields. The view from our bedroom, taking in plump cows, well-fed sheep and miles of crops, should have soothed my soul, but at this time of year my thoughts inevitably drifted to what might have been. My lost child, as I always thought of him or her, would be nine tomorrow. "I hope you're happy," I whispered.

Despite remaining true to my promise that I'd always look forwards, just once in a while I indulged in a fantasy of family life quite unlike the one I'd been plunged into... I dreamed of a world inhabited by two harmonious households, two fathers each with their child, and me flitting seamlessly between the two. On dark days like today, I choked on the choice I'd made. Had I known Charlie would live on for years, would I have done what I did? Who would I have chosen? I sighed at such a pointless circle of supposition – no one, especially me, could have read the future or in retrospect, taken a different path.

Raking a brush through my hair, I forced myself to return to the present and my irritation at being dragged to the Cotswolds. Lewis refuses to stay long in London, terrified his creditors will catch up with him, so we behave like gypsies, commuting between city and country. Esme doesn't seem to mind. She huddles in with Grandpops and they giggle together. Or Lewis takes her for riding lessons. She fell off a nippy little Shetland pony yesterday, made a dreadful fuss. Granny Fanstone and I do our best to avoid each other. She's taken to communicating with me via notes. Today's missive, delivered by Esme an hour ago, read: *Please meet me in the morning room at three o'clock for a talk.*

For a talk? I suppose she wants to discuss money. The lack of it. She's got hold of some notion that my books bring in hundreds of pounds. I expect she wants help paying for the cost of repairing the roof or the broken windows. The gall of it.

Well, it won't be for much longer. Once I announce my intentions, I doubt she'll want sight or sound of me. In her view, I've always been 'beyond the pale', an 'abominable woman'. She'll probably throw a party after I ask Lewis for a divorce. Although the idea of it breaks my heart, I can't keep flip-flopping between him and Charlie. It's not fair on any of us. Charlie was my first love, and he needs me so desperately. His recovery these last few years has been extraordinary and I'm running out of believable reasons to stay in London. And Esme is still young enough to adapt. At least in Guernsey, she'll be all mine. I'll explain her away somehow. Divorcing Lewis means I won't live in fear of discovery, constantly on the lookout for a friend or acquaintance holidaying in St Peter Port, and unmasking my duplicity.

Can I live without Lewis? Yes, I think so. He's not quite the bon vivant he was – the Depression saw to that – but he'll soon find someone else to warm his bed. And I'm sure we can come to an arrangement over Esme; now that she's old enough to voice her feelings in the matter it wouldn't be so easy to take her from me.

"Mummy?" A quiet little voice made me jump.

In the reflection of the mirror, Esme's head poked around the door. "Call me Arcadia, darling. Mummy sounds so *aging*. What is it?"

"Granny sent me. She said to say it's five past three." Esme hovered in the doorway, standing on one foot.

Oh, drat the woman. I picked up my hairbrush. "Tell her I hadn't forgotten."

Esme frowned, unsure what I meant, but knowing better than to question me. "Yes, Mummy." She retreated, backwards, a bit like an unctuous servant not wanting to give offence. She's quite gawky at the moment. All arms and legs. Teeth in a brace. Twelve is a difficult age. Something of nothing.

I fluffed up my hair and took time to reapply my lipstick. The collar of my blouse showed signs of fraying. I took a chiffon scarf and fashioned a bow tie to disguise the wear and tear. With a cameo brooch pinned at the centre, I deemed myself ready for war.

Shoulders back, chin up, I marched to the morning room and entered without knocking. Granny Fanstone was bent over a side table, buffing out a mark with her perpetual duster. She spoke with her back to me. "Sit down." A command, not an invitation.

I counted to seventeen while waiting for her to finish whatever didn't really need doing. Obviously she wanted to discomfit me. By the time I reached fourteen, she'd almost succeeded. Finally, she took the high-back chair opposite me – a stark, uncomfortable piece of Edwardian furniture – and placed her hands on its arms. I'd opted for the leather bucket chair and a more relaxed posture. Legs crossed, one arm across my waist, the other resting on top, hand dangling in the air. A cigarette holder would have completed the effect, but smoking isn't allowed inside until after dinner.

She tapped her fingers on the ornate woodwork. "You don't fool me, Arcadia. You may have gulled my son and your daughter with your lies and deceit, but I won't be an unwitting party to it any longer."

My foot began to tremble. I pressed my heel into the ground and a stab of pain shot up my tensed calf muscle. I stayed silent.

"Nothing to say?" Granny drew her already thin lips into an even tighter line of disapproval. "Of course not. What defence could you possibly have?"

What did she know? Or think she knew? "You appear to have spun your own narrative. Whatever it is."

Granny flashed a hard look at me. "A piece of work, that's what you are. A grubby piece of work."

I raised my eyebrow at that. Not the sort of language I expected Granny to use.

"It's perfectly clear you are having an affair of some sort." She spat the word 'affair'. "All those trips away disguised as research." She spat 'research' too. "I've checked your books. None of your settings show any familiarity with the places described. You've certainly never visited any of the towns you claim such intimacy with. I don't know where you go, and I don't care. But you're a disgrace as a mother and a wife, and I won't have my family shamed."

I sat back. What on earth did she think she could do to me that I wasn't already planning? In fact, maybe this little chat would make leaving Lewis easier. I'd deny – of course – any impropriety. But I could tell Lewis his mother's attitude was the proverbial last straw and I saw no point continuing a loveless marriage (I'd have to say loveless, I'd have to make him believe that) and living with a mother-in-law who made my life hellish. I'd tell him I want Esme to have the same idyllic childhood I had in St Peter Port...

"This is my offer." My ears pricked. Offer? "You will leave Esme here at the end of her school holiday. She won't return to London with you, or indeed ever again. You will not see her unless I am present. Do you understand?"

"That's ridiculous–"

"Equally, you will never *ever* do anything to let Lewis down. God save him, he seems fond of you and he's had enough bad luck these last few years without tolerating a philandering wife."

I saw my chance. "I'll divorce him–"

Granny leaned forwards, her gnarled hands curled like tiger's claws. "You'll do no such thing. Lewis is planning to sign up to the army again. There's a war coming, mark my words. Your high society lot may fawn over Hitler, but he's a dangerous man who will stop at nothing short of world domination. The forces of good will soon mobilise to extinguish him."

I thought her speech somewhat alarmist, but I had heard similar rumblings amongst the art elite. As for Lewis signing up, it must be something Granny Fanstone had decided on his behalf. He'd not mentioned any desire to serve King and country again. Not to me. He'd escaped the Great War unscathed, and at almost forty it seemed a mystifying choice.

"If Lewis performs well as an officer, and we oust those despicable Nazis, he may have a future in politics. But not as a divorced man. You will not stand in his way."

Politics? Lewis? He knew nothing about political life, beyond the day's headlines and pontifications with his chums at the club.

"I'll allow you to visit Esme when Lewis is home on leave, or on special occasions with my prior permission. Then and only then. If you decide to destroy your life and publicly separate from my son, be assured you will lose custody of Esme and not be allowed to see her until she comes of age. A punishment which will see you cast out of society and dropped pronto by those smart friends you value so highly." Granny paused. "I suspect the BBC wouldn't want you on their radio programmes, either."

My head spun, listening to her trap me. The courts rarely ruled in favour of a woman caught having an affair. I'd be branded an unsuitable mother and that would be it, Esme would be ripped from me. If I mounted a fight, Granny would marshal the establishment against me and I wouldn't stand a chance.

"That's blackmail," I spluttered.

"No, Arcadia. It's common sense. As I'm sure you'll come to

see, in time." Granny's mean lips parted in a smile. "I suggest you also desist from those trips away."

Not see Charlie? Oh, no, no, no. I'd find a way. Somehow. But she'd trapped me with Lewis, using my own daughter as a pawn. I wouldn't put it past her to set a private detective on me – except that she's low on funds after she helped to bail out Lewis after his stockmarket losses – so I'd need to be careful.

I rose with all the dignity I could muster. "This may come as a surprise, but I love Lewis. It is not a hardship to be his wife. Whatever you think you know about our marriage is poppycock. As for Esme – I've always favoured a country upbringing. I'm sure the new arrangement will suit everyone."

With that, I swept from the room.

22

ESME

GUERNSEY, AUGUST 1958

*E*sme pushed aside the bedclothes and drew back the curtains. A weak sun broke through the patches of cloud, glimmering on the slate rooftops of the terraces opposite. The milkman looked up and waved as he walked up the front path, carrying his milk churn. She waved back, pleased she'd remembered to leave out an enamel jug last night for him to fill, and went to the bathroom to wash her face. After pulling on slacks and a cotton shirt, she went downstairs, looking forward to a mug of fresh, creamy milk before knuckling down to work. The visit to the library to do more research on Bernard/Charlie could wait; after her visit to M. Mellon, she was eager to get on with Clara's story and her typewriter beckoned.

The hours disappeared while she mapped out scenarios and began drafting the facts as she knew them. A clatter at the door, mid-afternoon, interrupted her mid-sentence. Not wanting to break her thought, she quickly tapped out: *and purchased rat poison whilst on a day trip to Jersey*, and prepared herself for a visit by a travelling salesman, or a copy of the parish magazine. But there on the mat lay an airmail envelope with red, white and blue stripes around the edge, and her address penned in Hugh's green ink.

She took it to the dining table and for a few seconds sat staring at Hugh's handwriting before taking a breath of courage and slipping her finger under the sealed flap.

Dearest Esme,

I can't tell you how much I would love to hop on the steamer and come to visit you but it's not possible, my dear one. What with the tyranny of deadlines, no deputy editor (she left and went to Guernsey!) and preparations for the move to Philadelphia, I've barely time to sleep let alone take a jaunt to foreign parts.

Is cost the issue? Can I send you the fare to come here?

Don't disappoint me. Frankly, life is so much more complicated without you.

Hugh

Esme slumped back in her chair, dismayed. Was that it? His way or the highway? He'd need to do better than three short paragraphs if he seriously wanted to win her hand. It sounded more and more as if it was her organisational skills he missed most. If he couldn't find time to show he'd truly made a mistake, finally come to his senses, and make the effort to put her first, why on earth should she bother? As for paying her passage, didn't he understand she wanted to show him Guernsey, share her delight in St Peter Port and introduce him to the people and places she'd come to treasure? That she needed tangible proof of his love for her?

She shoved the letter back in its envelope and tossed it on the table. Blast Hugh, she wouldn't reply. Her silence would say what she didn't know how to express in words: that his overture was too little, too late – and irredeemably pointless.

To slough off her pent-up anger and disappointment, she hopped on her bike and headed to the Guille-Allès Library, relishing the damp breeze on her face and the smell of wet leaves. Whilst she harboured little confidence of uncovering anything substantive, at least her research would keep her mind off Hugh.

She'd just parked her bike, when she saw Anthony striding in her direction, his head down, hands in pockets, deep in thought.

"Anthony," she called out.

He came to a full stop, and nearly tumbled smack-bang into her. A broad grin broke over his face. "Hello, you. What are you doing in these parts?"

"I came to find you."

He squinted at her through his horn-rims, a ticklish smile playing at the corners of his mouth. "You've uncovered whodunnit?"

She laughed. How she'd missed his way of joking with her. "Not quite. I do have some good news though."

"Oh?"

"I think Clara Denier could be an excellent subject for my next novel. I've been poking around and it's possible she might be innocent. It would make a compelling story."

"Oh my goodness," said Anthony. "That's thrilling. How I envy you. All I get to do is dig up lists of things past and occasionally get a crumb of domestic trivia thrown my way. You, on the other hand, are clever enough to weave a story around a real event and bring it to life for hundreds, thousands of people to enjoy."

Pumped by his enthusiasm, Esme felt she must be on to something. "I'm not saying she is innocent, but there's definitely cause to be suspicious of Mellon, Clara's former employer." She was tempted to tell Anthony she believed he could have murdered both his wives to get their money, but if she was wrong, she shouldn't start malicious slurs on his name. "It seems he inherited a lot of money but now lives on his uppers."

"How do you know that?"

"I met him."

"You met him?" He sounded confused.

"Well, yes..." She realised an explanation was in order. "I pretended to be a reporter. In a way, it's not so far from the truth. The thing is, I need help."

Anthony spread his arms. "I'm your man."

"Is there a way to find out if M. Mellon has ever been charged with any crimes?"

"Easy-peasy. I'll get on to my police informant. Anything else?"

"I also need to track his financial affairs, find out where the money went. If he made bad investments, then I suppose he just had poor luck." Like her father who handed everything over to Lloyds, thinking he'd make his fortune, but instead saw all his shares take massive falls, leaving him penniless. "On the other hand, if debt collectors were after him then he might have been in a real bind. My problem is, I'm darned if I know where to get the evidence, if there is any."

"I've a friend who works at the bank. I could ask him."

"Really? I mean, how could he help?"

"Dunno. Those sort of records are probably confidential." He rocked on his heels. "Exciting stuff, Tuppence. And how's the search for your family going?"

"I've been a bit sidetracked by Clara..." And Hugh. "But I'm still keen to unravel the mystery, so I'm here to go through the papers again, see if I missed something." Her earlier research had focussed on Clara, but in her fascination for the murderous housemaid, maybe she'd overlooked news items about Bernard C Vautier. Or Charlie as she now thought of him.

"Good idea. By the way, I'm intending to order your book. Can't wait to get stuck in."

She lowered her head, caught off guard by his interest. "I shan't mind if you don't like it."

"Of course you will, you liar." He gave her a friendly bump with his elbow.

She laughed and they entered the library together.

"Come and find me when you've finished," Anthony said. "I'll be in my office."

The date of the letter sent to Arcadia, 6 October 1945, had fallen on a Saturday. The writer, M, had written... *it's been the most terrible two days*. According to Anthony's search of police records, Charlie was arrested in early October. Given the war had ended only a few weeks earlier, and officialdom was still in disarray, his initial court hearing may have been delayed, with M only learning of the arrest two days before reaching out to Arcadia. Esme decided to play it safe and examine the *Guernsey Evening Press* from the last week of September.

The librarian helped her locate four weeks' worth of papers, and Esme took the heavy folders to a long, wide table. Two elderly men, retired military types, were sitting at either end. One was poring over a large leather-bound book, the other busily made notes from a pile of moth-eared magazines. Esme sat between them and forgot their presence as she focussed her concentration on every article, no matter how small. She even scanned the long columns of advertisements for *Employment Wanted*, *Death* and *Marriage* notices.

At last, in the October 8 edition, she found a small mention. Bernard Vautier had been denied bail for assaulting a British officer. He was held over for a further seven days. No wonder she'd missed the story. It was in the same edition that carried the report about the sensational murder attempt on Francine Mellon. Alert for further information, she read the next week's papers even more closely. On Monday 15 October, buried at the bottom of page 7, she found one paragraph:

Assault charges dropped

Local man, Bernard Vautier, was released from custody after charges against him for assault with intent to cause grievous bodily harm were unexpectedly withdrawn. The court bailiff advised there had been an out of court settlement between Captain Lewis Fanstone and his attacker, and that no further statements would be forthcoming from either party.

Esme's mouth went dry. She reread the unfathomable words. Lewis Fanstone. Her father. How on earth did he know Charlie? What was he doing in St Peter Port? Why did they get into a fight? Why did he drop the charges? And, most puzzling of all, why was Arcadia called to Charlie's aid, rather than to her husband's?

With trembling fingers, she turned the pages of the remaining October papers but there was nothing further. After copying the article into her notebook, she returned the newspapers to the librarian and went to seek out Anthony in his office, her mind in a spin.

"Good grief." Anthony took off his glasses and pinched the bridge of his nose. "Good grief."

The look on his face mirrored Esme's own astonished reaction at discovering her father had been the army officer attacked by Charlie.

"What do you think?" She sat on the edge of his desk, impatient for his response.

"There must be a logical explanation."

"But why would someone – M – write to my mother saying she must come to Charlie's aid? Surely it would make more sense to urge her to rush to my father's side?"

With precision, Anthony replaced his spectacles. "You'd think so." He paused. "Did you know your father had been to Guernsey?"

"No. But by October 1945 I'd left the WAAF and taken digs, and I hardly ever saw my mother. My father's letters didn't talk about where he was posted, but I suppose the British Army sent him here. He'd hardly have come on a holiday." She took a deep breath. "I think I should go to England and see him." If she wrote, she doubted he'd respond given he'd ignored her request to accompany her to Arcadia's funeral. She must go to England, seek him out and appeal to his better nature. If her father refused to talk about Arcadia, her granny might know what led him to fight with a man called Charlie in Guernsey and why Arcadia became involved. Whatever the outcome, conscious Granny's remaining time was limited, she'd be glad of the opportunity to see her.

Anthony stood, paced, and then perched beside Esme. "Why don't you ask Mavis? She'd know, wouldn't she?"

"She might, but she won't tell me. Besides, she denied Charlie was ever arrested for any fight with an officer. Which is pretty stupid, given it was in the papers."

"Let's not try and draw a conclusion that suits us. It's possible your father and Charlie were old army friends who got into a spat, so of course he'd drop the charges when things calmed down."

"But the letter talks of a possible attempted murder charge. That's not a small spat." Esme became aware of the heat from Anthony's leg and she shifted slightly to one side. "When I see him, I can ask him. I also want to know why he was here."

Anthony lowered his gaze and fiddled with some paperclips. "I suppose you'll see Hugh as well."

Did she imagine it, or was Anthony trying very hard to sound nonchalant? "I'm not sure. Maybe." Perhaps she was being unfair to Hugh. In his letter, he had sounded busy and stressed. It was a let-down, that was the problem. She'd expected him to tell her when he'd make the crossing, and now he'd put her on the back foot. After fifteen years jumping at his every command and whim since she first reported to him during the war, if she turned up on his doorstep, it would look as if she were running after him. He'd never believe she'd made the decision to come to England for reasons quite independent of his request.

He swung around. "Why the sudden change of heart? You said you had to sort–"

"I just meant... My father lives in Gloucestershire. Hugh's in London." It sounded weak, even to her own ears.

Anthony gave her a piercing look. "It's only a short train ride. I want you to see him. I've given it a lot of thought. The fact is, Tuppence, you seem to me to be very happy here in St Peter Port... but if your heart is in London–"

"Philadelphia. He wants me to go to America."

Anthony swallowed. "Oh, I see... you're not sure about moving so far away."

"It's not that." She didn't want to tell him about Hugh's unsatisfactory letter. In a perverse way, she felt it reflected badly on her that she'd even consider seeing him after he'd refused her invitation to come to Guernsey. Yet being in England and not contacting him would be petty and not resolve anything.

He faltered. "Is it me?"

How typical of Anthony to see straight to the crux of her dilemma.

When she didn't answer, he persisted. "Will you return?"

"Yes. Whatever happens, I'll be back. I promise."

He looked about to say something, hesitated, then smacked his knees with a hearty slap and jumped up. "Good. By the time you come back I may have another lead to follow up."

His sudden change of subject broke the crackle of tension, and Esme exhaled in relief. "You secretive devil. What?"

"Not sure why I didn't think of it before. I checked the death notices and there's nothing recorded for Bernard Charleston Vautier."

"Mavis said she's certain he's dead."

"And you'd believe her? After all her efforts to stonewall you?"

Esme smiled. "So he could be alive?"

"If he is, I'll find his address and we'll pay him a visit on your return." He rubbed his hands together. "I rather think between your father and Charlie, we're on the cusp of getting some answers to the riddle your mother left behind."

And the riddle of my heart, thought Esme, *will that puzzle also be solved?*

23

ARCADIA

GUERNSEY, JUNE 1940

$\mathcal{E}$veryone said the fall of Paris was only days away. If they were right, Guernsey would become vulnerable to German attack and be cut off from the mainland. Even if I could only spend a day with Charlie, it would be worth the effort, so I took my chance and left on the first available ferry.

Arriving at his front door, I suddenly felt awkward about turning up unannounced. Although I had a key, and he never locked the door when he was at home, I knocked to give him a moment to prepare for a visitor.

I needn't have worried. When the door opened, it wasn't Charlie, but Mavis who was standing there, an enquiring look on her face. At least, until she saw me.

"Good grief. Jane. We weren't expecting–" She wiped her hands on her apron, but made no effort to let me in.

"I know you weren't. I wasn't sure a telegram would arrive in time, and if it did, you'd probably have tried to stop me coming." I peered over her shoulder and down the corridor. A shadowy figure moved around at the far end, in the kitchen. "How's Charlie?"

"Recovering from a bad cold, if you must know."

I tamped down a flutter of irritation. *If you must know.* Of course I must know. I'm his wife, for heaven's sake. "Seeing me will cheer him up, poor darling." I pushed past her, stopping at our bedroom to drop in my suitcase.

I heard Mavis sigh behind me. "I'll put the kettle on," she said.

I'd rather she left me alone with Charlie, but to ask her to leave would be churlish. Despite my fears, the ferry coming over had been filled with holidaymakers, to all intents unconcerned that war raged just across the water in France and invasion was imminent. But even so, every second with Charlie would be precious, and I didn't want to share him.

"Jane." Charlie's misshapen form filled the doorway. Light spilled from the picture windows behind him, shielding the expression on his face. "This is a—"

"Surprise? Shock?" I laughed and took him in my arms. He felt thinner – much thinner than when I'd seen him five weeks ago. Close up, I could see his pallor. "Mavis says you've been under the weather. Nothing too dreary, I hope?" Any illness worried me; he'd suffered so much, his system didn't cope with setbacks.

"Mavis exaggerates. Just a sniffle."

Mavis, fiddling at the sink, looked up sharply and shook her head. We both knew Charlie hated a fuss. I'd play along with the charade.

"Good to know."

Balancing on his stick, he shuffled to a dining chair. "You shouldn't have come. It's too dangerous."

"Don't be silly. The boat was full of tourists." I stroked his hand where it lay on the tabletop. Earth clung to his cuticles. "You've been gardening."

"More vegetables. Potatoes, carrots. Runner beans." His underlying meaning was clear: he was stocking up for inevitable shortages.

Mavis brought over a teapot, milk jug and two cups. "I'll be off." She untied her apron. "Will you see me out, Jane?"

She placed a hand on Charlie's shoulder. "Don't forget your medicine."

I led the way to the door, keen now to be relieved of Mavis's possessive attitude.

She joined me, stern-faced. "How foolish you are, Jane. What if you get trapped here?"

"Stop being so melodramatic. Nothing's going to happen overnight. I had to see Charlie while there was still a chance. I'll only stay a few days."

Mavis lowered her voice to a stage whisper. "How's Esme?"

I wished she hadn't asked. "I've not seen her in an age. Granny Fanstone has made her board at school and I'm not allowed to visit without permission."

"You get letters?"

"Oh yes. Full of girlish nonsense about hockey matches, the terrible food and how she hates carrying a gas mask everywhere. You know the sort of thing." An awkward pause hung between us. I shouldn't have said that. How did Mavis know anything of the ways of teenage girls?

"And her father?" Mavis couldn't bring herself to say 'Lewis'.

"He's fine." Lewis wasn't a subject for discussion. Mavis only asked to be polite. As it happened, I constantly fretted about him. He'd been assigned to some top-secret unit and couldn't tell me where he was posted. I received occasional letters – Lewis was never one for putting pen to paper, that was my department – with all the interesting bits blacked out. That was another reason I couldn't stay away for long. If he got leave, it might only be with forty-eight hours' notice and I couldn't risk missing him – and the chance to spend time with Esme as well.

I glanced back down the hallway before giving Mavis a quick hug. "I'll be back as soon as it's safe. Thank you for taking care of him. Let me know if anything–" expressing my fears for Charlie made them too real "–untoward happens."

Mavis squeezed my arm. "You can rely on me."

Her words rang in my head as I made my way back to the kitchen. How very true. Mavis: always dependable, always loyal.

Charlie had poured two cups of tea. "I can't pretend I'm not glad to see you. Even if I do think you're an idiot to risk your safety." His words slurred. "I've missed you."

Ever since Granny Fanstone issued her ultimatum, we'd seen more of each other, not less. With Lewis in the army and Esme under Granny's custody in the Cotswolds, my time had been more my own. Betting that Granny couldn't afford to put a private detective onto me, I ignored her veiled insinuation of some sort of hold over me regarding my trips. For the past two years, I'd visited every two or three months. Only short breaks, but the frequency brought us closer, and made our life together less fractured, more domestic and harmonious. It made the Nazi threat even harder to prepare for.

I came up behind him, wrapped my arms around his chest and rested my cheek against the top of his head. He smelt of carbolic soap. "What medicine are you on?"

He placed his hands over mine. "I haven't had any illness. That was a lie. I've been anxious. Afraid. Mavis found some tonic. I don't think it makes a difference."

I stiffened, and circled around to sit next to him, so I could read his face. "Tell me."

"Bad nightmares." He chewed on his lip.

I didn't ask further. I could guess. With Germany on the move, his time as a prisoner and the harsh treatment he'd suffered in the World War I camps would resurface like an unsinkable buoy. He'd only spoken of the torture he'd endured once, but in his sleep, he would often thrash around, yell out and beg for mercy.

"I wish I could take you back with me." We both knew that was impossible. And yet, the alternative was no better. If the Germans took Guernsey, Charlie risked being captured, which could mean imprisonment again, and all that might go with it.

For now, our time together was too important to waste on being maudlin. It might be several months before we would see each other again. I ran a finger down the front of his trousers and heard his sharp intake of breath. "Take me to bed," I said. "Undress me. Let's make memories."

24

ESME

ENGLAND, AUGUST 1958

*B*ack in the familiar Cotswolds sitting room with its sagging sofas, worn Persian rugs and side lamps with chintzy tassels, Esme was transported back to her teenage years. For reasons she'd never understood, she'd lived here for several years with her grandparents before and during the war.

They'd been happy days for Esme: sleeping on a camp bed in the cellar during air raids; the butter dish with her name on it for her weekly two-ounce ration; and when she was old enough, painting her legs tan and drawing on a stocking seam. Despite the deprivations, it had been exhilarating. Blacked-out windows, gardens turned into vegetable allotments, and delivering government leaflets in her Girl Guide uniform all added spice to growing up – as well as the curiosity of the East End children billeted in the attic.

Her mother, meanwhile, had remained in her and Lewis' partially bombed-out London home, and rarely visited. She'd claimed living in a small village under the same roof as Granny Fanstone would be 'worse than the front line of battle'. In return, whenever Arcadia's name was mentioned, Granny would sniff and declare, "Your mother doesn't give a jot for you," and with a brisk flick, snap her fingers under Esme's nose.

Older and wiser, Esme now wondered if there had been another reason why Arcadia had chosen to stay in London for the duration of the war, aside from her dislike of Granny Fanstone. Another man? Unlikely. Whenever Lewis was home on leave, he and Arcadia had seemed as lively as ever, wrapped up in happiness at being together for a short time. Well, perhaps this evening she'd get some answers.

These days, forced to live back in the Cotswolds with his mother, Lewis existed on a small pension. Grandpops was long dead, but Granny Fanstone soldiered on, albeit profoundly deaf, bones shrunken, and daily willing the gods to take her to heaven to join her beloved Henry. Seated across from him, Esme watched her father take a cigarette from a battered silver case, tap the end and light up. In his other hand he held a large tumbler of whisky. Neat. The way he preferred it. She examined his face, the criss-cross of fine lines testament to years of hard living. Few signs remained of the once good-looking army officer. The man before her was gaunt, clothes hanging limp on his bony frame, eyes sunken and sad. But when he looked up at Esme, a little of their sparkle returned.

"Nice to see you, possum," he said. He always called her possum. He'd caught the name from an Australian friend and it stuck. "You've cheered Granny up, even if she couldn't hear a word you said. She won't wear those blasted earpieces. Says she doesn't want to get dependent on them. I ask you! She's eighty-five."

"She's polishing more than ever, I see." No maids now, Granny kept a constant rag in her hand to clean any surface before it could harbour dust. The only exercise she managed these days was her daily circuit of the old house checking standards hadn't slipped, before she returned to her bed where she spent her days mulling the past, reading old letters and diaries, and talking to the ghost of Grandpops.

"It keeps her occupied, and the furniture gleaming." His voice dropped. "But put it this way, possum, your timing is good. She's failing fast but stays bright, although she says she's ready to join Grandpops."

Esme had adored her Grandpops. Confined by a thrombosis to his bed, he'd had a naughty sense of humour, and would terrorise the maids by pretending to have dementia. "Where's my breakfast?" he'd yell at dinner time. Or he'd call them all into his room and insist they line up on parade and salute him. Esme would be reduced to fits of giggles at his antics, which only spurred Grandpops on to bigger and greater pranks.

"I hope I feel that way about someone one day." As soon as she said it, Esme realised her wistful comment was tactless. Lewis would hardly want to join his ex-wife, Arcadia, in the afterlife.

Lewis took a large slug of whisky. "I'll be up there–" he looked skywards, "–reconnoitring with my fallen comrades for a few beers and a game of cards."

Typical of her father to see the life hereafter as one big party. "You didn't come to Arcadia's funeral." She didn't mean to sound accusatory, but her voice came out hard and resentful.

"No. I wouldn't be a hypocrite."

"It would have been nice for me."

"Sorry, possum."

Even in death, the day had been all about Arcadia, not the grief at her passing. It would have been the way Arcadia wanted it. Centre stage, the talk of the moment. A few of her old friends were there, swapping stories about their glorious youth, the good old days before the war when they partied and danced the nights away. *How amusing Arcadia was! What scintillating company! Such a talent too!* No one took notice of Esme, or offered condolences, and why would they? The daughter who was either taken care of by nannies or her grandparents, and would occasionally be seen at Arcadia's side when it suited her to play mother. No one asked after Lewis, the errant husband, either, although Esme heard their whispers. *Such a scoundrel! How he squandered money!* Esme, saddened by their superficiality, had been glad to place a bunch of bluebells on her mother's coffin and say her goodbyes.

"Aren't you going to ask how I've gone in Guernsey, looking for Arcadia's family?"

A heavy silence fell. Lewis took another sip of whisky and stubbed out his cigarette in the ashtray on the arm of his chair. "Did you have any luck?"

"It's like she never existed."

He nodded, as if unsurprised, but remained mute.

"But I did discover *you* were there in 1945. And got into a fight."

"Aha."

"Why?"

"I was stationed in St Peter Port for a few months. The British sent me to help with the liberation."

"I worked that out. I meant the fight with Bernard Vautier, otherwise known as Charlie."

Lewis shook his head. "Old news, possum. Leave it be."

"I want to know. I need to know. Why did you exchange blows? Did he attack you? Why did you drop the charges?"

"I can't tell you. I promised your mother."

Her mother? Esme stared at him, torn between frustration and anger. "My mother's dead. And to my knowledge, you never spoke to her after the divorce. Why would you need to keep your word to a woman you obviously hated? Despised even?"

Lewis tensed his jaw, the muscles taut in his cheeks. "I'm not doing it for her."

"Who then?"

"You, possum. You." He took another cigarette from his case. "So don't ask me."

"That's ridiculous. I'm a big girl, and having asked, I deserve an answer. Anyway, you can't keep a promise to a dead woman."

"I can and I will." He struck a match.

"But – she was so young when she left Guernsey. Sent to England, her father at war, her mother dying. When I was growing up, she never spoke of anyone, friends or family. If I asked, she changed the subject. No one I've spoken to has ever heard of her. I don't understand how she became so invisible when I know – I *know* – she kept in touch with someone because I found a letter, telling her Charlie was in trouble. That's what started all this."

Lewis's breath, tense and raspy, filled the air as he dragged on his cigarette. "Remember, your mother told stories for a living. Don't believe all she told you. She had her secrets. And some secrets are best left hidden, as I discovered to my peril."

Esme pressed on. "How did she know Charlie? Who was he to her? It can't be a coincidence you got into a fight."

"It was nothing. A misunderstanding."

"I don't believe you. And Arcadia – did she go to Guernsey in 1945?"

He blew smoke up to the ceiling. "Apparently she often went to Guernsey."

Esme frowned. How could she not have known? "Why did she go? Who did she see?"

His face closed down. "I can't tell you, because I didn't know. I thought she was off scouting locations for her books. We all did. Once or twice a year she'd take off, leave you with Nanny, and go chasing inspiration. Scotland, the Lake District, Cornwall. Or rather, as it turned out, Guernsey."

Her mother often went to Guernsey and yet no one there knew her? None of this made sense. Esme banged her fist on the side of her chair. "What's so terrible that I need protecting? Don't you realise you're making it worse? Please, don't stand on some old-fashioned platform of duty and honour instead of helping me learn more about my family."

Lewis took a deep drag on his cigarette. "I won't be the one to tell you. But if you plan on returning there, and you really want to know the truth, ask Charlie, if he's still alive. Or maybe that woman who's always been in love with him. Mavis. Perhaps one of them won't have as much *honour* as I." He spat the word with sarcasm. "And I won't have it on my conscience."

Mavis, in love with Charlie? That was a turn-up. Esme put it aside to think about later. "Can I ask you one more thing?" She would be risking rejection, but it was worth a try.

"You can ask. I may not answer."

"Why did you divorce? Surely you can tell me that now. I'm not a child – well, I wasn't then either – but I don't want to keep assuming she left you because she was tired of all your women and wild spending, when it might have been something else altogether."

He snorted. "Is that what she told you? Feasible enough, I suppose, given my track record. We always loved each other, in our way. She lit up my life until... until–" He paused. "Let's just say it was your mother who brought disgrace on this family, and her death should be the end of it. I don't want you tainted with her wrongdoing. Granny Fanstone was right about her all along. Arcadia only ever cared about Arcadia. As I said before, no good will come of you poking around in Guernsey. Drop it, possum." He drained his glass. "I'm for bed – and before you ask, the subject won't be reopened. Not by me." On his way out, he kissed the top of her head. A small apology, perhaps, for being tight-lipped.

After he'd gone upstairs, Esme turned over what he'd said, and not said. She'd never seen any indications that their marriage had been in crisis. Quite the reverse. They often spoke of longing for the day when they'd be able to resume married life and spend time on their own. And yet, they divorced shortly after the end of the war – and it now seemed clear the catalyst for their separation had its roots in Guernsey.

∼

The buzz of laughter and eager chatter over mugs of tea in the visitors' area was at odds with the cold, forbidding exterior of Holloway Prison. Except for the sameness of their white shirts, Esme found it hard to believe that the room contained convicted criminals. Although on closer inspection, she saw sadness in their eyes – women separated from their husbands and children, bravely trying to be cheery.

She'd brought Clara a package with foodstuffs, unsure whether anything more personal would be either allowed or appropriate. The guards took it from her, promising Clara would get it after they'd checked the contents.

Prison life had aged Clara; if asked to guess her age, Esme would have said mid to late forties. Her skin had dried into papery lines, her hands were gnarled with arthritis and her hair was completely grey. Sitting across from one another, Clara did her darnedest to put Esme at ease, sensing her visitor's discomfort to be in such alien surrounds. She talked about her job in the sewing room, the daily exercises the women undertook in the grounds, her burgeoning love of gardening and watching things grow.

"Here's me talking non-stop, I'm such a chatterbox, I am, and you've made this special trip to see me." Clara stopped for a moment to draw breath. "I was right chuffed when I got your request. I wondered to myself, now what brings Miss Fanstone to England?"

"I came to visit my grandmother; she's not got long left. Now I'm en route back to Guernsey but I thought it an ideal opportunity to meet you while I'm in London."

A faraway look shadowed Clara's face. "For all what

happened, I miss Guernsey. I know as most hated it when the Germans came but I found them days exciting. You never knew what would happen next. And I felt safer than I ever had."

"You must have been with the Mellons since the war began?"

"I went to them a few months before, straight from the children's home. Thirteen, I was."

Gosh, that meant Clara was quite a bit younger than Esme. The years had not been kind. "Why were you in a home?"

"My father, he was a drunk. Hit my mam, drank away all our money – what little we had – and then scarpered to France after mam died. He didn't want to look after a scrap of a girl like me."

"How old were you?"

"Four, I think. That's what they told me."

"What was it like in the home?"

"Oh, miss, you've no idea." Clara clasped her hands together. "It were awful. We was treated no better than rats. I tell you what, being there prepared me well for this place. At least here I get fed and sleep in a dry bed."

"And were the Mellons good to you?"

"As good as anyone else ever had been. They told me what to do and I did it. Stayed out their way most of the time. I was to be seen and not heard, that's what the mistress said."

"And M. Mellon? He was never harsh, or laid his hands on you?"

Clara laughed. "Good lordy, no, miss. He had his hands all over another, if you get my meaning."

It seemed Clara had little motivation to kill her mistress and jeopardise what must have seemed a comfortable life. "Did you have friends, Clara? Or a sweetheart?"

"There was a boy I saw on me afternoon off, but he skedaddled. Never even came to my trial."

"Do you have any idea who killed your mistress? In your letter you said you had 'private ideas'."

Clara shook her head. "I only said that to make you curious. I only know it wasn't me. Will you find who did it? Please say you will?"

Esme was loath to make a promise she couldn't deliver. "I want to write the truth of your life, Clara, and if that means I discover new evidence, it would be a great bonus. I can't say more than that."

A bell rang, signalling the end of visiting time. Esme thanked Clara for seeing her and shook her hand. "One last question... did you ever know someone called Arcadia, or anyone with the family name, Robin?"

"Like the bird, miss? No, can't say I ever did. Nor that other funny name. Arcade?"

The warden, a gaunt woman with a severe expression, came over and shooed Clara away. "Back to your cell," she said, then turned to Esme. "Good day to you."

"I'll let you know how I get on," Esme called over her shoulder, as she made her way to the exit. There was something endearing about Clara, with her ready acceptance of her lot whilst still retaining enthusiastic joy for her small life. Esme may not have promised Clara her freedom, but she intended to do everything possible to gain her release, because having met her, she now was certain Clara had suffered a miscarriage of justice.

Walking back into the Soho office gave Esme a charge of electricity. Her senses heightened at the clatter of typewriter keys, the smell of paper, the hubbub of voices. She held her bag close to her body and wove past desks of frowning stenographers, reporters with phones hooked under one ear busy scribbling notes, and editors flicking through the day's galley pages. One or two heads lifted and gave her a smile or nod of recognition. Delivery boys dropped off envelopes marked *Urgent*, whilst telex operators deciphered wire stories with furious intensity.

There was a bounce to Esme's step as she headed to the office at the end. She'd spent her life either trailing, heartsick, behind Hugh, or living in the shadow of her mother's literary envy. And now she had the opportunity to put an end to both, and carve her own way.

Through the glass wall, she could see Hugh – sleeves rolled up and held in place with a shirt garter – arguing on the phone, like old times. At this time of day, he'd be persuading some poor type-setter to replace the lead story with a more eye-catching head-line. He slammed down the receiver, lifted his hand in acknowledgement and waved her in.

"You look mighty happy." He made to kiss her cheek, but Esme gave him a warning glance. Too many curious eyes in the typing pool.

"I am." She glanced around. "This place doesn't change. The usual final edition mania."

"It's worse than ever without you here to keep everyone's toes on the line." Hugh laughed. "I can't tell you how thrilled I am to see you. I wracked my brains for a way to get to St Peter Port, but you beat me to the punch. Anyway, the main thing is you're here."

"I had to see my father."

For a second, Hugh looked crestfallen, then brightened. "And me of course." He grabbed his jacket from behind his chair. "Let's get out of here. Lots to talk about."

Her took her elbow, talking non-stop as he steered her to the exit. "I've hired a new deputy editor. Starts next Monday. Nowhere near as good as you, of course, but he'll step up as editor when we go to the States." He called across a row of desks. "Hey, Jimmy, that colour piece needs a haircut, too verbose, too many adverbs," then grinned at Esme. "Remember that secretary you took on; Anita? She's a gem, you really can pick them. I'm promoting her to office manager." A young red-headed lad passed by. "Nice scoop, Felix, keep that up and you'll be a fine journalist." In the same breath, he added, "I thought we'd go to the Duke of Argyll for a drink first. Okay with you?"

Esme found she didn't care she'd been replaced, although it was gratifying to know Anita had stepped up to the challenge. Nor was she interested where they had a drink. "If you don't mind, I'd like to collect my personal belongings. I left so suddenly–"

Hugh gestured for her to go ahead. "I need to sort tomorrow's lead. I'll see you in the lobby."

She took a sharp left turn. Her old desk, at the end of the row, had afforded some degree of privacy. Cleared of the usual daily detritus, it now appeared somewhat neglected, sporting only a telephone and a pot of pencils. There wasn't much in the drawers to gather up: a fountain pen given to her by her father on her twenty-first birthday, a spare pair of stockings, a photograph of her parents on holiday in Torquay, an *Oxford English Dictionary*. Everything else – old notebooks, stationery, reference books – now belonged to the new deputy editor. A quick double-check of the desk drawers yielded one more item: a letter from Hugh, dated September 1947.

76 Brewer St, Soho, W1

Dear Esme,

Sorry not to have been in touch for a while. Since I married Tomasina, there's been little time for letter-writing. But this is less of a letter, and more of an offer.

Cutting to the chase – will you come and work for me? Yes, I know you are writing a book but you can't live off that inheritance from your grandfather forever, sooner or later (until you become a famous author) you'll need income. And I need you!

Here's the thing. I'm starting a newspaper. It's to be called The Monitor and I intend to focus on how England's people are rebuilding

this nation of ours: the difficulties, the challenges, the bureaucratic
nonsense, coping with grief, coping with injuries.

I desperately need a secretary-cum-copy editor and who else can I
trust? You will be superb. Please, please say yes. We'll only be a staff of
three to begin with (Tomasina will write most of the articles) but it will
be fun. Starting salary, £230.

If the answer is yes, can you start immediately? Come to the address
above and we will work it out as we go along.

Best,
Hugh

She hadn't taken long to decide. The very next day, she'd
entered this building for the first time, although ten years ago
Hugh had only leased one small office. She remembered walking
in, telling herself to bury any romantic thoughts about Hugh and
make the sternest effort to like his wife. And largely, she'd
succeeded.

"What have you found there?"

At the sound of Hugh's voice, Esme jumped and thrust the
letter in her pocket. "Nothing important." She put her things in
the roomy shoulder bag she'd brought for the purpose, and
without a backwards glance, followed Hugh out to Brewer Street.

They walked past The Crown, the office's local pub, to the less
frequented Duke of Argyll where their conversation wouldn't be
overheard by Hugh's employees. Esme found a small table with
two spare chairs while Hugh bought her a gin and tonic. The last
time she'd been in a pub was with Anthony, for another tricky
conversation. She smiled, picturing the way his hair flopped on
his forehead, the distracted way he tapped his pipe on the back of
his hand...

"Bit of a queue." Hugh set down two gins and then half-filled
each from a bottle of tonic. He lifted his glass. "Here's to us, and
our next big adventure. Oh, I've so much to share with you. The
plans are progressing well. I've taken on an editor, super chap,

ex-marine, comes from New York. He's hiring a couple of writers, a sub-editor and a receptionist. I rather thought you could manage all the production side of things. You know the set-up we have here, and that will leave me free to wine and dine advertisers. What do you say?"

"Hugh–"

"I know it's a lot to take in."

"Hugh–"

He slapped his forehead. "I'm an idiot, aren't I? Worse, I'm putting the cart before the horse. I haven't even proposed properly yet and here I am, telling you about our new life together. By the way, I've already leased a marvellous house. Five bedrooms, white picket fence. There's even room for a swimming pool. Miranda chose it from the realtor's catalogue, but don't let that put you against it. You'll love it. And you can furnish it any way you want. Within reason, of course."

"Hugh. Stop."

"Sorry. Nerves. I'm babbling."

Esme leaned forwards and took both his hands in hers. His skin felt dry and cool. "Do you believe there's a time for everything?"

Hugh looked taken aback. "I suppose I do. And this is our time."

"Is it? I'm not so sure."

"Esme, darling. I know I'm a stupid man and I've been a bit slow on the uptake, but I realise how much you mean to me. All these years we've been together and yet it's taken until now for me to see you. Really see you."

"And what do you see?" Could it be his blinkers had fallen away, and at last he understood her needs, her passions?

"I see our future." He fished in his jacket pocket and placed a small box on the table. "Here's my commitment to you. Open it."

She looked at the box and back at Hugh. "I fell in love with you the first day we met," she said. "Did you know that?"

Hugh frowned and shook his head.

"I thought not. You probably don't remember it." He'd snapped his fingers and she'd followed him out of the typing pool. Another WAAF, ambitious and perky in her smart uniform, keen to do her bit for King and country. "One moment I was typing letters to bereaved family and the next, under your command, mapping every U-boat sighting." And ever since, she'd continued to do Hugh's bidding.

He gave a nervous smile. "You were good at your job. Always cheerful. Despite the long hours and lack of sleep. But, you know, there was Tomasina."

"And Pippie. Not to mention, Miranda."

"What are you getting at?"

"My point is, how well do you think you know me?"

"What a silly question. Like the back of my hand."

"As a colleague, yes. As a woman?"

Hugh sighed. "Smart. Organised. Reliable. That's it. Reliable. Someone I can't be without. Someone who keeps me steady." He pushed the box further towards her. "Go on. Open it."

She pushed it back. "You've missed your moment, Hugh. I don't want to be your right-hand woman, running your life for you. And my newspaper days are over. I want to be loved and cherished. Not be second, or even third, best."

"But – but – that's crazy. These things happen. It's never too late."

"That's where you're wrong. I'm a novelist now, living in Guernsey. Don't misunderstand. I enjoyed working for you. I learned a lot and met interesting people. But I've wasted my emotional self by being in love with someone who only noticed me when the office machinery broke down, deadlines got missed or no one remembered to buy coffee."

Esme saw a flash of irritation cross his face and in that instant she knew that anything they'd had in common, or whatever glue had held them together in the past, was now long gone.

"But I've already–" He checked himself. "Is there someone else?"

"No. That is, yes. Yes, there is." Anthony. If he'd have her. "And I must get back to him." She stood, her drink untouched. "I'm sorry, Hugh, because once upon a time this conversation might have had an entirely different ending. But I wish you all the luck in Pennsylvania." She leaned down and kissed his cheek. "Goodbye."

Head high, she exited into the bustle of Soho. If all the connections worked, she could retrieve her suitcase from the luggage locker at Paddington Station, be on the boat train departing Waterloo at nine o'clock, and dock at St Peter Port in the morning.

25

ARCADIA

LONDON, 8 OCTOBER 1945

*G*etting out of the Cheyne Row house for a couple of hours should have raised my spirits. Living in a partially bombed building, boarded up where it had taken a hit, was a constant reminder of what we'd all suffered. The chance to see Esme, though, always became fraught with the undercurrents of her resentment. She might be twenty-one but she still harboured a stiff, wounded edge where I was concerned. Generally, despite my best efforts, I managed to put my foot in it, say the wrong thing, or upset her in some unforeseen way.

Sitting across the table from one another at Lyons Corner House, we were separated by a plate of toasted teacakes and a large silver teapot. The conversation was stilted, even though I did my best to be gay and chivvy her along. As always, she was hard work.

At least now Esme had come of age, Granny Fanstone couldn't prevent us meeting. However, it was obvious Esme saw it as duty rather than pleasure. Perhaps I shouldn't be surprised. That poisonous old woman had doubtless created a whole parallel persona for me – a selfish, self-serving mother who preferred to enjoy the high life without the inconvenient encumbrance of a daughter. And all the while knowing I couldn't say anything in rebuttal.

I tonged a cube of sugar into my tea and scouted around for a subject to chat about, other than myself. "How's that young man of yours? Gerald, is it?"

Esme kept her eyes fixed on the tablecloth. "Jeremy. And he's not 'my young man'. He's just a friend."

"Oh? He seemed rather keen on you, I thought."

She shrugged. "You thought wrong."

"Oh well, plenty more fish as they say."

"Not really, Mummy. Given so many men have lost their lives," she said sharply.

Rebuked, I sat back and examined her. Out of WAAF uniform, she hadn't exactly taken advantage of wearing mufti. Her dress was a drab grey, relieved only by red buttons at the neckline, and not particularly fashionable. She still wore her hair long; to hide the scar, of course, but it didn't flatter the shape of her face. I moved to another, safer topic. "What are your plans, now the war is behind us?"

"I'm going to write a book."

"A book?" My voice came out as a strangled squawk. "What sort of a book? A schoolbook?"

"A novel, actually."

I felt my hackles going up. "No money in it, darling."

"I thought you'd be pleased. Following in your footsteps and all that."

"No doubt your father has said he'll help you get it published."

"He hasn't, and I wouldn't ask. If it's not good enough to find a proper publisher, then it's not good enough to be published."

Ouch. Esme had always been sniffy about Lewis paying to publish my books – vanity publishing, she had the cheek to call it. I slowly stirred my tea, absorbing her announcement, and tried to tamp down green darts of jealousy. "What's it about?"

"Do you remember those children from the East End who were billeted at Granny Fanstone's?"

I nodded. Two ruffian boys and a shy girl, aged between eight and eleven, who were scared of chickens and preferred to hide in the sheds rather than ride horses. They'd been housed for more than four years in the former maids' quarters. Esme wasn't allowed to have much to do with them. They were sent to the local school whilst she was parcelled off to Cheltenham Ladies' College.

"After they returned to Billingsgate, I often wondered how living in the affluent Cotswolds might have changed the course of their aspirations," Esme said. "I couldn't ask them because no one thought to exchange addresses and anyway their original home had been bombed to ashes, so I decided to invent their futures in a novel."

"It sounds like a good idea." I tried not to sound begrudging. "Though I'm not sure what you know about that sort of person?"

"No more than you do about eighteenth-century society," Esme snapped, "but at least I can go to the East End and talk to people about their war, and how it affected them. Maybe even speak to youngsters who were billeted." She looked at her watch, the one Lewis and I gave her for her eighteenth birthday. "Tell me your news."

I waved at the waitress for the bill; whenever Esme checked the time, it meant she'd soon find an excuse to be off. "The usual. I'm still giving my weekly book reviews for the BBC's *Woman's Hour*, and I've a new novel hitting the shelves in a few weeks. I'm planning a bit of a launch party. There will be lots of important people there, darling... celebrities, politicians. You should come along, do some networking. You might even meet some eligible bachelors." On reflection, I should see this business of Esme trying to write a book as an opportunity for us to enjoy a shared hobby and repair some fences.

"Not my thing, Mummy, but thanks anyway." She gathered

together her handbag and gloves, and before I could ask if we were heading in the same direction, she'd left me with a promise we'd meet again next month. These days, she shared rooms with two other girls. I should have adored her living with us, but bound by my so-called 'agreement' with Granny F, I'd had to deflect the idea when Esme first raised it. Once Lewis left the army, perhaps he could persuade her, although now she'd had a taste of independence I couldn't imagine she'd want to move back in with her parents.

Feeling flat after our unsatisfactory get-together, I didn't want to go back to an empty house, with no one for company. Lewis was still on an overseas posting – his letters were sporadic and not very informative about his whereabouts – and he wasn't due leave for several weeks. After Benson signed up, the only servant we kept was a woman who came in daily to clean and prepare very average meals. A blessing in some ways, as it was propelling me into learning how to cook – with the aid of Marguerite Patten, my BBC cohort who generously provided with me with copies of her on-air recipes.

I walked towards Knightsbridge and cheered myself up by browsing through Harrods. Then I went to the post office in the hope that a letter awaited me. With the Germans occupying the Channel Islands, ferries and postal services to and from the mainland had ceased. I'd been able to send Charlie short messages via the Red Cross – the 25-word quota just enough to assure him I was well and thinking of him – but they took months to arrive. Very occasionally I'd receive something back, in a terrible left-handed scrawl, but at least I knew he was alive, not detained by the Germans, nor suffering some other fate. Once in a while, Mavis wrote too. These were letters which I found hard to bear, knowing she saw Charlie all the time and had insinuated herself into his daily life. In her last one, dated in July shortly after liberation, she revealed the islanders had been near starvation and needed some recovery time from all the hardship, but that she'd write when it was feasible for me to visit. With that, I had to be content, but I was pursued by images of Charlie, skeletal and malnourished, traumatised by German gangs.

At the post office, I queued for twenty minutes before a harried assistant served me. I purchased some stamps and waited. The young man returned and passed across a letter addressed by Mavis in unsteady handwriting, as if she'd been in a hurry. Anxious to learn its contents, rather than tuck it into my bag to read at home, I moved away from the counter and slit open the envelope with the miniature penknife I carried.

October 6th, 1945

> *Dearest–*

> *It's been the most terrible two days. I so hoped to sort everything quickly and not bother you but things have gone from bad to worse. C has got into the most awful trouble and landed in jail. Now there's talk of an attempted murder charge. C's gone all mute and sullen and won't speak to any of us. You must get over here as soon as you can. The ferries are running again though Lord knows how reliable they are.*

> *Love, in haste, M.*

My mind went into overdrive, unable to fathom how on earth Charlie could have ended up in jail. He never left his house, so had some spectre from his past, a malignant spy who might reveal his dark secret, turned up and threatened him with exposure? There was only one way to sort whatever mess he'd become entangled with. Filled with a weight of dread, I walked from the post office and headed straight to Thomas Cook's travel agency, praying I'd be able to secure a berth on the next day's ferry.

26

ESME

GUERNSEY, 1958

*E*sme alighted from the steamer and hurried up the gangway, albeit hampered by the weight of her case. She'd telegrammed Anthony with her arrival time, hoping he'd pick her up. She scanned the early morning crowd – husbands eager to reunite with wives, parents anxiously checking for children, friends waving with mad enthusiasm at their buddies – but she couldn't see him. She hefted her case, heavier than on her outward trip thanks to her raid on Foyles bookstore, and made her slow way to the roadside. There was no sign of his cream MG amongst the waiting cars and taxicabs.

Disappointed, she walked the length of the harbour wall to the bus station, dropped her case and perched on top. Perhaps he hadn't received her missive. Perhaps he'd had to go away. Or perhaps he knew she'd returned but didn't want to see her. No, that made no sense. They'd parted on good terms, their friendship still intact. Perhaps he was ill... there'd been a nasty flu bug doing the rounds...

The arrival of the bus interrupted her disconsolate thoughts. By the time she'd paid her fare and settled in her seat, she'd become more optimistic. Quite likely he'd pop in on his way to work to say hello. Then they could make arrangements to see each other later and she'd tell him how she'd broken it off with Hugh.

She hugged herself in anticipation of the look of delight that would cross Anthony's face. His cheeky smile. The knowing twinkle in his eye. Would he jump up and take her in his arms? Or would he nod and probe for details, to be sure she really was over Hugh. Anxious knots caught in her stomach. Why, oh why had she been so stupid and not realised sooner her heart lay with Anthony? How could she ever have considered Hugh the man of her dreams? How come Arcadia had seen what Esme refused to acknowledge – that Hugh had no staying power? Certainly not the romantic kind.

She stared out of the bus window as the steep town streets gave way to narrow roads. Lavender, in a riot of purple, sprouted from cottage gardens. Glasshouses, one after the other, glistened under the rising sun, whilst here and there Esme spied hedge-boxes filled with tomatoes, potatoes and eggs. They weren't just familiar sights now. They signalled 'home'.

There were so many other things to share with Anthony. All that she'd discovered from her father: his promise to Arcadia not to reveal the reason for his fight with Charlie; her mother's regular trips to Guernsey. They'd discuss what possible reason she'd had to keep these trips from Lewis, and the increasing oddity of no one knowing her. Had she used an assumed name when she'd journeyed here? Esme sighed. That made no sense either, because she'd grown up here, so people would have recognised her. And she was keen to know what more Anthony had discovered about Charlie. Above all, whether he was still alive – and living in St Peter Port.

The bus driver dropped her at the end of her road. Esme dragged her case onto the pavement. The bus chugged off and she took a moment to enjoy the early morning peace, broken only by birdsong and a light breeze ruffling the trees. No one was about except for the postman, a portly young man with a shock of red hair peeping out from under his peaked cap.

"Here, love," he called across the road. "I'll carry that." He hurried over, swung his mailbag across his back and lifted her case as if it contained only feathers.

Esme made no argument, thankful for Guernsey courtesy. It wouldn't happen in London.

"Been off somewhere, eh?" he asked.

"England."

"Never been." He trudged on ahead. "Missed the war," he added by way of explanation, although he couldn't have been older than late twenties.

"Were you evacuated?"

"Nah. Mam kept me here. Said it was safer. I dunno. All them Jerries everywhere. I was a good scavenger though. Never got caught neither." His voice held an edge of pride. "Here we are." He turned up her path and put her case at the front door. "Welcome home."

Smiling at his words, she pushed her key in the lock, eager to get inside. She heaved her case over the step and picked up the small pile of letters lying on the mat. On top, an envelope with just her name: *Esme*. Still in her coat, she extracted the sheet of paper.

Esme,
> *Sorry, couldn't fetch you. Very busy. Be in touch in a week or two.*
> *Regards,*
> *Anthony Fellowes*

Esme felt sick. This wasn't a note from a man keen to know how things stood between them. It was a brush-off. Why? She read and reread his words. His whole tone was abrupt and dismissive, as if he'd lost interest in her. He hadn't even nominated why he couldn't see her. As for writing, 'Regards', and addressing her as 'Esme' – not even 'Dear Esme' – well, that seemed to speak for itself.

Or was she being silly? Reading between lines that didn't exist? Maybe she should take his words at face value. Something had cropped up to take his immediate attention. A family emergency, perhaps. If that were the case, he'd apologise profusely, wouldn't he?

Stumped, she slowly walked through to the living room and dropped onto the sofa, blinking back tears. What on earth happened to cause such an about-turn? And how could she put things right? She couldn't go chasing him down, but the idea of waiting for him to contact her – *in a week or two* – was excruciating. She could only guess that Anthony had been angry at her decision to see Hugh, and as a result, she'd blown it with him. Failing a cupid with a magic bow, she'd have to accept her feelings weren't reciprocated. Yet again.

If Mavis was surprised at opening her front door to Esme, she didn't show it. Instead, she invited her in, asking in a casual tone, "Any particular reason for your visit?"

Esme only hesitated for a split second. "Yes, there is. You see, I saw my father, Lewis Fanstone–" she scanned Mavis's face for a reaction, but she kept her chin high and her expression impassive, "–and he told me I should speak to you. Because you know why he got into a fight with Charlie back in 1945." Mavis remained silent. "I found a letter in my mother's flat, asking her to come to Guernsey, because C was in terrible trouble. You wrote that letter, didn't you?"

Mavis crumpled slightly and Esme could see her battling to make a decision. Finally, she took Esme's arm. "Come in. I'll make us tea." Her voice had softened, almost apologetic.

While Mavis busied herself in the kitchen, Esme looked

around. Mavis's house was like Mavis; austere, clean lines, and plain decoration. No florals or vivid colours. An oak sideboard displayed several half-filled crystal decanters and a tray of glasses, but there were no other ornaments. The effect was startling. Modern and chic. Mavis favoured deep maroon for her soft furnishings, Scandinavian-style leather armchairs, and whitewashed walls relieved by dozens of framed landscapes of the Channel Islands. No people, just views of the sea, fields, battlements and bunkers, rows of glasshouses. Each signed *M. Lucas.*

Finally seated with cups of tea, Esme noticed how Mavis's brusque, controlled demeanour had been overtaken by a more anxious, yet conversely, more relaxed, person. When she spoke, her voice was soft with yearning. "I couldn't wait to meet you after I learned you were in town, asking questions."

Esme frowned. "But you pushed me away, refused to help."

"Because your presence here stirred up the past and threatened to expose what we all agreed would stay buried. I can't deny it's a relief your father has lifted that burden of secrecy from my shoulders," she said. "Besides, you deserve to know the truth. We are all a lot stronger than people give us credit for, actually."

"Did you know Arcadia?"

Mavis smiled. "Oh yes, I knew Arcadia. She was my sister."

Esme was incredulous. "But my mother had no siblings."

"Did she tell you that? How strange. Well, given what transpired, perhaps not."

Esme examined her aunt's face. "I can see the likeness now. It's the eyes. And cheekbones." Mavis had the same smoky grey eyes – Arcadia lined hers with kohl – and plump cheeks, which Arcadia accentuated with rouge. "It's rather eerie."

Mavis drew herself up. "There were three of us. Ginia, me and your mother, Jane."

Arcadia was once called Jane? Surely not. "It can't be. Jane died. After the war, you said."

"In a way, she did. Her heart died, and she had no taste for staying here. To be honest, I thought her selfish, abandoning Mother, me and Ginia to go and live the life of Riley in London. Over time, she dropped contact with everyone, bar the occasional Christmas card."

A frown creased Esme's forehead as she grappled with this latest bombshell; the facts incompatible with what she'd always believed. "But Arcadia told me she left here when she was about thirteen, before war broke out. She was sent to live with an aunt in England because her mother – oh, Elizabeth, of course – was sick with TB."

Mavis peered at Esme under raised eyebrows. "Pure fabrication on her part. She wanted to erase those years, pretend none of it happened. But Jane was long past her teenage years when she left."

"So she was running away?"

"As it turned out, yes. Though of course, the real reason she never wanted to return was because she was so *ashamed*–" Mavis sat back in her armchair and stared into space, as if grappling with something. A memory? A confidence? Her conscience?

Another thought struck Esme. "Elizabeth is my grandmother... why didn't she acknowledge me when I saw her?"

"Quite simply, she never knew you existed. Only I knew Jane went by the name Arcadia in England. So when you turned up asking about Arcadia Robin, naturally Mother had no idea who you were referring to."

"And until I told you, you hadn't known Arcadia had died, had you?"

With the edge of her index finger, Mavis flicked away a spontaneous tear. "It came as quite a shock. After what happened later, in 1945, I'd vowed never to speak to – or speak of – Jane again. But when all was said and done, Jane was my sister, and to die alone..."

Yes, thought Esme, Mavis had suffered these past few weeks, grappling with sadness at discovering her sister's passing. "Some good has come of it though, hasn't it? For me, anyway. At least I've found my family, even if I don't understand the reason for all the secrecy. And what of Ginia?"

"Ginia, like your mother, has a restless soul. She fights for the rights of women where she sees injustice and we never quite know where she'll pop up next. Her last letter – two months or so ago – indicated she was raising funds to start a maternity hospital for unmarrieds. Ethiopia, I think."

"Is she married?"

"Oh no. She's not one for men."

Esme put that cryptic comment aside to delve into at a later time. "You said Jane's heart died. What did you mean?"

Mavis took Esme's hands in hers. "Shortly after the end of the war, a letter came from the War Office advising Bernard Charleston Vautier was presumed dead. Charlie. Jane's husband."

"Husband?" Esme sat bolt upright. "My mother married Charlie?"

"They were childhood sweethearts and married a few days before he left for the front. They both went, Charlie and my William. Inseparable they were. Fought side by side."

"I can't take it in." Esme covered her face with her hands, trying to unpick what it meant. She should have been shocked to learn Arcadia was married before she met Lewis, but she was more surprised that her parents had kept it secret from her. Arcadia may have been many things, but she wasn't the shrinking violet type. She was a snob, though, and ambitious. Perhaps she thought being a divorcée would hinder her public popularity. She looked at Mavis. "But Charlie wasn't dead. Twenty-five years later he got into a fight with my father. What on earth happened when he returned from the war to cause him and my mother to separate, and for her to leave Guernsey?"

The light was fading. Mavis turned on the sidelights and closed the heavy brocade ivory drapes, blocking the late-afternoon sunshine and giving the room a sombre hue. She poured sherry from one of the decanters, handed a glass to Esme and sat back down. "My dear, you have it all quite wrong." She took a sip. "Much of this is Charlie's story to tell but I doubt he'll see you."

Esme stifled a gasp. She hadn't held much hope of Charlie still being alive. "Oh, but he must."

"Please understand, he's still very angry. But he's a good man. And sensitive." Mavis twisted her hands until her knuckles went white. "It gets complicated. But know this – your mother loved Charlie dearly. It was a terrible day when the letter arrived in 1918, stating he was presumed dead. She went into herself, feeling she couldn't share her pain when so many people had suffered losses and had to cope with terrible grief. All she said was that without Charlie, everything seemed pointless." Her voice was flat.

"Go on," Esme said.

Mavis sighed and took a deep breath. "Some years later he reappeared like a ghost at his mother's funeral. Frightened and maimed, he was. People stared at him and his father wept." Mavis choked. "I'm sorry, my dear, I still find it hard to think of those times. You've no idea. He hobbled on crutches with a stump for a leg and his face half blown off. It was a terrifying sight."

It all defied understanding. "And Arcadia?"

"She arrived a few days later."

Esme felt a cold hand pass over her heart, unsure if she could bear to hear what happened next. "Exactly – *exactly* – when was this?"

Mavis bit her bottom lip. Her voice was low and gentle. "1924. She'd married your father several months earlier but hadn't told us. She feared it would be too upsetting for Charlie's parents, that they'd think she'd forgotten him. She later told me she'd planned to let the family know once the baby was born, but as things turned out, she never told anyone."

"The baby was me?"

"Yes. Precious Esme." Mavis smiled and her eyes crinkled with warmth, but Esme only saw deceit as disbelief morphed into cold realisation.

Her head pounded like a jackknife and she stared at Mavis. "She never divorced Charlie, did she? Rather than face the consequences, she denied my existence. My own mother. How could she? And you let her."

"My dear–"

Esme raised her hand. She wanted no more of Mavis's revelations or excuses.

From somewhere in the house, a clock chimed the hour. A cuckoo chirped a merry alarm. Time kept up its inevitable pace, ticking to another tomorrow.

~

Esme pedalled at speed away from St Martin, the wind whipping into her face. No wonder Mavis had been horrified when she'd turned up in St Peter Port; the tangible, living proof of her sister's criminality. No wonder Arcadia kept her at arm's length, the daughter who wasn't Charlie's. No wonder her father never spoke to her mother after 1945, when somehow he'd found out the truth about his sham marriage.

My mother was a bigamist. I am therefore illegitimate. And Mavis conspired with her to keep the truth from both Charlie and Lewis.

Her anger brewed into a frenzy, and she pumped the pedals faster, tears streaming down her cheeks. She turned into The Queen's Road, dreading being on her own in the cottage with only the walls to talk to and no one to confide in – for how could she bare her heart to Mavis?

Without pausing to consider the pros and cons, she made a swift decision. Instead of heading up the hill, she veered onto Mt Durand. After a couple of false turns, she arrived at The Plough Inn and propped her bike against the wall. Heads turned when she walked into the low-ceilinged bar, but none of them

SARAH HAWTHORN

belonged to Anthony. Oh well, there'd only been the slimmest chance he'd be here, and anyway, she must look a fright with her hair matted from the wind and probably a bright-red nose from crying. Silly idea.

"It's Miss Fanstone, isn't it?"

The voice caught her unawares and she turned to see the publican sporting a broad grin, waving her over. "You must be wanting your Anthony," he said. "He just left. You'll find him at home." He winked. "Number thirty-eight."

"Well, I'm not–"

"And hopefully you'll put the smile back on his face. He's been a bear the last few days."

She took the publican's words as a sign – permission, even – to seek out Anthony, thanked him, and left the bar. She smoothed down her hair, retrieved her bicycle and wheeled it up Allez Street, past the row of terraced houses. Unease crept in. Maybe it wasn't a good idea to knock on his door if he was in a disgruntled frame of mind. What if he refused to see her? Well, she'd insist. She badly needed to sort things between them and find out what had caused his sudden coolness. Mostly she needed a friend.

Standing outside number thirty-eight debating what to do, the door swung open to a laughing couple. A moustachioed man held back the door for Esme. "Do you know where you're going?"

"Anthony–"

"Top floor." He grabbed his girlfriend's hand, and they were gone.

She made her way up three flights of stairs, rehearsing her opening line... *Sorry to barge in on you... I was passing and...*

"Hello there."

She looked up.

Anthony leaned over the bannisters, a quizzical expression on his face. At his feet, a dog's head poked through the bars, her spotted ears pricked in anticipation. "I thought I heard footsteps," he said. "What brings you here?"

It was all a muddle then. Esme burst into tears. Anthony came rushing down and pulled her into his arms. She sobbed in uncontrollable, unladylike gollops until he gently led her into his flat and to an incongruous floral sofa, where he put his arm around her, and stroked her hair. Judy ran around in frantic circles, finally settling on the floor with her paws resting on Esme's feet.

At last her breathing slowed, and she took in the woody aroma of Old Spice aftershave and rough texture of Anthony's tweed jacket against her cheek, the soft pressure of his body next to hers, and the calming rhythm of his hand caressing her unruly hair.

"Tea?" Anthony asked. "And then we'll talk about it. Or not. Sometimes a good old cry is all that's needed. People put too much store on talking."

She lifted her head, glad of his understated empathy. "Tea and talk."

While he fussed in the tiny kitchenette – a cupboard really, comprising a counter with a Baby Belling cooker, a kettle, a sink and shelves above and below – Esme took in her surroundings. The cramped living area housed a desk stacked high with folders and papers, the floral sofa and a leather bucket chair, a side table with a record player, a worn tapestry wall hanging, and two bookshelves laden with books, records, boxes of all sizes (labelled *Letters, Photos, Ma and Pa*) and trophies. She picked up a small tarnished silver cup. *First in Algebra. Form Two.*

"Bathroom's down the hall," he sang out. She took it as a hint and went to tidy up. Refreshed and less dishevelled, when she returned, Anthony had brewed two steaming cups of tea.

He sat in the bucket chair, not next to her on the sofa. "Where would you like to begin?"

"Mavis has turned my life upside down and I don't know how

to make sense of any of it. I'm sorry I blubbed all over you. I feel drained. And there's Hugh. I have to explain—"

Anthony averted his eyes and focussed on his tea. "No you don't. I said I'd be your friend, remember? It's me who should apologise for not collecting you from the ferry. Childish of me. My excuse is that it was a bit of a shock, seeing the announcement of your engagement in *The Times*. Anyway, congratulations." He cleared his throat and looked up. "What did Mavis say?"

Esme blinked twice. What on earth—? Confusion gave way to a slow fury. How dare Hugh. What presumption to place a notice in the paper as if her acceptance of his proposal were a foregone conclusion. She had to set this right. Not be deflected down a different path.

She pulled back her shoulders. Whatever happened, she wasn't going to allow herself to be let down all over again. Not without a fight anyway. "We're not engaged. We never were. He asked me but I never said yes. In fact, I said no. He'd assumed I'd trot after him to America and manage his life. But I'm not. I've told him. I wanted to be back here. In St Peter Port. Don't you see? I wanted to be back here because – because—"

Anthony leapt up, spilling his tea down his trousers. Droplets flew through the air, landing in a brown arc on Esme's pink skirt. "Oh, drat."

"It doesn't matter."

He took her in his arms, laughing. "It doesn't, does it?" And then he kissed her. A slow, decisive kiss, quite unlike any kiss Esme had ever experienced. *I've come home,* she thought, and relaxed into the luxury of his lips.

"Oh, Esme, I can't tell you how I've longed for this," Anthony whispered. He pulled her closer to him, took her head in both hands and kissed her again. "When I thought you'd been swept out of my life by Hugh, I was gut-wrenched."

Esme marvelled how two hours earlier she'd never felt so

miserable; now, she tingled with joy and a sense of peace. "I'm so glad you were here. You've calmed me down."

"Are you up to telling me why you were so distraught?" He hugged her to him. "I'm here to listen. And help."

She smiled and nestled into the warmth of his chest. "It's not a pretty tale."

He listened without interrupting while she went through everything Mavis had revealed, and her difficulty in rationalising her mother's behaviour.

"I'm still struggling with how I should feel," she said. "Part of me is furious Arcadia callously left me to discover for myself I was born illegitimate. She had thirteen years after the balloon went up to tell me. Never a hint, never a word. Did she think it didn't matter? That I wouldn't care?"

"Don't judge her too harshly," he said. "Not until you have all the facts."

"Is that all you can say?" She expected him to be shocked at the turn of events and indignant on her behalf, but all he did was kiss the top of her head and espouse his theory that people were inherently good and should be cast in a positive light unless the evidence pointed otherwise.

"It makes no difference whether your parents had a valid marriage certificate," he said. "What matters is they both believed it was legal at the time they made their vows."

His words gave her pause. She stared up at the grimy ceiling, well overdue for a repaint, and tried to put herself in her mother's place. Losing the love of her young life, rebuilding her dreams with another man, a baby... her lover's return. Arcadia can't have been the first woman to be taken by surprise when her supposed dead husband returned from the front in one piece. It had been an honest mistake, and surely one which the authorities would have quickly forgiven. So why did she place herself in such jeopardy, risking discovery and dire legal consequences? Certainly, a lengthy jail term. Not to mention the consequences for the rest of the family – Esme, Lewis, even Granny Fanstone – tainted by the scandal and publicity. Perhaps not Granny Fanstone. She would have been triumphant in victory, her instincts proven right. Esme could imagine her furiously polishing silver, saying, "I always knew that woman would come to no good."

Anthony stroked her thigh. "Penny for them, Tuppence?"

"You've been storing that up, haven't you?"

"Too irresistible. Like you."

She sighed. "I was thinking about what I'd have done in my mother's situation."

He traced a finger down her scar. "She had to make a decision on the spot. It can't have been easy. Once she'd said nothing about having a daughter, she must have got caught in her own lie."

"Finding out Charlie was still alive must have been horribly confusing for her. I expect she thought she'd return to London and that would be that, but my father told me she came often to Guernsey. Once or twice a year. That's what I don't understand."

"Then you must see Mavis again. Find out why. What happened."

Esme grimaced. "I was rather rude. I ran out on her."

"She'll understand. There's Susan and Elizabeth too."

"I promised not to see Elizabeth again." That was before she knew Elizabeth was her grandmother, but in fairness to the old lady with her erratic memory, it would be best not to take her by surprise. "Her friend Susan is another matter."

"You may have to wait a few days. Strong winds are forecast so the ferries to Herm will be cancelled."

The excuse to delay immediate action appealed to Esme. It would give her time to adjust to her new world view. And not just her discovery about Arcadia. Anthony too. "There's no rush."

"What about seeing Charlie? Are you up for it?"

She baulked at the idea of confronting a broken-down war

veteran who chose to live a hermit existence. "How could I explain myself? As far as I can tell, he doesn't know Arcadia – or rather, Jane – had a daughter. Yes, we know he got into a fight with my father but it would be wrong to draw too many conclusions, wouldn't it? I don't want to be responsible for piling more misery on him."

"Good point. Susan first, then Mavis to see how the land lies, and we'll take it from there."

Esme snuggled into Anthony. *We.* There was a great deal of comfort in being *We.*

But as quickly as that thought brewed, it led her to consider her parents and their sudden separation in 1945. They'd always seemed so suited, so happy. How had they managed to remain a tight couple – *we* – when for more than twenty years, Arcadia hid her marriage to someone else? Or had her father known, and gone along with the deception?

For the next few days, while the summer storms raged, Esme holed up in Junction Cottage with her typewriter – and warm thoughts of Anthony – for company. When they'd parted, she'd deliberately made no arrangement to see him again, wary of rushing things. Arcadia's droll advice haunted: *Stay aloof, darling, don't wear your heart out there for all to see.* But Anthony had made it clear he'd be knocking on her door as soon as the weather cleared and they could get to Herm.

On Wednesday, the wind dropped and a pale sun emerged through the clouds. Clara's predicament continued to deepen, which Esme found quite thrilling, and she pounded away on the keys, making her perilous situation even worse: *You are a slut, a dirty maid, a servant with attitude beyond her–*

A sharp tap on the front door roused Esme from Clara's

showdown with Francine Mellon. Her heart took a small leap. *Anthony.*

She checked her reflection in the mirror above the hall table. Her hair stuck out every which way from her frequent attempts to push it out of her eyes. She smoothed the wayward strands as best she could and pinched colour into her cheeks. In lieu of lipstick, stupidly left upstairs in the bathroom, she moistened her lips and flung open the front door.

A formidable-looking woman clutching a mottled green carpet bag and wearing an ill-fitting raincoat was standing in the porch. "Esme?" She thrust out her hand. "Virginia Robin."

"Oh." Caught off guard, Esme stared at the strange woman. "Of course. Ginia." She shook her hand. "How do you–"

"Are you going to invite me in?"

The woman's tone brooked no option. "Yes, of course, please–" Esme took a step back to allow her to pass.

Ginia marched in, taking in her surroundings with a sweeping glance. "Nice place. Too many knick-knacks."

"It's not mine–"

"I know." She sat at the table, her bag on her lap, and peered at the sheet of paper sticking out of the typewriter. "A writer, eh? Not sentimental slush like Jane, I trust."

"No, well, I–"

"No time to chit-chat. I'm only here for a day. Duty visit to Mother. Mavis told me you'd turned up. I expect she's being tactful when you want answers, eh?"

Esme examined her other aunt. "You look so like my mother."

Ginia snorted. "Without all that muck on my face. And a few stone heavier." She pulled back her shoulders. "Heard she died."

"Yes. Her heart–"

Ginia snorted again. "Her heart. Appropriate."

Esme dared not ask what she meant for fear Ginia would snort again. "What can you tell me?"

"Mavis *advises* me I'm allowed to reveal the secret Jane and I had." Her voice was thick with sarcasm. "How kind of her. I will. But not for Mavis's sake. For yours. And Jane's. God bless her misguided soul."

Esme experienced a fleeting moment of dizziness, much as Alice must have felt when she tumbled down the rabbit hole. "Tea?"

"Filthy stuff. No thank you. Sit down."

Too surprised to do anything else, Esme pulled out a chair and plonked herself down.

Ginia briefly shut her eyes. "It was my father."

Esme hadn't expected that. "My grandfather?"

"That scum." Ginia pursed her lips and thrust her chin upwards. "He was a nasty piece of work. Used to come into my bedroom. Made me do things. Said if I didn't let him, he'd visit Mavis or Jane. Couldn't have that."

Oh God. "Did your mother know?"

"She knew all right. Tried to stop him, but he'd beat her. Clever about it. Never any bruises."

"Were there–" She paused, unsure how to phrase the question. "Others?"

Ginia nodded. "Young lads. Boys in his care. Poor little devils."

"Why didn't your mother tell someone? Go to the police?"

"There's the catch. He'd forced them into a corner. Her and Susan."

"Susan?" The conversation was turning stranger with every twist. Esme struggled to keep up.

"He accused them of being more than friends. Said it was a criminal act."

Lesbians? "Goodness."

"He knew damn well there was nothing going on. But Mother was trapped. She couldn't risk him saying something. Funny thing was, it brought her and Susan even closer. He unwittingly opened the door to their feelings."

"Was this another secret between you and my mother?"

"No. It was years later, after Susan's husband died, that they finally got together."

"So?"

"Jane found out about the boys. She'd looked through the keyhole of Father's study. Thought he might be beating them. One boy always left in tears. Father had his pants down and – well, safe to say, she saw what no young girl should see. We told Mother, who said Jane was mistaken and asked us to tell no one. So we didn't. Then the war came."

"And he was called up?"

"One of the first to go. Kitchener's Volunteer Army." Her mouth set in a hard line. "Good riddance."

Esme shuddered at what young Jane had witnessed. "How unimaginably awful. And confusing."

"Jane often talked to me about it." Ginia took a deep breath. "It was her way of trying to find out. She suspected he might be abusing me too. I never told her. Never told anyone. Not even Mavis. You're the first." Her shoulders started to shake. She gripped the handles of her bag. Esme watched, horrified, as a low, keening sound escaped from deep within her. She rocked back and forth, gulping for air. Then the tears came in great rolling waves.

Esme leapt up and clasped her tightly until the torrent of grief finally gave way to exhausted, heaving breaths. "You poor child. You poor, poor child."

Ginia raised swollen, reddened eyes and gave a wan smile. "Seen worse in Africa. Silly of me. Forgive me."

"Nothing to forgive. I'm glad you shared this with me. It's a terrible thing your father did." Esme found a crumpled handkerchief in the ironing basket and handed it to her.

Ginia blew her nose and checked her watch. "Have to go. Promised to visit Mother. Then off to France." She stood, absent-mindedly shoved the handkerchief in her coat pocket, and edged towards the front door.

Esme placed a hand on her arm. "Did Jane know about Susan and your mother?"

"Good question. If she didn't then, she did later. We all know. By unspoken agreement, no one mentions it."

Esme opened the door. "Have they been happy?"

"Aunty Susan and Mother?" A huge smile broke over Ginia's face. "Blissfully." She clasped Esme's shoulders and kissed her, continental-style, on both cheeks. "I hope you find such happiness."

Such tenderness from the woman who looked like Arcadia, but with none of her bitter edges, cut to Esme's core. "Will you write? Stay in touch?"

Ginia looked at Esme as if she were a foreign animal. "Not one for letters. Come and visit. I'll be in France for a few months. I'll put you to work, mind you. Hospitals don't build themselves."

With a wave, she was gone, leaving Esme breathless from her whirlwind visit which covered so much territory in less than fifteen minutes. Her grandfather's despicable bullying was a sickening discovery. And Ginia's brave protection of her sisters from his abuse had obviously left her with terrible emotional and physical scars, which had shaped the course of her life. Small wonder she'd become a fervent supporter of the suffragette movement, never married and now worked tirelessly to help women abandoned by their societies. An aunt to be proud of. An aunt Esme would cherish.

27

ESME

HERM, 1958

Susan threw open the door, her bulky frame blocking the entry, a scowl on her face. When she saw Esme and Anthony, a large smile lit her features and instantly changed her from a curmudgeonly woman into a homely sort.

"Ginia told me to expect you."

Susan directed a cautious glance at Anthony, and Esme quickly introduced him. "Anthony's been helping me locate my family."

Susan wiped her hands on her apron and took his outstretched palm, but kept her eyes on Esme. "I'm sorry I wasn't so nice to you last time," she said, but didn't invite them in. "Wait there."

They waited awkwardly on the doorstep, not speaking, while Susan disappeared for a few minutes. When she returned, she'd taken off her housecoat and put on a light-blue jacket. There was a worried look on her face, and she held a dilapidated brown handbag. "We'll go to the White House. I've left your grandmother listening to *Mrs Dale's Diary*. I shouldn't leave her on her own but dredging up the past gets her all distressed."

"Are you sure? I could sit with her," said Anthony. "So you and

Esme can talk." He patted his pockets and pulled out a wad of envelopes. "I've been meaning to read this lot. Perfect opportunity to catch up on the family news." He flipped through the letters, frowning.

Susan looked dubious. "It's very kind, but she's not used to strangers."

"What if I sit in the garden? You can leave the front door open so if she calls out, or needs anything, I can tell her I'm here to do some pruning." Anthony looked around. "Those roses need deadheading, for starters. Leave it to me."

Esme shot him a grateful glance. He always seemed to know exactly the right thing to do or say. And Susan's acknowledgment of Elizabeth as 'her grandmother' had reassured her that her presence on the island, her position as Jane's daughter, had been accepted.

They walked the short distance to the hotel, talking pleasantries. How nice to see the sunshine. What a bumpy ferry ride. Such pretty pink wild flowers in bloom.

Susan held open the back gate for Esme. "I worked here for so long, this is my second home. We'll sit and have a cuppa. No one will mind."

Esme settled in one of the handsome, golden-fabric armchairs cloistering the unlit fire in the foyer, while Susan bustled off to the kitchen. Within minutes she returned with a tray of tea and biscuits, and without preamble asked: "What did Ginia tell you?"

Keen not to break Ginia's confidence, Esme chose her words with care. "She spoke about her father's abusive behaviour. To young boys, and herself. And the way he silenced Elizabeth by threatening to tell the authorities about her relationship with you. I don't mind, by the way. I'm happy you both found each other. I'm just sorry you have to keep it hidden."

Susan squared her shoulders. "That's as things are. One day it will change. Well, that's what Elizabeth and I say." Her face fell. "Used to say. Poor dear isn't one for political activism these days.

It's all I can do to keep her from knocking into things and falling over. As for her bad memory, it's as well she's forgotten most of it. The shame of Frank nearly killed her."

"Can you talk about it? Is that why my mother – Jane – fudged about her childhood and told me she'd left here as a teenager?"

"Did she?" Susan raised her eyebrows. "Hardly surprising." She nursed her teacup. "Elizabeth and I, we breathed a sigh of relief when Frank volunteered. It meant everyone was safe. Those poor boys, and Ginia. Jane and Mavis, too, if he'd a mind to hurt them. When the telegram came, we tore it open, thinking he'd be dead like all the others. Killed in action. It would have been best if he had. But no, it told us he'd been court-martialled and sentenced to hard labour for gross indecency. Two years."

"Oh, my heavens."

"The whole town knew, thanks to the gossiping postmistress. She'd taken down the telegram, of course. Somehow we kept it from the girls, explained things away by saying their father had been captured, which wasn't so far from the truth, but they knew something had changed. People would whisper and point at them in the street, or stop talking when they entered a shop. As for Elizabeth, she was ostracised, called names, made to live his shame. I was her only friend."

"What happened?"

"We never knew the exact charge, but we guessed he'd been up to his old tricks. Especially when a few months later, Elizabeth received a letter from a young corporal. Claimed he'd been in some sort of liaison with Frank and only kept his mouth shut because Frank was a superior officer. He said a hundred pounds would keep him quiet, otherwise Frank would go back on trial for buggery, and likely get the death penalty. Elizabeth screwed up the letter and threw it on the fire. *Go to hell,* she said. I never knew if she meant the corporal or Frank. Less than a year later, Frank died anyway. He was beaten up by a gang of other prisoners. We were told that they were 'coming to the aid of a young man' but it didn't take Einstein to work out what that really meant. Elizabeth told the girls their father had died of Spanish flu, and they believed it. So many lost fathers, brothers, sons that way. It came as no big shock. To this day, Ginia and Mavis don't know the real truth." She leaned forwards. "And I'd rather you said nothing. Sleeping dogs and all that."

Esme thought of what Ginia had suffered, and her anguished tears when she finally spoke out. "Don't you think it might be healing? Particularly for Ginia, to learn that in the end, he was punished for what he did?"

"I never thought of it that way. But what good would it do to rake it all over? Far as I know, Ginia's long put it all behind her."

Esme shook her head. "She's never forgotten. It's affected her whole life. Didn't you consider it strange she's never had a romantic attachment?"

"How ignorant, how unfeeling of me." Susan looked crestfallen. "Let me dwell on it. I wish I could ask Elizabeth's permission but that's out of the question."

"I'm going to visit Ginia in France. I could tell her."

"I'd take you up on that, but it's shirking responsibility. If she's going to know, Ginia has a right to hear it from us. Me. That way, she can ask her questions and hear our answers."

"And Mavis?"

"Dear me, what would be the point?"

"Because you've all kept these secrets for years." Esme exploded with exasperation. "It's time to clear the air. *Please.*"

A couple came clattering down the wooden staircase, bumping their suitcases, and Susan paused until they'd passed through to reception. While they waited, Esme nibbled on a shortbread biscuit. Although the truth about her grandfather's Great War was disturbing, and must have been devastating for Elizabeth, she felt better for at last owning some of her family history. Living through it, however, must have been vastly more oppressive.

"Is all this connected to why Jane... my mother... cut herself off from the family?"

"In a way," said Susan. "There was a terrible row. She accused Elizabeth of doing nothing to stop Frank molesting young boys, or to protect Ginia. The next day she left for London and even after Charlie returned, she avoided her mother and me on her visits here."

Esme tried to put herself in Elizabeth's place. She may not have understood the depths of Frank's depravity, or known what really went on behind his study door or in Ginia's bedroom. Perhaps it was a sign of those times: that on one level Elizabeth knew he was strict and sometimes overstepped the mark, but her limited life experience couldn't conjure dark places of sexual deviance or believe him capable of more than a brutal beating.

"I'm truly, truly sorry," Esme said. "It's too late for my mother to reconcile with you, but I hope I might on her behalf. I can only think once she'd made her position clear, she was too stubborn to budge. That was always her way."

"Whatever her reasons, I'm very glad we've had this chat." Susan brushed crumbs from her skirt and picked up her purse. "Now, I must get back to Elizabeth and release Anthony. Will you come too, pop in and say hallo? You deserve to get to know your grandmother, and in her lucid moments, she still has a tale or two to tell."

Deep in conversation, sitting in wicker chairs on the small patch of lawn in front of the house, Anthony and Elizabeth's heads were almost touching. A large stamp album lay across Anthony's knees. As Susan and Esme approached the gate, Anthony leaned forwards and whispered in Elizabeth's ear. She patted his knee and said, "The Germans weren't as clever as they thought." Anthony looked up, noticed Esme and closed the book before sliding it under his chair.

Susan opened the gate and called out. "*Lizzie*. This is Jane's girl."

Elizabeth swivelled her head in the direction of Susan's voice, her failing eyes squinting as she tried to make out the figures coming up the path.

Esme raced over and took her hands. "I came a few months ago."

"Jane. Dear Jane." Elizabeth reached up and stroked Esme's face. "A restless soul. Never stuck at anything."

"She married Charlie. You told me."

"Voile and lace, her wedding dress. What a radiant bride. What's your name, dear?"

"Esme. Jane was my mother."

Elizabeth's dry, powdery hand hovered on Esme's cheek. "She didn't have children. I should know. I'm her mother."

"I was born in London." It was plain the details of her birth and parentage would be too challenging, and unnecessary now, for Elizabeth to unravel and accept. "Jane told no one."

The old lady dropped her hand, blinked, and snapped to attention. "I remember. You fell off the swing and cut your face. Baby Esme. Of course."

Esme looked from Susan to Elizabeth and back to Susan. "You mean I've been here before?"

"We didn't know it was you," Susan said. "Mavis made a good job of covering up. Said she was looking after you while your mother was in hospital in London."

"Mavis?" Esme flopped into the chair next to Anthony.

"You stayed with her for a few weeks. None of us pieced together the coincidence of your arrival and departure on the same ferry as Jane. It only happened that one time, to my knowledge. I've no idea why she risked bringing you with her. Sentimentality, perhaps?"

Esme disagreed. Knowing Arcadia, it was far more likely she had no choice in the matter. Maybe the nanny fell ill, or took a vacation. "How old was I?"

"Three, maybe four."

Pieces fell into place. No wonder Mavis had seemed familiar when they first met. There were other things too. "I played bowls, didn't I? At La Collinette, walking in the garden, I had a memory of rolling a ball along the ground. I wore a white dress." She ran her fingers down the scar on her face. What a legacy from a trip she'd never known about.

"Such a pretty child," said Elizabeth. "We patched you up as best we could, didn't we, Susie? Eight stitches the doctor gave you."

"He did a grand job." Anthony leaned forwards and kissed her cheek, then pulled sharply away. *He's embarrassed,* thought Esme. *How adorable.*

"You were so brave." Elizabeth clapped her hands together. "Mavis gave you a lollipop."

Spontaneous tears clouded Esme's eyes. "Can I come and see you again?" She'd found her family and in return, they were giving her some childhood memories. Could they forgive Arcadia who never told Elizabeth she had a grandchild – her only grandchild? Was it too late to mend that bridge?

It was as if Susan read her mind. "Come often. We've a lot of years to catch up."

"Baby Esme," said Elizabeth. "Well, I never." A broad beam of pride brightened her face, peeling away years of regret. "A granddaughter, Susie. Whatever do you make of that?"

~

Their visit to Elizabeth and Susan ended with affectionate farewells, and promises to visit Herm again soon. Esme bounced with euphoria as they headed back to the jetty. "I can't quite believe it, Anthony. What started as a bit of a lark to see if I could make sense of a mysterious letter, has turned up a whole family of grandparents and aunts. Not to mention a plethora of scandal."

Anthony didn't reply but kept his eyes fixed on his feet plodding along the path. She took his arm, surprised at his change of mood. He'd been so keen to find her relatives, she'd expected more enthusiasm. Perhaps he was tired. He'd been champion at keeping Elizabeth company, and following her meandering thoughts couldn't have been easy.

She tried another tack. "I expect you want to put your feet up and relax. I made mushroom soup. The fruit and vegetable man in the market told me what to do. With any luck, it might actually be edible."

When he remained silent she nudged him. "Did you hear me? I've prepared supper for us. I can tell you everything Susan told me, and you can share whatever it was you and Elizabeth were talking about so intensely. I want to know what she meant by the Germans not being so clever."

"Supper? Excellent. Onion soup, you say? My favourite. But I can't. I have to, um, go to the office. I've spent too long today chasing down your relatives. I need to catch up."

The promise of an intimate evening drained away, and Esme made an effort to hide her disappointment. "Mushroom, not onion," she said brightly. "Of course. I've been taking up too much of your time." But the feeling of having been rejected, and Anthony's lack of remorse that they wouldn't spend the evening together, stung.

They reached Rosaire Steps, the ferry visible in the distance.

"Ten minutes," said Anthony. "Time for a smoke." He took out his pipe and went about the business of tapping out dead leaves, opening the blue tobacco tin, rubbing and kneading flakes, filling the pipe and slowly lighting the bowl with deep intakes of breath. To Esme, it was a stalling tactic to avoid conversation. He'd been quiet ever since she and Susan returned to the house. Was it something she'd said or done? Perhaps obeying her mother's advice to remain aloof had sent the wrong signal.

"Is there something on your mind?" she ventured.

"Not really. Well, yes, there is. But nothing to worry over."

"Come tomorrow night. The soup will keep."

"Look – I've a few things to attend to. I'm going to be rather busy for the next few days. You understand, don't you?"

She didn't, but then again, was hardly in a position to complain. They'd not made any commitment to each other, however–

Anthony pointed his pipe ahead. "C'mon. Ferry's docking." He took off down the steps, leaving Esme to follow, churning over what it was she shouldn't worry about. Was he sick? Had there been some bad news from home in one of those letters? Or had he plain gone off her?

ESME

GUERNSEY, 1958

*S*eated at the dining table in front of her typewriter, Esme chewed on Travis's offer: the cottage owner's contract in Geneva had been extended a further three months, would Esme like to stay on? Oh, how she'd love to, but she'd almost unearthed all there was to discover about Arcadia's family. If there was nothing to remain for – she dared not formulate the name 'Anthony' into her thoughts – then she must make plans to return to England and find a job. Although... the cottage cost her nothing and was a lovely place to write – and staying meant more time getting to know her new-found family.

Her savings and small inheritance from Arcadia were all but gone. The rent from Arcadia's flat gave Esme a small cushion of financial comfort, but was about to get eaten away by unexpected bills for rewiring, a chimney sweep and the installation of a telephone. Her six-monthly royalties were due from sales of *The View From Here,* but if the last cheque was any guide, she'd be lucky to net five pounds.

Maybe she could find a job. A waitress? A shop assistant? She could see if the *Guernsey Press* or *The Star* had any openings for a copy editor. She'd easily be able to find employment if she returned to London – which, she was surprised to note, made her heart sink – but she'd need a place to live. Not Arcadia's flat. She baulked at the idea of living with the spectre of her mother at her shoulder.

She strummed her fingers on the table. "What do you think, Jasper?" The cat, from where he lay curled in the rocking chair, lifted then dropped his sleepy head, disinterested. "I need a miracle."

She stared at the typewriter and the sheet of paper poking up above the roller, with the words:

```
Clara huddled in the corner of the dank
cell,   thin   arms   wrapped   around   her
shivering body —
```

"Oh my heavens," she whispered, and ripped it out, replacing it with a clean sheet. "What an idiot."

Dear Mr Jennings-Smythe,

My apologies for being out of touch for so long. I hope you've not forgotten me! As it happens, I'm in Guernsey, researching my latest book. I've attached the first few chapters for your critique. It's loosely based on a scandal that occurred in St Peter Port in the 1920s. I should have the final manuscript ready to send you in a couple of months.

She paused. Dare she ask? She hovered her fingers above the keyboard – her mother wouldn't have hesitated, so neither would she – and resumed typing.

Any advance, if Chatterworths Publishing can oblige, would be welcome.

Sincerely,

Esme Fanstone

She gathered together pages one to fifty, pinned her letter to the front, slotted the bundle into a large manila envelope and propped it on the table to post later. If Mr Jennings-Smythe replied in the affirmative, her decision was made, independent of Anthony. All weekend she'd tried not to think of him, with only moderate success. His face kept winkling its way to the forefront of her mind together with his parting words, *I'm going to be rather busy for the next few days.* She wanted to give him the benefit of the doubt because he *had* looked downcast when he left her, and his hug *had* been warm... But if only she'd been more forthright, questioned why he wouldn't confide in her.

She stared out of the front window at hectic bees swarming around clumps of lavender bushes, envious of their frenetic activity and annoyed at her own inertia. Would her mother have waited in the shadows to be noticed or called upon? Of course not. She'd have taken matters into her own hands. When impatience brewed in Arcadia and threatened to boil over, she'd leap into motion, declaring 'doing nothing is tantamount to frittering one's life away'. Esme could still hear her tart admonishment about Hugh, 'If you allow yourself to be walked all over, you'll become downtrodden'. Her words had stung but how right she'd been. Thank heavens she'd escaped the trampling of Hugh's size nine boots and seen sense before becoming trapped in domestic drudgery.

In a flurry of determination, Esme hastened into the hallway. She snatched up her beret, secured it on her head, opened the door and wheeled her bike away before she changed her mind. She didn't care if Anthony were cross with her for seeking him out, she wouldn't sit about any longer biting her nails and listening for the click of the gate. No. She'd bail him up and demand to know how things lay between them.

She pedalled with furious intensity along the street and freewheeled down the hills, working herself into a frenzy. At the

Royal Court building, she flung her bike against the wall and dashed inside. A creaky old usher, stooped with arthritis, stopped her. "Yes, miss?"

"I'm here to see Anthony Fellowes." Her breath came in sharp gasps.

The usher wasn't to be hurried. He picked up a clipboard, licked his index finger and scanned the first page, the second, and then the third. "He's not here."

That was a blow, but she'd wait. "When will he be back?"

"Doesn't say. Indefinite."

Indefinite? Esme felt a sick twist in her stomach. "Where is he? I mean–"

"Abroad."

"He can't be–"

"That's what it says here. I'm not at liberty to say any more. Excuse me." He looked over Esme's shoulder. "Yes, sir, can I help you?"

A man spoke over Esme's head. "I'm here to see the head clerk."

The usher bowed and gesticulated down the hall. "This way, sir."

Dismissed, Esme retraced her steps out of the building. What on earth did it mean, Anthony had gone abroad? He'd not said a word about going away. Just that he needed 'a few days'. Not an indefinite break. How long was indefinite anyway?

Too despondent to ride her bicycle, she walked back up the hill, head down, while considering her next move. She rejected the idea of returning to Junction Cottage. She'd only brood about his whereabouts. Someone must know where he was, and when he'd return. Funny he hadn't left word at his office. Maybe he left word with the publican at The Plough? Or one of his neighbours. Perhaps the friendly couple who lived on the floor below? And who was looking after his dog, Judy? Or had he taken her with him?

Just in case Anthony had already come back – or not gone, just a silly clerical mix-up – Esme took the bus to Allez Street. She'd collect her bike later. At his house she rang all the doorbells, but the building remained silent and unresponsive. No anxious dog barked, no hurried footsteps came to answer her knock. She looked up at the windows facing onto the street, but no curtain twitched, no curious face peered out. She checked her watch. Almost five o'clock. The Plough would soon open, and within the hour some of the residents would return home from work. She'd come back.

The pub showed no sign of life either. Esme sat on the wooden bench in the side courtyard, trying to stem her anxiety. Just before five thirty, the ruddy-faced publican appeared, carrying a watering can.

At the sight of her, he stopped short and a spurt of water caught the hem of Esme's skirt. "Aha, it's Mr History Man's friend," he said. "Am I glad to see you."

Esme jumped up and flapped the droplets away. "Whatever for?"

"One night, Mr History said. That was Sunday. Now it's Tuesday. Run off me feet, I am. That darn dog of his is a machine. I spend all day feeding it, walking it, cleaning up its–" He floundered for a word. "You-know-whats." He tipped the can above a hanging basket.

"It's your turn now."

"Mine?"

"You're his girl. Not me." He thrust the can at Esme. "Finish watering them baskets. I'll get her lead and the key."

He stomped off and ducked under the low doorway, leaving Esme more worried than ever. So Anthony only intended to be away one night. Wasn't it a concern he'd been gone for three days? What if something had happened to him? An accident?

$\sim$

Entering Anthony's flat with Judy bounding ahead in excited leaps reminded Esme of the day she went to her mother's London apartment after Arcadia had died. She had that same feeling of being an interloper, trespassing on someone else's territory. Being here uninvited was all wrong, but she hadn't been given much alternative. Judy, however, appeared unconcerned at being glad-handed around and brushed up against Esme's legs, giving gentle nudges with her snout. Esme took the hint. In the tiny galley kitchen, she filled a bowl with water and found some dog biscuits, which Judy demolished with gusto.

The flat yielded no clues of Anthony's whereabouts. Esme perched on the edge of the sofa and looked at its bachelor disarray. Plates in the drainer, cushions needing plumping, jacket flung over a chair back, pipe tobacco in the ashtray. Nothing signalled sudden flight or, indeed, a planned departure. No convenient note to the milkman advising dates of absence, or neatly packed and dated food parcels left for Judy. One night, the publican said. Abroad, the usher said. Both scenarios seemed mutually exclusive, although in theory, she supposed a fleeting overseas trip was possible.

What on earth was she to do? She couldn't stay here, but equally she couldn't take Judy to Junction Cottage. Jasper would never tolerate the competition. Could she leave Judy on her own here, overnight? What if she barked, annoyed the neighbours? Or needed to go out? No, she couldn't be left alone. Who could she ask to take her? Travis? Even if he might, Esme didn't feel she could ask. It placed him in an awkward position if he wanted to refuse.

It made sense, Esme concluded, that Anthony hadn't done his homework very well. He'd only been gone two nights, after all. He probably hadn't allowed for travel time, ferry connections, or flight availability. In all likelihood he'd turn up later this evening. She'd wait for his return.

She raided his cupboards for something to eat, figuring it was the least he could provide in return for her ministrations, and heated a tin of baked beans. She sat at the small table which doubled as a desk, pushed aside a pile of papers and files, and ate her frugal meal. Supper finished, she scoured his bookcase for something to read. It was evident Anthony prioritised military history over fiction, but she spied a copy of Hardy's *Tess of the d'Urbervilles*. As she'd read it twice before, she kept checking his limited library in case she saw another option.

"Oh my goodness." Sandwiched between *Is War Hell?* and *From Harlem to the Rhine* poked a copy of *The View From Here*. Her novel. She pulled it from the shelf, checked the spine and saw it had cracked in several places. Anthony had obviously read it all the way through. Page 236 had been turned down at the corner and she tutted. Didn't he know one should never deface a book that way? If their friendship survived, she'd buy him a bookmark. A piece of paper slipped out from under the inside back cover. A receipt from W & G Foyle in Charing Cross Road. So he had got around to ordering it, but as he'd never mentioned it again, it was safe to assume he hadn't been impressed. Downcast, she replaced it, tugged out the Thomas Hardy and curled up on the sofa with Judy beside her. The book failed to hold her concentration. Perhaps it was the strangeness of being alone in Anthony's flat, or an uncertain sense of rejection, but she couldn't settle.

At ten o'clock she took Judy for a walk. The street was quiet, and she saw no one. In lieu of a better plan, she walked back to the flat, left a note on the mat in case Anthony came back – *I'm here looking after Judy, and I'm sleeping in your bed. Esme* – undressed to her undies and pulled on a blue-striped pyjama top. It smelt masculine, of his familiar aftershave mixed with soap suds. She read one more chapter and turned out the light, wishing Anthony were beside her and praying nothing had gone awry between them.

Some time later, a banging woke her. Confused, she rolled over and pulled the bedclothes around her ears to block out the noise. Another knocking and she opened her eyes. Pitch dark, it must be the middle of the night. And she wasn't in her own bed. A warm lump lay next to her. Of course, Judy. The knocking must be Anthony. She turned on the light and threw back the blankets. The alarm clock read twenty past twelve. Odd he hadn't let himself in.

"Coming, coming," she called out.

Judy bustled ahead and pressed her muzzle to the gap under the front door, sniffing and pawing.

Esme yanked on the door handle. "I didn't think you–" She tailed off at the sight of a slight, blonde woman, a suitcase by her side. She wore an elegantly tailored cream suit and black stilettos, which struck Esme as a bizarre choice of shoes for Guernsey's cobbled pavements. A black leather handbag dangled over the crook of her arm. Judy barked and circled the woman, trying to jump up.

"Can I help you?" Esme felt ridiculous, standing in the doorway in Anthony's too-big pyjama jacket, in front of this smart mannequin.

"Is this Tony's place?" the woman asked in a clipped, British accent.

Wrong flat, thought Esme. "Tony? Er, no." She tugged on Judy's collar. "Down, girl."

The woman frowned. She had startling blue eyes and a pouty mouth. "But this is Judy, yes?"

"Oh, you mean Anthony." Who on earth was she? "Come in." Esme stepped back, feeling like an inferior servant, as the woman swept in, her gaze taking in the cramped apartment. "I'm afraid Anthony's not here. Is he expecting you?"

"And who might you be?"

Esme bit back a rude response. After all, she'd been the one woken up; she was the one looking after Anthony's dog; and this midnight visitor presumed superiority? "I'm a friend."

The woman eyed her from toes to hair and back down her semi-clad body. "Well, I'm his fiancée."

"I b-beg your pardon?" Esme stuttered.

"His fiancée. Belinda." She thrust out a manicured hand, which Esme took in mechanical response. "I'm paying Tony a surprise visit."

Her words rang like discordant scales around Esme's head: *Fiancée? Tony? Surprise visit?* Everything sounded wrong, out of place.

"I say, I'm sorry to wake you up so late. I've had the most terrible time getting here. It's taken *days*. My ferry was cancelled yesterday. High winds. Finally we left late today and when I arrived at the horrid little port, the town was empty. I had the most awful to-do finding a taxi. I thought for a ghastly moment I'd have to *walk*." She shrugged out of her jacket and tossed it on the sofa. "Judy-pudy, Judy-pudy." She leaned down and rubbed Judy's ears. "I don't suppose you've got a gin? Or whisky? I could use a settler for my nerves."

Without her jacket, Esme could see how thin Belinda was, like a skeleton. She paced the flat in abstracted, jerky movements.

"I don't think so. I could look–"

"Don't bother." Belinda snapped open her bag and withdrew a silver cigarette case.

"Light, darling?"

Esme retrieved the box of matches next to the oven. "Here." She tried to gather her composure as she watched Belinda set a match to her cigarette with a trembling hand. A raft of emotions beset her but uppermost, anger. Anger at herself for being a fool – again. Anger at Anthony for being too weak to tell her the truth about Belinda. Pretending he'd broken it off. Leading Esme on. Her head throbbed and she yearned to scream or throw something or slap – yes, slap – Belinda.

But she did none of these things. "I'll get dressed and leave you. I'm not sure when Anthony – *Tony* – will be back but I'm sure you can manage Judy. You seem to be best of friends."

Belinda took an agitated step forwards. "Don't leave. Please. Sit. Let's chat. Actually I'm thrilled you're here. You're just the person I need." She waved her cigarette in the air. "An ally."

"An ally?" Esme couldn't help being intrigued.

"Thing is, I'm here to give the boy a bit of a giddy-up. Mummy and Daddy are getting rather fed up that we won't land on a date. For the wedding, you know."

Esme blanched. "I don't."

Belinda squealed with laughter. "That's *exactly* my point. Tony is hopeless. Even you don't know and you're obviously a friend. Look at the way you're taking care of Judy. How kind is that?"

"Look, I think you've got the wrong end–"

"What I don't get – and maybe you can help me out here – is why on earth would he keep stretching out his time on this benighted island? I mean, he was supposed to be back three months ago. Honestly, if I didn't know him better, I'd start to think he'd met someone else. So here I am, determined to bring him to his senses and drag him back to Cambridge." She winked. "And I'll persuade him the way we women do best."

The throbbing in Esme's head intensified. It was Hugh all over again. Anthony, the two-timing bastard, had been playing with her affections whilst all the while stringing Belinda along. How had she not realised? For goodness' sakes, all those years being convinced one day Hugh would fall into her arms and she still didn't recognise a man who could be bewitched by lipstick and guile? What did that make Esme? A brain on a body, that's all, interesting but lacking social charms. What, in turn, was Belinda? A sex bomb, a wife to parade like a trophy. No contest.

She shook her head. "I can't help you. I barely know him." She edged into the bedroom alcove and gathered her clothes.

Belinda followed her and slouched against the wall. "Can you take Judy with you? I'm not really equipped for dog walking."

Esme gritted her teeth, zipped her skirt and buttoned her cardigan. "I have a cat." She stepped into her shoes. "You'll cope."

And before she burst into tears, or said something she'd regret, she let herself out.

ESME

GUERNSEY, 1958

*C*harlie's house was quite unlike Esme's expectations, except for its secluded location at the edge of a bluebell wood near a cliff path. Had she been asked to describe who lived behind the pretty frontage with its whitewashed walls and Wedgwood blue window and door frames, Esme would have said a house-proud woman who carefully tended the overflowing baskets of freesias, clipped the hedges and kept the path swept of leaves or debris. The drystone wall around the house and the shingled tiles on the roof were in tip-top condition. The paintwork gleamed, free of cobwebs or muddy splashes. A polished brass sign, *Woodland Corner,* confirmed this unlikely house to be the correct address.

Although Mavis had assured her that Charlie was happy to meet, Esme was wary of what reception to expect. Mavis had said his first instinct was always to avoid meeting new people, for fear of being viewed like a freak show. But even though she'd steeled herself for Charlie's physical appearance, her worst imaginings hadn't prepared her for the man who opened the door. Her first impression was a face with a massive poorly patched hole beneath the cheekbone, jagged deep scars pitting his blotchy, reddened skin, and his left eyelid pulled down over a shuttered eye. He wore a yellow bandana around his head, to hide – what? A faded, baggy grey shirt failed to disguise his emaciated torso, which twisted awkwardly to one side. She was too shocked to gasp – and too determined to show no revulsion. It was hard to conjure him as the handsome boy of her mother's dreams, who Arcadia had continued to love without reservation despite his disfigurement.

"I'm not a pretty sight." Charlie's words slurred as he struggled to make the sounds, paralysis evident down one side of his face.

"But you're a welcome sight," said Esme. "I'm so pleased you agreed to meet."

Charlie grunted and gestured for her to follow him. He leaned on a crutch and hopped ahead with a surprising lightness of foot. His left trouser leg was tied in a loose knot below the stump of his leg, and the flimsy material flapped in the air.

If Esme had expected gloom, the home's interior was an equal surprise. The walls along the hallway were painted white and led to a glassed-in conservatory. Light streamed in, leaving shards of summer rays dappling over the simple furniture: a wooden table surrounded by four bentwood chairs, two art deco armchairs covered in pale-green fabric and in the corner, a piano and a cello beside a music stand. Landscapes and seascapes – she recognised the artist as Mavis – peppered the walls. A folded wheelchair leaned against one end of a counter that housed a serviceable kitchen: sink, oven, cupboards. Everything neat, not a speck of dust to be seen.

Through the window, she spied row upon row of garden beds lush with a variety of plants. Vegetables, many on trellises: beans, peas, cucumbers. At ground level, strawberry beds, the ripening fruit visible under protective nets. Beyond, a giant-sized greenhouse, sun glinting off its sparkling glass panes, crops of tomato plants shining red and plump from within.

"Sit." Charlie pointed to one of the armchairs. He sat in the other, and placed his crutch on the floor. On the table between them lay dark-blue and gold-edged china teacups, milk jug, sugar bowl and plates alongside a teapot covered in a knitted cosy. Charlie passed her a platter of scones and nodded to the pots of butter and jam.

She took one, still warm from the oven. "Did you make these?"

"I did." Without asking, he poured her a cup of tea, then one for himself. "I talk slow. Easier for you to understand."

He'd deliberately seated her away from his bad side. His good eye sparkled with warmth, but there was something else. A slight look of trepidation.

"I'm not sure where to begin," said Esme. "This is rather an unusual situation."

"Aye." Charlie fell silent for a few seconds. "I never knew about you. Any of it. Until 1945. It's a rare day when you learn your wife is a fraud."

"Mavis told me you're still very angry with my mother."

"Angry? I'm long past angry. Just sad she didn't trust me. She didn't tell me about you, or your father. I had to find out for myself. So did he, poor bloke. It made me wonder about love." Charlie shifted in his chair and rubbed the end of his stump. "I can still feel my foot. Invisible nuisance."

Esme buttered her scone and took a small bite. Delicious. "How did you find out?"

"A trick of coincidence. One Jane never planned for. Clever woman, your mother. She had it all worked out, and except for the war, she'd have got away with it and we'd all have lived happily ever after."

"I found out by accident, too, only recently. When my parents separated at the end of 1945, I was twenty-one and living in London. No one told me anything, other than they were getting a divorce, and I assumed my father's affairs or his gambling were to blame."

Charlie put a straw in his teacup and took a long sip. "Your father was posted here at the end of the war. Sent to help liberate the island from the Nazis. While he was here, he decided to look up his wife's family. I suppose he thought Jane would be pleased he'd made the effort. Although to his knowledge she'd not stepped foot in the place since she was a young girl."

"We always called her Arcadia."

"That gave me a jolt. When we married, we vowed we'd build a house after the war – the Great War, that was – and call it Arcadia. A place of harmony and beauty. But to me she was plain Jane. Your father knew her real name, of course." He cleared his throat. "It was on their marriage certificate."

The slow timbre of his speech gave each word emphasis, and time for the meaning to permeate.

"You never knew she wrote books, did you?"

"No. She told me she published school textbooks. Another lie." He paused to suck on the straw. "I've never read any of her books. Too afraid of what might be in them." His voice faltered, and Esme swiftly changed the subject.

"Tell me about meeting Lewis."

"Ah." Charlie took a few moments to refill their cups, and Esme let him take his time. This couldn't be easy. "He went to the post office and asked where he'd find any of the Robin family. He introduced himself as Jane Robin's husband. 'No you're not,' the postmistress said. 'Jane's husband is right here, in St Martin. Been married since 1917'. Jane being a common enough name, Lewis apologised for the mix-up, asked for my address and decided to pay me a call thinking I'd be a relation, a cousin perhaps. He claimed to be a family friend and we made pleasant small talk. Until he saw Jane's photograph on the sideboard."

Esme instinctively looked across the room, but the sideboard was now bare of any photographs.

"He asked how I knew Jane. I assumed they were London pals,

and I was eager to hear news of her. I hadn't seen her since 1940. You can imagine, I had questions aplenty."

"Five years... and virtually no contact. I don't know how you stood it."

"There were worse hardships. It was safer for her in England. That thought kept me going."

"And Lewis?"

"It's all a blur. He said they were married, and I said he'd got it all wrong. The long and short is we got into a fight." Charlie balled his hands. "I may only have one leg, but I've strong arms and fists. We brawled in the street and I swung a punch that knocked him out stone cold. Neighbours called the police and I got arrested. They told me if he didn't regain consciousness, I'd be facing a murder charge. I didn't care. I sat in that cell, unable to believe it. Jane was my world, the reason I'd kept going. And it all turned out to be smoke and mirrors. But thanks to you, sense prevailed."

"Me?"

"Jane caught the ferry over, but I refused to see her. Lewis visited me in jail. Told me he and Jane had a daughter, and for her sake, a scandal should be avoided at all costs. We made a deal. He'd file for divorce, even though the marriage was void, to keep the paperwork straight. Jane would be told never to set foot on Guernsey again, or contact any of the family, and we'd both keep our mouths shut. If she ever returned, we'd report her to the police. You were never to find out."

"And no one else ever found out? Not Elizabeth? Or Susan?"

"Mavis knew, of course." He looked away. "It's a terrible thing, but we told everyone Jane was dead."

Esme clasped her hand to her mouth. "Did Arcadia – I mean, Jane – agree to that?"

"She had no choice." Charlie slumped in his chair. "I regretted it later. I missed her. Decisions made in the heat of the moment always come back to haunt. By the time I'd got my head together, it was too late to redress any of it."

"So you never saw her again?"

Charlie shook his head. "No, to my own detriment. I often thought of writing, but what would have been the point? I couldn't go to England, and she couldn't come back here. I realised she'd only tried to do what was best for everyone, and over time, I forgave her. Her visits were the high points of my year, when my small world came alight for a short time, and I missed her." His words, strained and raspy with exhaustion, hung in the air. "I hope you and I can be friends, Esme, and right some of this dreadful wrong."

"Whatever I can do, Charlie. Say it."

"Tell Jane I remember every moment of our life together. Tell her how proud I am of her for raising such a wonderful daughter. Tell her I'm sorry for my own failings, and not accepting hers."

Esme closed her eyes and took a deep breath.

"What is it, child?" Charlie placed his hand on her knee.

Esme grasped his hand between hers. "I can only be a poor substitute, I'm afraid. My mother – Jane–" While she struggled to find words to tell him he'd lost his beloved Jane for all time, Charlie tensed, as if preparing himself. Esme held firm, and said, "She's gone."

A low groan escaped him. He rocked back and forth, eyes fixed to the floor. Esme sensed his agony, felt the hardened skin of his strong grip, and in an unbidden rush, she broke into heaving sobs. Ferocious tears that had refused to flow when her mother died, now overwhelmed her. She clung to Charlie, glad of his comforting presence and knowing he, too, grieved for all that would never be voiced, all that would never be shared.

When her weeping finally abated, Charlie gently wiped her wet face with the edge of a serviette. With a tired sigh, he slumped into the corner of the armchair. "I need some time to myself," he said, his words even slower now. "But come back soon. Ask Mavis to visit too. There's something I should have told her a long time ago. We mustn't leave anything else until it's too late."

～

Esme wheeled her bike away from Charlie's house feeling lighter of spirit and closer to her mother than ever before. Yes, Arcadia had made a wrong decision, but she'd done it for what she perceived to be the right reason. It gave Esme heart, knowing her mother acted to protect her. What a choice she'd had to make: between the boy she'd always loved and the fun-loving husband with whom she shared a child. No wonder she was torn into bits over what to do. No wonder she kept herself on a tight rein, watchful for any slip-up, dodging between England and Guernsey, keeping both lives separate and both men in the dark. And ultimately, for naught – she lost both of them. Yet her intervention had kept Charlie from jail and Esme from ignominy.

Would Esme have discovered her mother's one unselfish act if she hadn't come across that letter from Mavis? That question pummelled her thoughts as she made her way back towards the village of St Martin. Mavis's house wasn't far out of her way and she decided to pop in on the off-chance she'd be there. The detour would also postpone closing the front door of Junction Cottage and facing the prospect of another lonely evening without Anthony.

A grim-faced Mavis greeted her. "Come in. I've bad news, I'm afraid."

Had something happened to Elizabeth? Esme's heart quickened and she followed Mavis to the kitchen. "What is it?"

"Steel yourself, my dear. Something quite unpleasant has occurred."

Esme, her legs shaky, plonked herself down at the table.

Mavis looked quite rocked, unlike her usual calm demeanour.

"A telegram came to Elizabeth's house from a stamp trader in London. Susan brought it over to me." She waved a sheet of paper at Esme. "Here."

"What does it say?"

"They are checking the provenance of a stamp which has come into their possession. The person who brought it in wishes to sell it and is claiming it as their own."

Esme knew nothing about stamps, and still less why this letter had caused such consternation. She nodded encouragingly at Mavis, urging her to continue.

"Due to the value of the stamp, they need to be reassured it's not stolen goods."

"Oh, being fenced, you mean?" Anthony's voice popped into Esme's head. *Good sleuthing, Tuppence.*

Mavis stiffened. "I suppose so. The dealer says records show the stamp – a Penny Red from some rare plate number – as registered to Frank Robin. They ask for confirmation of owner-ship, because as far as they can discern, it's never been sold since he acquired it from a private collector in 1909."

Frank. Elizabeth's husband. Of course – it was one of the few things her mother had ever mentioned about him, that he'd hide away in his study cataloguing his stamps. "He collected stamps as a hobby, didn't he?"

"He did. After he died I wanted to throw them all out. Dust collectors, that's all they were. But funnily enough, Elizabeth refused. She said they might be worth something and after that, they got shovelled into a drawer and forgotten."

"It sounds like a mistake by the dealer."

"I thought so too. Until Susan told me Elizabeth and Anthony had been looking at one of the albums, that day you both visited. Susan asked what prompted her to show him, what was Antho-ny's interest, but Elizabeth was vague. Alarmed, Susan pulled out the album and sure enough, she found a few gaps, but the paper was yellowed and aged as if the stamps had been missing some time. Possibly years, she thought. Then she found a space where it looked like a stamp had been recently removed, as the paper underneath hadn't weathered. It was a clean white oblong. Worse, it had the notation P.R. written in faded ink below."

Penny Red. Sick realisation hit Esme. "And she thinks—"

"Anthony. He's the only one who's been anywhere near those albums."

Esme's mouth felt dry. "Can you be sure? He's never mentioned any interest in stamps."

"He's an archivist, my dear, and a historian. He's interested in old things and understands their value. Most small boys collect stamps at some time in their childhood and I'd be most surprised if Anthony didn't know there are some very sought-after Penny Reds."

What was it she'd overheard Elizabeth say to him? Something about the Germans... *they weren't very clever*. Had Elizabeth been showing off? Demonstrating how Frank had hidden a nest egg in plain sight? Anthony's abrupt change of attitude towards her that day meant she'd never had the chance to ask. Not that he'd have told the truth, if Mavis's suspicions were correct. It all started to added up.

"He's gone overseas," she said. To London? To a stamp dealer? "I mean, he may be back, I don't know, I haven't heard from him. I don't want to hear from him—" Her gullibility over Anthony, how he'd hoodwinked her, made her look so foolish.

"Really?"

Esme didn't want to discuss Belinda. Their encounter lingered, raw in her memory. "We had a falling out." What a child she sounded.

"I'm so sorry, my dear. I know how fond you are of him but I have to go to London and see if I can establish – though heaven knows how – whether the stamp is Frank's. Apparently it could be worth up to ten thousand pounds."

Esme's eyes widened. Ten thousand pounds was a small

fortune. It could buy a very nice house. A mansion. Could Anthony be so criminal? "Let me come with you." If it weren't for Esme, he'd never have seen the stamp album. "Please. I feel responsible."

"Well–"

"I'd like to see my father anyway. And I'd welcome an excuse to get away for a few days." Any illusions she'd clung onto regarding Anthony were now shattered into tiny pieces. A liar, a two-timer and a thief. The idea of seeing him, with or without stiletto-heeled Belinda clutching his arm, was noxious. She didn't want to hear his excuses, his weak apologies, his pathetic explanations.

Mavis hesitated, but only for a moment. "I'm catching the 10.15 Southampton steamer in the morning."

"I'll be there." Esme's mind already raced ahead. She'd ask Travis to feed Jasper, take in the post and cancel her milk deliveries. As soon as she got home, she'd write to her father and prepare him for a visit. And she'd try, with all her strength of mind, not to dwell on Anthony. The rat.

ARCADIA

LONDON, 1949

*D*ivorce came with a high price tag, stripping me of everything I'd treasured. And what divorce hadn't taken, the war had. When I should have been at Ascot, joining the others in the Royal Enclosure, I found myself working the sewing machine at the kitchen table in this poky flat. Society had excommunicated me and aside from an occasional whisky sour with a past acquaintance, I saw few of the old crowd. Friendship, I had learned, followed money and status. A divorced woman was not only impossible to seat at the dinner table, but she might target the man next to her as a future new husband. She certainly couldn't be allowed to rub shoulders with royalty at the races, or take a first night box seat at the theatre for the gossips to peer at through their opera glasses. Not that I could afford it anyway; these days I could only run to a last-minute discounted seat in the upper circle.

I manoeuvred the needle to the end of the seam, eased my foot from the treadle, and snipped the thread. I held the fabric to the light – a shimmering satin the colour of marshmallow – to check for any pulls in the material. Satisfied, I examined the *Vogue* photograph to ensure I'd emulated Dior's New Look as closely as possible. Whilst it pained me to pull apart my designer ball gowns – glorious concoctions from Schiaparelli, Lanvin, Balmain, Vionnet, Chanel – I had no use for them anymore. I also had no wardrobe space. My bedroom could only fit a minimum of furniture, like every room in this doll's house. At least I had a Chelsea address, but if I wanted to maintain it I'd have to keep on restyling old frocks for Moira's Fashion Boutique. With book royalties dwindling now that the BBC had 'released me of my obligation' – yet more fallout thanks to my divorcée status – and with my star fading from the public eye, I had to make income where I could. Those years of resizing hand-me-downs from Mavis and Ginia were finally paying unexpected dividends.

At the harsh sound of the doorbell, I started. Unannounced visitors were rare. Probably a tradesman looking for work, or a door-to-door salesman. I set aside what would soon be a facsimile of Dior's classy new season A-line skirt with cinched waist, then went down the narrow hallway and checked the peephole. Goodness, it was Esme, what a turn-up.

I smoothed my hair and opened the door. "Esme, darling. What a lovely surprise." We duty-kissed on the cheek and I waved her in, leading the way to the sitting room. At the kitchen, I paused to pull shut the door but I wasn't fast enough.

"Whatever are you doing?" Esme's eyes widened. "Sewing? You?"

"Just taking up a hem, darling," I said. "Keeping abreast with fashion." I looked her up and down and bit back a rebuke about the passé nature of her coat, instead taking it from her. "Go through. Tea?"

She declined. "I just dropped by on my way back to the office from the printers. I can't stay long."

The sitting room was the largest and best furnished spot, the place I spent most time – either writing at the roll-top mahogany desk, or lying on the chaise longue where I deliberated on thorny plot issues. When Lewis and I separated, he allowed me some sticks of furniture, and a few worthless abstracts which he hated, but they brightened the walls. Funnily, he kept one copy of each of my books, whether for sentiment or as proof of our publishing endeavours I never knew; the rest I used to decorate the shelving along the wall facing the picture windows.

"How's your father?" I asked. I still missed him terribly. Despite everything, and even taking account of his playboy antics, he was always so much fun; no one made me laugh so much, not even Charlie. "Has he taken up with anyone?"

Esme gave me a sceptical look, obviously misunderstanding my motive in checking on her father's welfare. "Why would you care when you chose to leave him?'

"I want him to be happy." That was true, but equally, it would be hard to accept he'd moved on.

She raised her eyebrows at that. "There was a woman called Ingrid. She came from Sweden."

"How exotic."

"Not really. She was rather mannish. Not Daddy's type at all and when she began making hints about marriage, he dropped her." A cheeky smile crossed her face. "I think being married to you cured him of giving it another go."

I laughed. Not at her observation, but at her refreshing attempt at humour. "Talking of marriage... anyone on the scene?"

She immediately clammed up. "No. Too busy at work."

"You're not still moping around after that publisher fellow, are you? He's not the catch you think he is." I'd never taken to Hugh, although Esme seemed to think him marvellous. When I'd suggested to him that I write a series of commissioned articles, he'd dismissed the notion with no discussion, saying he was only interested in subjects that hit a nerve with the common man.

A rosy blush crossed Esme's cheeks. "He's still in mourning."

Oh yes, the bluestocking wife who died a few months ago. "Nevertheless, don't be taken in by him. His sort look after number one first, mark my words."

Esme rifled in her handbag, pulled out an envelope and handed it to me. "For you. It's an invitation to the launch of my book, *The View From Here*. Please say you'll come."

I can't deny, I was touched. "Will your father be there?"

"Yes, and Granny, but don't let that deter you. You can stay opposite ends of the room."

"I'm sorry darling, I have to decline. It's your day and I don't want the focus on me, and my presence spoiling it for you."

"For heaven's sake," Esme exploded. "Do you really think because you've penned a few racy books, you'll be the bigger drawcard? The majority of people there will never have heard of Arcadia Fanstone, far less read any of your novels."

"Darling, calm down. That's not what I meant." I felt on the verge of tears. This was a deliberate ploy of Granny Fanstone's. By attending, she knew it would be impossible for me to be there too. I could handle keeping my distance from Lewis, but Granny F was the loose cannon who might go off and cause a scene. At the very minimum, she would publicly snub me. "You don't need people whispering and watching to see if Daddy and I get into a fight. It's better I stay away. Give me a signed copy and we'll have our own private celebration. How about that?"

I could see Esme wrestling with her feelings. "I suppose you're right..."

"I know I am." To make up, I'd speak to my old pals at the BBC to see if someone would interview Esme and help promote her book. "I hope you've spoken to Hugh about featuring you in a profile piece?"

She visibly bristled. "I couldn't possibly put him under that pressure. It would be quite wrong of me to try and influence his editorial choices." She stood. "Time for me to go. I'll be in touch."

After she'd left, I returned to my faithful Singer sewing machine, but I couldn't concentrate. I'd seen from the way Esme reacted at the mention of Hugh's name that she was besotted, but I feared she'd never find happiness until she gave up on him. I had to stop pressing the issue, as my advice obviously irritated her, but it was hard to stand by and see one's daughter's youth passing her by. At her age, I'd known the joy of Charlie, with his wondrous sensitivity, and then Lewis, who taught me to push my boundaries.

It may have been complicated and imperfect, but I'd known the love of two wonderful men, and nothing could erase those memories which would go with me to the grave. I wished I could tell Esme about it, but perhaps it was better my secret must remain hidden. Even thinking about Charlie punctured my veneer. If only I could have said goodbye to him and had the chance to explain myself – how I got caught in my own web of lies, and once I'd started I couldn't stop, but got buried under more lies. And how easy it is to lie when you know you are implicitly trusted.

31

ESME

ENGLAND, SEPTEMBER 1958

*T*he man behind the glass-topped counter at Harcourt and Sons, *Purveyors of Philately*, wore a brown suit which hung, ill-fitting, on his string-bean frame. His bald pate, poorly disguised with a few combed-over dull-brown hairs, shone with a gleam of perspiration.

"The name is Fortescue." He clasped his hands in a prayer-like pose. "How may I help you?"

While Mavis explained their mission to the obsequious dealer, Esme strolled the floor of the Strand establishment. Within glass cabinets, rows of stamps were neatly lined up and labelled with meticulous attention to their provenance. Floor-to-ceiling book-shelves of orderly albums were arranged next to slender drawers, marked by date. Solemn collectors examined the contents with magnifying glasses. Quiet murmurings between customers and stamp traders buzzed through the air, creating an intense atmosphere. A group of small boys in school blazers and caps examined packets of well-priced mixed stamps on a revolving stand and counted out handfuls of coins under the watchful gaze of their form master. Stamps, Esme concluded, did not flare her interest but she tucked away the small experience of visiting this dusty museum-style store for future reference. One day she'd write it into a book.

"*Esme.*"

She spun around to see Mavis waving her over. Fortescue had a peculiar expression on his face, cheeks sucked in and one eye twitching. Somewhere between cock-a-hoop and disapproving. Mavis took her elbow and steered her away from the counter. She kept her voice low. "I can't believe it. It wasn't a man, but a woman who brought in the stamp. That Fortescue–" she hissed his name "–said she left her name as Miss Robin."

Relief and horror swamped Esme. So it can't have been Anthony after all – but Miss Robin must be a relative of some kind. But who? "How strange. I mean – one of us? A family member?"

"Let's not jump to conclusions," said Mavis. "It seems far more likely to be an imposter. Someone claiming to be a Robin. For the time being, I've instructed Fortescue to do nothing. Ownership of the stamp, however, is reasonably conclusive. It fits the space perfectly in father's album and circumstantial evidence points to it being the same one, especially given there's no record of it ever having been auctioned or sold privately."

"How can they be certain it's your stamp?"

"Father had it valued in 1909. Harcourt's have the documentation. Fortescue says it's the real McCoy not a forgery, and as there are only seven known to be in existence, we can assume it belongs to us." She looked around to check they weren't being overheard. "There's another twist, however. It may be nothing, but the day before the woman came in, a man asked if any Penny Reds had come onto the market recently. Said he was a collector."

Perhaps Esme had discounted Anthony too soon. "Did he describe him?"

"Medium height, medium build, youngish. He wore horn-rimmed spectacles and had a pipe poking out of his breast pocket."

"Oh dear, it sounds like Anthony." Esme could picture him, earnestly asking for information.

"I'm afraid it does. Fortescue said the man stuck in his mind because of this so-called Miss Robin bringing in a Penny Red the very next day."

"If it was Anthony, why would he ask if any were for sale? If he was in possession of our Penny Red, why not request a valuation then and there? I think it's a red herring."

"I tend to agree." Mavis further lowered her voice. "Another thing, the woman claimed she'd provide Harcourt's with a signed letter, confirming ownership."

"Did she say it would come from Frank's widow?"

"Apparently not. Elizabeth wasn't mentioned."

How odd. Such an omission likely meant 'Miss Robin' was indeed a charlatan, as Mavis reckoned. "If this woman said she'd give Harcourt's proof of her right to the stamp, why did the dealer bother to write to Frank? I mean, I'm glad he did, but what prompted him?"

"The woman seemed to be in a hurry, and when she advised she'd have the letter sent by post, rather than personally bringing it in, Fortescue became suspicious. To satisfy himself Harcourt's wasn't in possession of an excellent forgery or stolen goods, he decided he'd better contact the owner direct. By having a third party independently verify the claim, he would be more comfortable about Miss Robin's authenticity."

His caution seemed justified. "What do we do next?" Esme asked.

"The woman left an address. The Regency House Hotel in Bloomsbury. Do you know it?"

"It's a small private hotel. Quite unassuming and respectable." Not a robber's den, at any rate.

"We'll take a black cab." Mavis faced Esme, her expression stern. "Don't think this exonerates Anthony. Be prepared, Esme. He might have put this woman up to it. They could be in league."

It sounded far-fetched and overly dramatic. Esme tried to picture Anthony and some moll – possibly Belinda who really came to St Peter Port to set up an alibi? – as a pair of stamp thieves, operating an illegal ring. The idea was ludicrous. And yet she'd believed in his honesty, his genuine interest in helping find her family, and the tenderness between them, hadn't she? A façade that had proved fake. In truth, he was another Hugh, flirting with her affections, filling time until he wed Belinda. Such duplicity meant he could also be a clever trickster, who'd known about Frank's stamp collection and used Esme to get access to the albums. All the while in cahoots with Belinda, going by the alias Miss Robin.

"Should we call the police?" she asked.

Mavis cocked her head. "No." Her decisive tone left no room to argue. "We'll check this woman out first. I hardly think any harm will come to us in a hotel in Bloomsbury. If by chance this turns out to be a family matter, we don't want publicity. If, on the other hand, a fraud is being perpetrated, we will contact the authorities."

They were silent on the journey to Gower Street, for which Esme was grateful. It enabled her to prepare herself for whatever – and whoever – awaited them at the hotel. Of course, the woman might have checked out and they'd be none the wiser. Except she'd have to return to the trader in the Strand, given she'd left the stamp there while they checked its authenticity. Esme envisioned a sordid, drawn-out investigation, which would bring nothing but stress and unhappiness. What a horrid turn of events.

The man behind the desk in the Regency Hotel's wood-panelled reception barely looked up from his newspaper. Esme peered over the counter to find out what was so riveting and saw he was reading the sporting pages. Mavis coughed twice to attract his notice and with an air of extreme resentment, he raised his head. "Yes?"

"We're here to see Miss Robin." Mavis spoke with authority.

He went back to the cricket results. "Number eight. First floor on the left."

Mavis walked smartly ahead, leaving Esme, heart thumping, to trail behind. What if Anthony – or Belinda – answered the door? How could she face them? How could she bear it? The whole scheme was ill-thought-out. She tugged on Mavis's sleeve. "Are you sure about this? What if it gets violent?"

"We're dealing with a stamp thief, not a murderer, dear. But if you want to wait downstairs, I quite understand."

She certainly wouldn't leave Mavis on her own. They'd confront this together.

Mavis rapped on the door of number eight. "Room service," she called out.

Esme half-prayed there'd be no answer, but within seconds she heard the security chain being unlatched, and the door opened. Swathed in a voluminous navy-blue dressing gown, her face covered in cold cream with only those familiar smoky grey eyes peering out, appeared–

"*Ginia.*" Mavis's voice boomed out, like cannon fire. Esme stared, gobsmacked.

"Good heavens." Ginia's eyes popped like two smouldering fires in a snowstorm. "What are you two doing here? You might have telegrammed first. Come in, come in." She held back the door and the two women entered. "And what's all this room service nonsense?"

Esme had to hand it to Mavis. She recovered her equilibrium with grace, removed her hat, and sat on the desk chair with it in her lap. "We weren't sure who – or what – to expect."

"Why did you come then?" asked Ginia.

"Do wipe that stuff off your face. It's like talking to a panda bear."

Ginia bristled. "If I'd known to expect visitors—" But she went to the basin and rinsed the cream away with a facecloth. Esme perched on the end of the bed, watching the sisters spar.

"How did you know where I was staying? I never told anyone." Ginia, her face rubbed clean and shiny, leaned against the window ledge.

"The stamp trader. A Mr Fortescue," said Mavis.

"At Harcourt's?" Ginia's voice shot up an octave. "How funny. I only went there at the suggestion of a young man. How could you possibly have known?"

"Was he called Anthony?"

"Anthony. That's right. Charming. Historian. From Cambridge."

Esme couldn't believe it. Ginia and Anthony were in this together? Not only that, but Ginia seemed unconcerned at being found out.

Ginia looked from Esme to Mavis and back to Esme. "What on earth is this?"

"Anthony has told us nothing," said Mavis. "We're here because of a letter Mother received from Harcourt's trying to authenticate a stamp of Father's which we had reason to believe Anthony stole—"

"Oh, how ridiculous." Ginia snorted. "Why would Anthony steal a stamp? He's not an idiot."

Esme interrupted. "It all pointed that way."

Ginia crossed her arms. "You are a pair of numbskulls. But I'm very glad to see you. You can tell that Mr Fortescue that I am who I say I am. And we can clear this up. I want to get to France."

"Not without an explanation." Mavis turned her steely glare onto her sister.

"I'd hoped to surprise you."

"Surprise me now."

"There's no need to look quite so priggish, Mavis." Ginia wrapped her gown around her body and circled the room. "A couple of years ago, when I helped clear Mother's house before she moved to Herm, I put aside Father's stamp albums to throw out. Mother got very agitated and said I mustn't. Said they were valuable."

"Yes," exclaimed Mavis. "She said the same thing when I tried to get rid of them after he died."

"Did she mention hiding them from the Germans?" asked Esme. "During the Occupation?"

"Hiding? No. She left them on the sideboard. In full view. The Germans were too stupid to be double-crossed, she said. Twice they raided the house. Mother hid a pot of disgusting nettle jam – no sugar, rationing you know – at the back of a cupboard. They were thrilled to find it. Never checked the albums."

"Go on," said Mavis.

"A few years after the war, I was home for a short visit, and I took some of the stamps to that antique trader on The Pollet. He said they were worth a few bob, nothing more. 'If ever you find a Penny Black or a Penny Red, then you'll be talking,' he said. That young fellow, Anthony, was in the shop. He overheard and introduced himself. Explained he was a stamp enthusiast. 'If you find one, take it to Harcourt and Sons of the Strand in London,' he said. 'They'll get you the best price.' We all laughed. 'Wouldn't that be fine?' I said. 'Imagine how many starving mouths in Africa I could feed'."

"What did you do?" Esme leaned forwards, fascinated.

"Nothing. Had no time. I was off to Africa. Made sure the albums were safe in a cupboard. Knew they'd be there when I got back. Once, in Addis Ababa, I came across a philatelist. Asked him about Penny Blacks and Reds. He said some were valuable, most not. Forgot all about it until I got back."

"How does Anthony come into all this?"

"I've no idea. That's all your making." Ginia turned and circled in the opposite direction. "After I met you, young Esme, you may recall I went to Herm to see Mother. While I was there, I took a closer look at the albums. Wasn't expecting anything. Lo and behold. A Penny Red. Didn't say anything. Just took it. Thought I'd get it valued. Remembered that young man's advice. Decided to visit Harcourt and Sons before I sailed to France."

"But why didn't you tell us?"

"No one had looked at those albums in decades. No point stirring up excitement. If there was money to be made, I'd find out. That Mr Fortescue has stirred up a hornet's nest. I told him I'd get a signed affidavit. You had no need to rush over here in a panic. Goodness, no."

"He's being prudent," said Mavis. "He thought you were a shady character. It's those eccentric clothes you wear, Ginia. I can quite understand he'd not auction off a stamp, which could be worth thousands of pounds, just on your say-so."

Ginia took two long paces and opened the door. "Wait for me downstairs. I'll get dressed and we'll go back to Harcourt's. Put an end to this nonsense. You can confirm my identity to Fortescue. Let's get a valuation and talk to Susan and Elizabeth about selling." Her face hardened. "I'll never forgive Father for what he did to me and Mother, and all those poor boys–" Her face clouded. "But if finding this stamp means some recompense can come at last – well, that's some comfort. All I ask is ten per cent of the proceeds go towards building my hospital in Ethiopia."

"Ten per cent?" said Mavis. "I don't think so."

Her sister's face fell. "It's a small price–"

"Since Esme arrived I've learned some unpalatable truths about our childhood; the terrible things Father inflicted on those who trusted him, and how you and Jane shielded me from knowing about his abuse." Emotion rippled through Mavis's voice. "We'll build the entire hospital, and if there's anything left over, we'll donate it to war veterans. What do you say?"

A tick of silence, and Ginia pulled Mavis to her in a fierce hug. The sisters swayed in the doorway, holding each other tightly. Esme backed quietly down the corridor, sad for their years of trauma, but glad at last they would share the pain and maybe find some peace.

~

Esme didn't return to the stamp emporium with Ginia and Mavis. They didn't need her tagging along, but more importantly, without her presence, they could have a good talk. Ginia had booked her passage to France for the next day, so this would be the sisters' last chance for many months to have a heart-to-heart about their father, bring all they'd suffered into the open and clear the air.

She wired ahead to announce her arrival and caught the afternoon train to Charlbury. To her surprise, her father waited on the station platform, looking spruce in a tweed suit, jangling car keys. She'd expected to call for a taxi.

"Hallo, possum." He took her case, flung an arm around her shoulder and smacked a kiss on her cheek.

She was pleased to see her father in good spirits. "Thank you for coming to fetch me."

He led the way out to the car park. "Glad to see you, as it happens. I've thought a lot about your last visit, and often wondered what you'd since discovered?" A wary, questioning note crept into his voice. "Now your mother's died, and it's all come out, perhaps the time has arrived to heal old wounds."

Esme grinned, delighted he'd had a change of heart.

Lewis stared with studied concentration through the windscreen. "Because I was so furious with Arcadia when I found out about her marriage to Charlie, one of my biggest regrets is that I never had the chance to find out why she didn't tell me about him."

"She was afraid how you'd react, of course."

"But we'd have worked it out. Somehow. There was you to consider."

Esme shook her head. "You're dreaming, Daddy. You're saying that in hindsight. It could all have got very ugly. Especially once Granny Fanstone found out. Can you imagine the uproar? She never approved of Arcadia. You know jolly well when you got divorced, it confirmed all her prejudices. I don't think Arcadia could risk confiding in you. This may be hard to hear, but she loved Charlie and I believe she felt the commitment to her marriage vows very strongly."

"In sickness and in health."

"To you too."

"Yes. Odd, isn't it?"

Odd indeed, thought Esme. But to Arcadia it had made sense. "I can see how angry and hurt you must have been when you discovered she was still married to Charlie. I can't conceive how you could ever trust someone who'd lied so much, even though it seems she thought she had no choice. But there's something I still don't understand. You said she did it to protect me. And yet all my life, she never showed me affection. She often left me with you. She resented my book being published. She was harsh about my choices, particularly men."

Arcadia had swept through Esme's childhood in a series of divine gowns, pausing to give her a goodnight kiss at cocktail hour, and demanding she dress nicely when guests were invited. It was her father who bathed her on Nanny's night off and read her a goodnight story; who introduced her to C S Lewis; and took her to Regent's Park zoo for an ice cream. When it suited her, Arcadia would lavish affection and attention. She'd buy theatre tickets and send for Esme, with the promise of a new frock. On a whim, she'd parcel up Esme and her father for a weekend trip to the coast, always where a dance band or jazz trio performed on the pier, so she could party.

Lewis tapped the steering wheel. "I'm not sure I have the

answer. She must have lived on this nervous tightrope of panic, constantly worried about being found out. And she couldn't admit to having family, after telling me they didn't exist. I suspect, once you were born, she desperately wanted the comfort of her own mother but all she had was Granny Fanstone who criticised her mercilessly." He pulled into the driveway, switched off the engine, and turned to Esme. "On Guernsey, she pretended to be Charlie's childless wife. In London, she had no idea how to be a mother, and wanted to be the darling of society. The result? I stepped in, you became Daddy's little girl, and Arcadia let it happen. During the war, rather than live with Granny, she stayed in London whilst you came here. When she tried to be a mother, it was awkward. Neither of you knew how to communicate. When she did make an appearance – usually when I was home on leave – she didn't fit in and was jealous of how close we were."

"Jealous?"

"Think about it. Her daughter is doted on by me and indulged by Granny Fanstone, who hated Arcadia and never made her welcome. Arcadia reacted by staying away even more, thus driving a bigger wedge between the two of you. Meanwhile, she's operating this double life all in order to protect you – the daughter she struggles to connect with – and there's no one she can confide in." He sat back. "That's my opinion."

"I only ever saw her as selfish and distant, which of course, she was, but now I realise she'd trapped herself and couldn't find a way out."

Lewis opened the car door. "You'll find Granny much changed. She's only holding on by a whisker. Go and see her, we can talk more later."

The bedroom glowed in the afternoon sunshine, but the light couldn't disguise the dark shadows of pain on Granny Fanstone's face. Esme held her hand as she slipped in and out of consciousness, waking only to briefly smile at her granddaughter, but Esme didn't want to leave her alone. She'd never forgive herself if Granny faded away with no one by her side to comfort her.

To pass the time, Esme pulled up a chair to the side of the bed, and opened one of Arcadia's earliest novels, *Miles From Home*. Despite the corny plot and clichéd characters, she couldn't stop turning the pages. Her mother had a knack for building tension with unpredictable twists and surprises. She knew how to tell a gripping story and wasn't shy of drawing on her own experiences in these fictional melodramas.

The hero of *Miles From Home* went travelling the world, leaving behind his wife and child, only to almost die in the jungle until rescued by a forgotten tribe. Ten years later, discovered by missionaries, he returned home to his wife who had remarried and had two more children.

Keen to learn how Arcadia resolved the problem of a wife with two living husbands, Esme eagerly flipped the page.

"What are you reading?" Granny Fanstone's voice, weak and phlegmy, diverted Esme's attention.

Esme showed her the cover and loudly enunciated her words so Granny could hear. "I'm reading one of my mother's books." There was little point lying. "It's... eye-opening."

Granny opened one eye. "I'll tell you a secret. Come here."

Esme leaned in closer for Granny to whisper in her ear. "What is it?"

"Don't tell your father." She coughed. "I've read most of them. Lovely stories."

"But you–"

"Shh. Our little secret." Granny relaxed back onto the pillow. "*An Affair for All Time*. My favourite."

That novel followed the torturous love between a man and woman constantly separated by one disaster or another, but always finding solace in the memory, and occasionally the arms, of each other. Hardly her grandmother's taste.

"Granny, you can't be serious."

"I liked *The Voyager Returns* too."

Esme sucked in her cheeks to stop the giggle which threatened to erupt at this startling disclosure about a penchant for lurid romances. Granny? Drawn to a bodice-ripper, set in the sixteenth century, about an explorer determined to overcome all obstacles and find his way home to his one and only love? She had to know more. "I don't understand. You despised Arcadia."

"Silly woman. Vacuous. Treated your father abominably. Sent him penniless. Say no more." Her breathing deepened. She'd fallen back to sleep.

Esme tucked the blanket around Granny's withered neck. Why had she really read the books? Because they were irresistible page-turners? Or to gain insight into Arcadia?

It was nonsense to claim that Arcadia had stripped Lewis of his wealth and lifestyle. According to Arcadia, Lewis had been an inveterate womaniser, and hopeless financier who gambled away what little remained at the card table – including his pride – and eventually it broke them. In truth, stupidity and bad investments were to blame for the loss of his fortune. So why pretend otherwise? Unless Granny, Arcadia and Lewis had each woven their own versions of history. And as a result, it became left to others to sift the tiny shards of truth from the pool of falsehoods.

Esme laid the back of her hand on Granny's brow. Hot. Feverish. She took a face flannel and dipped it into the water bowl on the bedside table and dabbed it on her papery skin. Her breathing became shallow and uneven; a struggle even while she slept.

As the minutes ticked by, and the clock on the tallboy chimed each hour, Esme kept reading. At eight o'clock she finished *Miles From Home*. In the final chapter, Arcadia neatly wrapped up the heroine's conundrum: husband number one shot husband number two. Appalled, the wife packed up the three children and left him.

With a satisfied sigh, Esme turned on the side lamps and opened *Love Found Me* – the tale of a young girl who leaves a trail of broken hearts in her wake, until she finally meets her match who, naturally, appears immune to her charms. With the book on her lap, Esme mused on how she'd been wrong about Arcadia's talents – sure, her books were trite, but they had pace and energy. When she returned to her cottage in Guernsey, she'd get stuck into Arcadia's last manuscript. It wouldn't take long to type out and edit, and then she'd send *The Art of Artifice* to be published. As for the proceeds, it would be hypocritical to keep them after years of disparaging her mother's works. She'd donate them to the Royal Literary Fund to help new, struggling writers.

There was something else. Her conscience. In her youthful arrogance, she'd dismissed Arcadia as a serious writer and, aside from a cursory skim of the dust jackets and a few saucy paragraphs, she'd never read any of her books. She'd believed anyone who couldn't secure a proper publisher – one who paid an advance and royalties – didn't deserve the public's reading energy, or money, for their efforts. It was an insult to real authors like Esme who slaved to write, edit, then edit again and again; who placed their work before ruthless reviewers and a discerning readership.

It was time she redressed her oversight. Maybe reading Arcadia's final book would fulfil her worst forebodings, but at least she'd have done her the courtesy of a considered opinion.

Granny stirred. Esme laid the book face down and took her hands. They were cold and unresponsive, as if already slipping from this world to the next. To get her circulation moving, Esme gently rubbed the wrinkled skin, freckled with age spots.

Granny Fanstone's eyes flickered, watery and vague. "We sat in the buttercups," she murmured. "Nanny made sandwiches."

"A lovely picnic?" Esme ventured.

"Lewis has chickenpox. He must be kept warm." Granny squeezed Esme's hand. "Tell his father to stay away."

"Yes, Granny." For what was the point in anything other than agreeing?

"Give him the paper. *The Times*." Her breathing became raspy and laboured.

Esme stroked her fingers. "He's waiting for you."

"We skated on the lake. Figures of eight." Granny closed her eyes and gave a contented sigh. "Ask Jennings to buy beeswax."

A deep rattle gurgled from her chest. Her head lolled to one side. And then, silence.

32

ESME

GUERNSEY, SEPTEMBER 1958

*A*t a few minutes past seven, Esme turned the oversized front door key in the lock and pushed her way in, dragging her case behind her. Jasper slinked from the kitchen and curled his body around her ankles, mewing and purring.

"You pleased to see me?" She leaned down and ran her hand along his sleek fur. "Or hungry?"

The cottage smelled musty, closed-up, even though Travis had come in every day to feed Jasper. Everything was exactly as Esme left it. Her manuscript stacked on the table next to the typewriter. Several plates and a mug in the drainer by the sink. A tea towel over the back of a dining chair. Looking around, she felt disconnected, a stranger in an alien habitat.

She dropped her handbag on the rocking chair and wandered into the living room. Dark and shuttered, she moved to the window to let in fresh air and daylight. Rays of sun caught motes of fine ash swirling in the air, blowing up from the fire's grate. She'd dust and vacuum later. The thought conjured Granny Fanstone, who'd never again polish her bannisters or buff the cabinets. Without Granny she felt adrift. Returning alone to Guernsey – because there was nowhere else to go – only highlighted she had no home of her own, no husband to comfort her, no busy career. The last two weeks had been filled with sadness and days closeted indoors whilst she took charge of Granny's funeral, then sorting and packing her belongings, managing her father's grief – not to mention her own – and making the decision to sell the Cotswolds house. It was too big and the upkeep too expensive for her father, but it signified the loss of Esme's last tie to her childhood. On the bright side, Lewis had offered to buy Arcadia's flat. "It'll suit me, possum," he said. "And it solves a problem for you, eh?"

She gathered up the post, went through to the kitchen and filled the kettle; a cup of tea was in order. With trepidation, she opened an envelope from Chatterworths Publishing and a cheque fluttered to the floor. Her eyes widened when she read and then reread the amount. "Wow," she muttered and flopped onto the nearest dining chair. The advance was not only large, it was life-changing: enough to finish *The Trial of Clara Denier* without the worry of finding a job, with some left over towards finding a more permanent place to live.

The kettle whistled and she scurried to the kitchen, her head in a whirl, grinning broadly. No sooner had she filled the teapot than she heard a rat-tat on the door. "Coming," she called out, before popping a tea cosy over the pot.

Still smiling, she threw open the front door. Anthony. "What on earth?" Her face fell and she took a step backwards.

"Can I come in?" He shifted from foot to foot.

Esme regained her composure. "How dare you? No, you most certainly may not come in."

She made to close the door, but Anthony wedged his body in the opening. "Please, Esme. I need to explain. It's been hell waiting for you to return."

"How did you even know I was back?"

"Travis told me you were expected this morning." He pushed his hair back, a worried frown creasing his forehead. "I know what it looks like, I know what you must think of me, and I can't blame you. I should have told you, trusted you. Oh, please, Esme. Let me in."

A couple walked past the front of the cottage, staring with open curiosity at the scene on the doorstep. Esme, not wanting the whole neighbourhood to eavesdrop, held the door back. "Just for a moment."

Anthony lowered his head and slipped past her into the dining room.

Without thinking, or perhaps to cover her confusion, Esme took two mugs from the drainer, wiped them dry and poured tea. "Here," she said. "Sit."

Despite her determination to remain unmoved by whatever excuses he might proffer, seeing him seated at the table – tousled hair, smuts on his glasses, button loose on his jacket – caught Esme as *right*. Without him had been all wrong. She shook herself. *Don't fall for his charm.*

"You must despise me." Anthony's eyes traced her face. "I despise myself, actually."

"You told me you'd broken it off with Belinda. That was hardly the impression she gave."

Anthony bit his lower lip. "I know."

"And you went to Harcourt's trying to find out about Penny Red stamps. Rather a coincidence, given Ginia tried to have her father's valued the next day. What did you have in mind? I know you got Elizabeth to show you Frank's albums. Why the interest? Was that why you left Guernsey in a hurry?" Her questions sprayed in a volley of anger.

His head whipped up. "Oh no. That's not it at all."

"So tell me. Explain." She sat back and crossed her arms. "And then leave."

Anthony took a deep breath. "Let me start by saying I never told you this before because it might have been nothing. I didn't want to make trouble. Thing is, that day when we went to Herm and I kept an eye on Elizabeth, she started talking about Frank's stamps. She said, 'Frank said sell the Penny Red but we never have'. My ears pricked up when she said Penny Red. Some are quite rare and valuable. She asked if I'd like to see it. I was fascinated and said of course I would. She sent me inside, told me I'd find the album on the desk in the front room. 'Ginia likes to look', she said, which I found a bit odd, but Elizabeth does get muddled. We sat together – you know that, we were still looking when you got back – turning the pages. But there was no Penny Red. Elizabeth got a bit flustered. 'We never sold it', she kept repeating. And then I came across a gap. A new gap, I'd say, with the letters P.R. underneath. That got me worried. Had someone recently taken it, I wondered? Ginia, perhaps? I asked Elizabeth, but she kept saying, 'We never sold it'."

Esme didn't move a muscle. So far, it all fitted with Ginia's explanation. "Go on."

"I'll be honest. I didn't know what to do."

Esme thought back to how quiet he'd been on the ferry home, how he'd dashed off and refused her invitation to supper.

Anthony scratched his head. "Then I remembered a conversation with Ginia–"

"That if she ever found a Penny Red or Black to take it to Harcourt's."

"Yes. She told you?" Relief flooded his face. "I knew she'd already left the island, so I thought my best bet was to see if a Penny Red had turned up on the market. An awfully long shot, and I wasn't sure what I'd do if it turned out Ginia had stolen it, but better to find out first rather than raise the alarm unnecessarily and involve police and cause a lot of upset. So I decided to go to London, which turned out to be a waste of time. Harcourt's hadn't had a Penny Red in months. I realised things would have to take their course, and it was best I kept my nose out of it."

So that was his involvement. Nothing sinister after all. And yet... "Why didn't you tell me all this? I understand you'd not want to say anything to the others, but there was no reason to keep me in the dark."

"If I'd told you I had suspicions about Ginia, and then it all turned out to be a mistake, it would leave a nasty atmosphere. You wouldn't think much of me. If – as turned out to be the case – it was a misunderstanding, there'd be no harm done. If not, I'd talk to you and let you decide whether you wanted to pursue the matter. I certainly wouldn't have interfered in what essentially was a family affair."

Esme reluctantly saw he'd been right to keep quiet until the full truth became clear. "It was good of you to try. Rather rash, though, to go racing off to London." Esme stood, her tea untouched. There was no point prolonging the conversation. Nevertheless, she was glad Anthony didn't turn out to be a thief, merely a misguided good Samaritan.

Anthony remained at the table. "Please sit down. Visiting Harcourt's wasn't the only thing I did in London. I also went to Belinda's flat."

"Stop–"

"No, listen – she wasn't there–"

"Of course she wasn't there. She was here. As you well know. No doubt she told you all about how marvellous I'd been, caring for Judy. And how she asked for my help with getting you up the aisle." Esme couldn't keep the sarcasm from her voice.

"She had no business being here, Esme, and if you'd be quiet for a moment and let me speak, I'll explain."

Esme blinked, surprised at his hardened change of tone. "Go ahead."

"I admit, it wasn't strictly correct when I told you it was over with Belinda. I liked you so much, I didn't want there to be any barriers to getting to know you, so I fudged the truth in case you straight out rejected me. From my point of view, the engagement was off. But Belinda refused to accept it. She bombarded me with letters, telling me I didn't know my own mind, suggesting I take time to rethink and clear my head, and that she would go ahead with the marriage plans anyway. Copious times I replied saying I couldn't see a future for us, it wouldn't work, we'd grown too far apart. She begged me to reconsider, said she'd come and live here if that's what it would take. I stopped replying, hoping she'd give up.

"Then I met you. I knew there was something there right away, a connection, we clicked. It was easy between us, no tension." He sighed and removed his spectacles, twirling them around his thumb and forefinger. "In my heart, I knew I shouldn't pursue you. Not until I was certain I was a free man. It was weak and unethical but as the weeks drifted on with no word from Belinda, I relaxed."

"Had you really ended it? Or had you led her to believe you were only here for a short time and then you'd be home to get married? Because that's what she seemed to think." Esme badly wanted to trust Anthony, but why would Belinda lie? Had he led her a dance? Played on the emotions of both women?

"The day I decided to go to London and chase down the Penny Red, I'd also received a letter from Belinda." A snapshot came to Esme of Anthony, with a pile of letters to read whilst Elizabeth slept. "She issued an ultimatum, either I returned and married her, or she'd be on the next boat over to have it out with me. She ranted, made silly threats, and didn't sound very stable. The letter decided me. I'd go and see her when I was in London – stop her nonsense – and if I had to, I'd see her parents. I'd been too patient, too nice. Time for mister tough guy to take over."

Without thinking, Esme took his glasses and polished the grimy lenses. "But you crossed paths."

He winced. "I deliberately gave no warning of my visit. I wanted to take her unawares, not give her the opportunity to dream up an elaborate plot or create a drama designed to guilt me into staying with her."

Esme handed back his glasses and folded her arms, unimpressed.

"Not that I would have," he added hastily. "I merely wanted to avoid an escalation of her hysterics." He replaced his spectacles. "Oh, that's better. I can see now."

"Go on."

"I went to her flat twice. And her office. She works for a modelling agency. They hadn't seen her for a few days. Apparently she took off without a 'by your leave'. So I went to her folks' place. Only her mother was home, and I didn't exactly get a friendly reception. She told me I should hotfoot it back to Guernsey if I wanted any chance of salvaging Belinda's affections. That got me worried, I can tell you. The idea of Belinda on the loose in St Peter Port, wreaking God knew what havoc and telling everyone she'd been jilted, didn't bear consideration."

Esme maintained a poker face. So far, so good. But she wasn't ready to capitulate yet. Let him squirm.

Anthony ploughed on. "When I returned, I found her in the flat and learned you'd been there, waiting for me. I was furious. Furious she'd dared to land on my doorstep and frightened at what on earth she might have said to you. To my shame, I yelled at her, threw her things in her bag and dragged her out to my car. During the drive to the ferry, I made it absolutely clear I was in love with another woman–"

"What? Say that again–"

He spoke slowly and softly. "In... love... with... you... Esme."

"Oh." *In love with you, Esme.* "Oh."

A crooked smile creased his face. "Is that all you can say?"

In his eyes she saw warmth, passion – and hope. Either Esme could remain wary and distrustful of Anthony's sudden declaration, or she could accept him at face value and risk being wrong. Which would be worse? Turning her back on the nicest man she'd ever known, or discovering he was human and had faults?

He took her face in his hands and stroked the outline of her scar with the edge of his thumb. "Dear Esme, I want to love you for the rest of my life. I want to come home to you, take care of you. Always. So before we take this any further... will you do me the honour of becoming my wife?"

Esme looked deep into his soft brown eyes. Ever since they'd met, he'd helped with every twist and turn of finding her family and unravelling the mystery of Arcadia's letter. He'd put her first, sheltered her from unpleasantness. Unlike Hugh, he made her feel safe and protected. Unlike Hugh, the notion of being a team meant sharing their domestic life, not organising his business affairs. A lifetime with Anthony stretched out, an adventure, an unknown future filled with pitfalls and joys they'd encounter together.

"I would be so very, very delighted," she said.

33

ESME

GUERNSEY, 1958

*E*sme's fingers trembled as she opened the notebook – an ordinary specimen with a dark-red cover – hoping her mother's last work would be a triumph, fearful it might be a dud. After everything she'd recently discovered, the title page intrigued her with its bold declaration, *The Art of Artifice*, a warning that this might not be in the usual vein of Arcadia Fanstone's works. And when she turned the next page and read the dedication, *To my daughter, Esme*, her anticipation increased. She resisted the temptation to turn the page and read it, there and then, standing by the dining table; it wouldn't do to flick through the contents, rushed and unconsidered.

"Shoo." Esme gently pushed Jasper from the rocking chair, and took his place. Sunlight streamed through the window onto her lap, illuminating the bleached ink of Arcadia's theatrical scrivenings; her distinctive loopy letters and her 'e' formed like a backward '3'.

Esme curled up her legs and began to read...

The Art of Artifice
To my daughter, Esme

#

CHAPTER ONE
Guernsey, August 1914

On 5 August 1914, my childhood ended. Not just because we learned of the looming threat of invasion and feared losing our men in the mud-soaked trenches of France – us girls never thought of such things. No – something far more sinister occurred in our household that day. Looking back, I think being the youngest meant until then I'd been somehow sheltered from the ugliness. Or perhaps I just didn't notice until my nose was pressed firmly against the reality of what went on under our roof. Or maybe I blithely believed the people who said: *How lucky you are to be the daughter of the headmaster! What a wonderful education you and your two sisters must have! How marvellous that the three of you are such good friends!*

~

Late afternoon turned to evening. The sun went down and Esme turned on the lamps. Not a novel, but a memoir. Like a voyeur, Esme watched Jane turn from a carefree girl into a resolute young woman with ambition and dreams, to a bride waiting for war's end, and then become Arcadia – a woman trapped between two loves.

Past midnight, Esme turned the page to the last chapter...

CHAPTER THIRTY
London, February 1958

The Harley Street rooms were larger than my entire apartment – and more expensively furnished. By my calculation, I'd need to sell about five hundred books to pay the consultant's account. The mere thought was exhausting. And impossible. Sales have dwindled away to a few hundred a year. Despite my back catalogue, which by now must number more than fifty novels, no one seems interested in good old-fashioned romance anymore. They want murder, mystery, mayhem and sex.

"Your specialist is running a few minutes behind." The receptionist wore a tan Jaeger wool suit and had matching dyed hair, thinning and patchy. It looked like a home bottle job – more orange than tan.

I sighed and rummaged through the magazines splayed on a glass-top coffee table next to a circular vase of hothouse roses. None of the available choices appealed, so eschewing *Esquire, Model Railway Constructor, Good Housekeeping* and *Home Chat*, I sank into the corner of a plush, modern sofa. A young man was sitting opposite, twiddling his trilby hat in an agitated manner, staring at his feet. I assumed he was waiting for the patient with the doctor, poor boy. I tried to occupy myself by concocting scenarios to explain the worried look on his face, but my mind kept slipping. Too preoccupied with the funny pains in my chest and what they might presage, I didn't care that his mother may have a terminal disease, or his girlfriend required assistance on what to do about a poorly timed pregnancy. Except for measles as a child and an occasional cold, illness of any kind had largely passed me by. I found sitting in the doctor's waiting room a confronting and unwelcome experience. One I wanted quickly over.

The clock above the receptionist's table – she was far too grand for a desk – chimed three o'clock. Already I'd waited fifteen minutes. My hands became clammy and caused the pleats in my skirt to crumple. I had to restrain myself from leaping up when at last the balding receptionist nodded to me and beckoned, "Come this way, Mrs Fanstone."

I followed her along a beige, thick, wool-carpeted corridor, lined with 19th century prints of scarlet-jacketed horsemen and women out on a hunt. We passed a dowdy middle-aged woman wearing a tattered hat pulled down over one eye. She smiled in greeting and I turned to see her hurry towards the young man. A domestic? Given the all-clear? I'd never know. I could hardly ask.

The receptionist held back the door and a portly, waistcoated man gestured to the chair beside his desk.

"Good afternoon, Doctor," I said, a bit put out he'd not shaken hands. Germs, perhaps.

"It's Mister," he said. "I'm a heart specialist." He opened a folder and placed spectacles across the bridge of his nose, carefully adjusting the wire arms around his ears. "Ha, hmm. Yes, hmm." He fingered the paperwork, tutting and blinking.

I waited in silence until the great man swung around, whipped off his glasses and assumed a serious expression. "Your test results don't paint a pretty picture," he said. "No cause for immediate alarm, but I'll be prescribing medications, and a strict diet."

My heart – the cause of all this – went into a panic, soaring and beating against my chest. "What do you mean? What exactly is the problem?"

He spoke slowly, as if I were of subnormal intelligence. "The blood isn't pumping sufficiently from your heart. This is why you feel tired and lethargic. We call it systolic heart failure. In your case, I estimate you may have as little as twenty per cent heart function. The good news is, if you look after yourself, you could easily live another year or more. Perhaps five, even ten, in some cases."

One year? My pulse galloped again, and my head spun, woolly and incapable of computing his words. "It's a death sentence."

"As I said, if you look after yourself–"

"And if I don't?"

He straightened my paperwork. "I can't say. You're a ticking time bomb."

I didn't want to hear any more and abruptly stood. "I have a lot to do and you've already kept me waiting a quarter of an hour." Time was indeed short, now. "Please write my prescription and I'll be on my way."

"Mrs Fanstone, there's more to discuss–"

"Or you can post everything to me." I didn't want to remain a minute more. His comfortable rooms, his superior attitude and rehearsed bedside manner, grated. I slid my handbag over my arm and left, pleased in a rather ridiculous way to have bested the pompous Mister.

Out on the street, I hailed the first black cab. An extravagance, but I couldn't face the walk to Oxford Circus to catch the number twenty-two bus. I directed the driver to my Chelsea flat, leaned into the corner of the back seat and watched the early rush-hour traffic as my heart returned to its normal pace.

"You all right, darlin'?" The driver looked at me via his rear-view mirror.

"A little breathless." An understatement. Even the most normal activities strained me these days. And now I'd been told there was no cure. Just a year if I were lucky. And if I were unlucky? It didn't bear consideration.

As the cab slowly wound through Mayfair and Knightsbridge, I gazed onto the familiar imposing buildings: Wigmore Hall, The Dorchester Hotel, Harrods. How would I spend my time? What mattered most?

In the end, it came down to family. But all of them except Esme – and that relationship maintained only a tenuous hold – had long discarded me as unwanted goods. Mother, Susan, Mavis... Charlie, dear Charlie... Lewis, even Granny Fanstone. Who would want to see me? Who would care when I died?

By the time we reached Sloane Square, I'd come to a

decision. A realisation. They all knew what I'd done. Apart from Esme. I should tell her, mend our fences. That very evening I would write and invite her for afternoon tea next week. Somewhere special. The Ritz. And I'd take my courage in both hands to tell her how I started my life as Jane Robin, and all that followed.

For a long time, Esme sat in the dark. Tears streamed down her face – tears of anger, empathy, loss. But mostly, tears of grief for a mother she'd never truly known, but who had now reached out to her via the power of words, to tell her story from the grave.

And yet... not all the pieces had fallen into place. Esme roused herself, turned off the side lamps, and went upstairs to retrieve Arcadia's jewellery box. She sat on the end of the bed, staring at the two photographs which had been hidden under her mother's last remaining trinkets: surely, a young Charlie. And as for the baby? It must be the child she gave away. A boy or a girl? Arcadia had requested not to be told her baby's sex, so it seemed Esme would never be any wiser about the identity of her half-sibling.

Another thing... Esme pondered on what had happened to Charlie in those intervening years from the end of World War I, until his return in 1924. Clearly, he revealed things to Arcadia that he'd asked she keep secret, and she'd abided by her promise. She'd only written about the scant facts that Charlie allowed to be made public, but even those might not have been the truth.

Too many secrets had blighted their lives, thought Esme. But she wouldn't ask, either. People were entitled to their secrets – if Charlie wanted to die with his intact, so be it.

34

ESME

GUERNSEY, OCTOBER 1958

*I*nspector Allbridge's windowless office, in the new police headquarters at St James's Chambers, was cramped. Esme had to edge her way around shelves spilling over with manuals and folders, and boxes piled high, to the uncomfortable steel-backed visitor's chair. The inspector didn't live up to Esme's idea of a crack investigator. Not that she expected a clone of Hercule Poirot or Sherlock Holmes, but the shabby man wearing trousers that nearly fell down his hips and a shirt with mismatched buttons, didn't inspire confidence.

Allbridge leaned back in his chair, barely visible behind the mounds of files on his desk, eyes closed while Esme explained her mission. Until he made a low grunt, she wasn't sure whether he was listening or had fallen asleep.

"So there you have it," she said. "M. Mellon was deep in debt and his only way out was to quickly raise money to pay the hoons who were after him. His bank records clearly show that after the deaths of both his wives, he sold their respective houses and withdrew all the money. In cash. It was a large sum, Detective."

Anthony's friend had been only too pleased to help; he'd

never believed in Clara's guilt. It hadn't been hard to track down the bank where Mellon conducted his business, but the police had never bothered to investigate him. Hopefully, Esme's efforts would redress that oversight.

The unshaven man before her slowly opened his eyes. "And you say the bank manager is willing to hand over Mellon's banking records?"

She clasped her hands in a tight knot and held her breath. "Yes. He said he'd raised concerns with the police at the time, but by then Clara had been arrested and nothing was done. He's more than happy to assist." The inspector remained silent, drumming his fingers on the desk. "I mean, it all adds up, doesn't it? M. Mellon was in a fix, he had debt collectors after him threatening who knows what, and his only way out was to murder his wife and inherit her money. And then it happened all over again."

"It's only supposition, I'm afraid, and not enough to charge him on." Allbridge smacked his lips together. "But I'd say it warrants reopening the case. The evidence against Clara was thin, to say the least." Then to Esme's surprise, he smiled. "We have a few things on our side though. In October 1945, the police force here was in a manner of flux, you might say. Because of the Occupation, procedures had changed and the force was being reorganised to bring it back in line with the English police force. And of course, more modern policing means we have better detection methods these days." He gestured around his office, although Esme failed to see how the jumble of paperwork represented a new way of doing things.

"So what happens now?" she asked.

Allbridge grunted. "A lot of form filling. And if we get lucky, an application to release Clara on insufficient evidence will be favourably received."

"And M. Mellon?"

"As I said, short of a confession, I can't see how we'll get him.

But if we get the go-ahead, I'll have him in for questioning. And believe me, it won't be pleasant."

Esme exhaled a large breath; she hadn't realised how tense she'd been about this meeting. "Thank you so much. I can't tell you how thrilled I am that you've taken me seriously."

Allbridge stood and extended his hand. "No, Miss Fanstone. The thanks are all from the Guernsey Police Force. If there's been a miscarriage of justice, then we must be seen to right the wrong."

She shook his hand. Knowing Clara would get a second chance to be proved innocent of her crime was a huge step forwards. All Esme could do now was wait.

Charlie and Esme sat in his garden, soaking up an early October heatwave. Esme wore a light cotton dress, and Charlie had donned a short-sleeved shirt, revealing yet more scars and ugly burn marks along his arms. His fortitude made Esme ashamed for ever being self-conscious about her unsightly cheek.

She leaned back to feel the sun on her face and luxuriate in its warmth. The air, scented with lilies, rippled with a light afternoon breeze. Baby sparrows clustered around the stone birdbath, dipping their beaks in the water. Overhead, an airplane left a vapour trail in its wake. She couldn't remember a more perfect day.

Charlie passed her a glass of home-made lemonade. "Are you and Anthony going to make your life here, on Guernsey?"

"We hope so. Anthony's research will keep him busy for some years and I can write anywhere. Besides, we both love it here."

"I asked you here for a reason." Charlie shifted in his chair. "I've told Mavis something I thought I'd never tell another living soul. And I'm going to tell you too."

"You don't have to."

"I must. Arcadia knew and she still stayed by my side." His voice sounded gravelly and tired. "I'm taking the chance you won't abandon me either."

It was why she came to Guernsey in the first place, wasn't it? To learn the mystery behind that cryptic letter to Arcadia? Having come so far, and uncovering both the unpalatable and joyful, she mustn't falter now. Whatever else there was to learn, however shocking, she needed to hear it. "Yes, I'd like a full picture of the past. Without it, how will I ever come to terms with who my mother really was?"

He took several sips through a straw. "Raspy throat," he said. "Too much talking."

"We can leave it for another–"

"No. Best said. Then it's done." He took one more sip. "Don't judge me too badly."

"As far as I'm concerned, you're part of my family now. Take your time. I'm not going anywhere."

He rubbed his stump. "I want you to try and imagine what it was like for us young lads sent to the front. We were scared, we missed our mothers and girls, we were living in muddy trenches with only our mates for solace. Who knew when our last day was about to come? There was nothing heroic about being sent over the top to face the enemy, and worse besides." His breathing came in short staccato gasps.

Esme remained still, waiting for him to gather himself.

"William – Mavis's husband – and I had stuck out the war together. We'd become superstitious about always fighting side by side. This time, our unit had been blocking the German advance for two days and nights. Casualties were massive. Fighting was relentless and we were exhausted. By the third day, William couldn't stop shaking. He cried and said he felt woolly-headed. Told me he couldn't go over again that night. I had to push him through the barbed wire and into no man's land. We ran towards the German line. It was mayhem. Shells, artillery fire. Men falling." Charlie began to tremble.

"Don't, if you can't." Esme laid a hand on his shoulder.

"I caught a blast in my face and legs, and stumbled. William turned to me and was shot in the back. I crawled to him. Poor bastard was screaming in pain. He grabbed my collar and whispered, 'Do for me'."

Tears streamed down Charlie's cheeks, and he hung his head. "I took my pistol and shot him in the head."

The horror of the scene played out in Esme's imagination: the noise of gunfire, the stench, the mud, the howls of dying men – and Charlie's pain. There was nothing she could say to erase that day for him, and she stayed silent, for who was she to judge?

Shadows lengthened. A bird – a thrush? – sang out. Esme kept her hand on Charlie, hoping to give some comfort.

He inhaled and expelled the air from his lungs. "I didn't know if I was a hero or a coward, but it was William's last wish. Had anyone seen me shoot him? I didn't know. I acted on instinct. My face hurt like hell, I couldn't feel my leg and I was bleeding. I dragged myself forwards on my belly. I wanted to scarper. Run away from what I'd done. Whatever happened, I'd be dead. Either killed for desertion or shooting a comrade. More likely, from my wounds."

"Oh, Charlie."

"I buried my identity tags in the mud, so if they found me no one would know who I was or what I'd done, and kept edging onwards. Whizz-bangs hailed down. I was hit in the arm just before I fell into a German trench and passed out. Next thing I knew, I was in a German field hospital. They'd taken off my leg. Chap on the stretcher next to me said we were lucky. They shot most of the wounded. He gave me a letter from his mother. 'I'm for it', he said, 'let mother know'. He died an hour later and I took his tags. The Germans never knew. Just another unknown soldier. I became John Ferris."

He coughed and took another long draught of lemonade. "They patched me up and after a few weeks sent me to a camp. Conditions were harsh, but I was strong and kept my head down. After a few months, we knew the war was on the turn. Word had reached us from prisoners taken at the front that the Germans were in retreat. Our captors were no longer so cocky. Our boys' morale improved. We just had to sit it out."

"What happened at the end of the war? Why didn't you come home?"

"Couldn't. My papers said I was John Ferris and so far I'd got away with it, but once I returned to England, it would get complicated. I imagined a letter to his mother from the authorities saying her son had returned. I couldn't do that to the poor woman. If I confessed my real identity, I was scared I'd be arrested for William's death because I didn't know if anyone had seen what I'd done and reported it. Decided it was best to keep my head down. Presumably I'd been declared dead. And I looked such a mess, I didn't want to face people."

"Where did you go?" A young man, brutalised by war and terrified of the consequences of his actions, would have had few options.

"Scotland, up north, Inverness way. Lived in a shepherd's hut where no one came. The laird gave me food in exchange for herding his sheep. I couldn't get Jane from my mind, but I told myself even if I dared go back home, she'd run away at the sight of me. Winter of '23 I got caught in a blizzard. Couldn't find my way to shelter. Ended up with pneumonia. Decided my time was up and I'd take my chances. I had to see Jane one last time."

"And you arrived back on the day of your mother's funeral. How awful."

"Dark days."

Charlie must have expected a difficult homecoming but nothing as wrenching as the loss of his mother and shortly after, his father's suicide. It was hard to imagine his longing for Jane, his self-hatred at his mutilated body, and his guilt at seeing Mavis, the widow of the man he'd killed.

"When I arrived and Jane wasn't here, I despaired. My mother and father were dead, and I could see no future. I hid in the shed, thinking to join them."

"But you didn't."

"Someone up there was looking after me." He smiled. "My luck turned for more than twenty years. That's the way I see it now. Jane came back and we patched together our marriage. I never asked about her London life. I didn't want to hear her lies. But it was Mavis who really looked after me."

"How did you explain your absence after the war?"

"Said I'd lost my memory. Shell shock. As for the authorities, no one seemed much interested. All it took was my birth certificate and I became Bernard Charles Vautier again."

"How did Mavis take it? When you told her about William?"

"I should have trusted her years ago. She thanked me for ending his suffering." Charlie made a small choking sound. "And then she told me how she and William never – well, it had not been happy between them, put it that way. They'd never really been man and wife. Not in the proper way. That was her guilt." He reached up and clasped Esme's hand. "I need to rest."

She sensed he also wanted to be alone. "You go inside. I'll clear up these things." She passed him his stick.

Charlie balanced his weight and eased out of his seat. "Make it count with Anthony every day. You never know when happiness will be snatched away."

Esme put her arms around him and held him close. "Reach out to Mavis," she murmured. "She's been waiting for you a long time."

35

ESME

GUERNSEY, DECEMBER 1958

*A*nthony by her side, Esme scanned the passengers disembarking the ferry. A stream of hugging families, reuniting couples, and chattering groups of friends surged along the jetty. Standing on tiptoes, Esme searched for the familiar face she prayed would be amongst the arrivals. Anthony squeezed her hand, and she felt the band of diamonds on her ring finger press against his palm.

"She'll be here. Don't worry, Tuppence," he said.

Esme grinned up at him. "I haven't felt this excited or nervous since I started kindergarten."

Anthony pointed over her head. "Is that her?"

They both peered at the lone figure stepping onto the gangway. A woman with a slight stoop and a bewildered expression, carrying a battered holdall, walked in their direction.

Esme waved in big swooping movements to attract her attention. "Clara!"

A beam spread over the woman's face and she hurried towards them. "Oh my, Miss Fanstone. Can you believe it? Here I am, back in St Peter Port and it's all thanks to you."

Esme made the introductions and Anthony took Clara's case. "How was the journey, not too bumpy?" he asked.

Clara didn't answer, her gaze riveted on the skyline of the town ahead. She sighed. "Just as I remember and never thought to see again. Oh, miss, it's a dream come true."

"You two wait here," said Anthony, "while I put Clara's bag in the car."

A flash of fear crossed Clara's face. "You can't take my things—"

"It's all right, Clara, you're coming to stay with me until you get settled," Esme said. "I want no argument, so don't even try." Now the moment had finally arrived, Esme realised how overwhelming it must be for Clara: the sudden change in her circumstances from her cell in Holloway Prison to being back in Guernsey and an uncertain future. She needed time to adjust. "Anthony, why don't you go on ahead? We can't all squeeze in the car anyway. Clara and I can get the bus." Anthony gave an understanding nod and Esme gave him a discreet thumbs up. Then she took Clara's arm and led her to the parapet at the edge of the harbour, facing the town. "Shall we sit for a moment?"

Clara acquiesced without a murmur, possibly glad of some time to reorient. "I don't know how I'll face it," she said, worried lines puckering her forehead. "I know as how I've been pardoned, but how will it be for me? To most folks, I'll still be a murderess."

"You mustn't think it, Clara. The newspapers have been full of the terrible miscarriage of justice you've suffered. I think you'll find people are sympathetic and kind."

"I hope so, but not everyone has a heart like yours." She picked at her fingernails. "As soon as I find work, I'll pay you back."

"Pay me back? Whatever for?"

"The room, miss."

Esme laughed. "Don't be silly. You're my guest. As for work, my neighbour, Travis, has said he'd be glad of your help. He's a widower and needs someone to keep house and cook for him. He'll give you a trial and if all goes well, it will be a permanent position."

"I won't let you down, I promise."

"But first, you need a few days' rest. And there must be so many things you want to do, things you've missed out on."

"Not so much. Except..." Her voice trailed off.

"Yes?" prompted Esme.

"I'd like to find my parents."

Esme frowned. "But you told me your mother had died, and your father was in France."

"They was my adopted parents. I mean my real ones. I kept thinking about them, when I was locked up in that place, wondering what they'd make of me." She turned her careworn face to Esme. "Foolish of me, I'm sure. But behind them bars, I had plenty of time to think about how my life might have been if my real mother had kept me."

"Do you know anything about her? Or your father?"

Clara shook her head. "I only know she was sinful. That's what Mam told me. As for him, nothing was ever said."

An unmarried mother, thought Esme, forced to give up her baby. Or else burdened with too many children already, and unable to feed another mouth. "I'm not sure where to begin to look." She'd found her own family, though, on only slender clues. Perhaps she could do the same for Clara. "Do you know anything at all about her?"

"Just her name, miss, as was on my birth certificate. Jane Vautier."

Seagulls cawed. Children playing hopscotch on the foreshore giggled and squealed. A car honked its horn. But Esme only heard a soundless moment as the pieces slotted into their rightful places. *Jane Vautier, née Robin.* Holding back tears, she took Clara's hands and spoke gently. "I can't unite you with your mother, I'm afraid. She died a little while ago but I do know she loved you very much. She even dedicated a book to you, *Smuggler's Cove.*"

Clara's eyes widened and her mouth dropped into a surprised O. "You knew her, miss?"

Esme nodded. "And I can take you to meet your extraordinarily special father, and your grandmother. You've two wonderful aunts, as well." Clara's jaw fell a little further. "And a sister – well, half-sister." Esme traced Clara's face, searching for the similarities: a shade of Arcadia, a whisper of Charlie. "It's a long story, Clara, but Jane Vautier was my mother too."

THE END

ACKNOWLEDGEMENTS

When I reflect on writing this book and the myriad people who helped bring it to life, the key highlight was time spent on Guernsey undertaking research, and the wonderful assistance I received from the local community.

Before making the trip, I reached out to various Channel Islands Facebook groups to help with thorny items of social history. My queries were regularly answered by Alan Solway, whose deep knowledge of the island was invaluable. On arrival, Alan took on the role of tour guide, giving up hours of his time to squire my partner and me around every inch of Guernsey. He related history and anecdotes; laughed at some of my assumptions; shared the colour and essence of the island and how it had been shaped by both World War I and World War II. Then, months after I returned to Australia and had been offered a publishing contract by Betsy Reavley at Bloodhound Books, Alan stepped up again and meticulously fact-checked the text.

Many others on the island welcomed my questions, opened up their archives and went out of their way to explain Guernsey's history or locate the answers I sought. Special thanks to: Andrew Chantrell at Old Government House Hotel (and my apologies that along the way, the chapters set at the hotel were deleted!); Andrew Chambers and staff at La Collinette; Lesley Bailey and Cheryl Latter on Herm; the librarians at Priaulx and Guille-Allès libraries; and everyone who shared stories, insights and memories.

As ever, I'm deeply indebted to my writers' groups. Lynn Hightower, Mark Hoffman and Emily Stokes, thank you for being there at the beginning and workshopping the first chapters; Andrea Barton for valiantly reading every draft; Women's Critique Group for pulling apart all the inconsistencies; Julia Kelly for once again being my first reader; Sue Anderson for her editorial wisdom; and my editor Caroline Garner for whipping The Dilemma into final shape, together with Tara, Betsy, Fred and all at Bloodhound Books.

A big shout-out to my mum, who tape-recorded her childhood memories of growing up during the war, and whose own grandmother inspired Granny Fanstone: it was wonderful to draw on such a rich repository of personal family recollections.

Thanks to the judges of the Grindstone International Novel of The Year for sending me one of the best emails ever, announcing the manuscript had reached the 2019 shortlist, and setting me on the path to finalising the story.

To my readers... thank you for putting aside many hours to read The Dilemma, it's truly appreciated. If you have any comments or thoughts, I always love hearing from you: sarah@sarahhawthorn.com.au

Lastly to Brett, my chief cheerleader and biggest critic: our daily walks with Lulu and Alfie keep my brain fresh, the reliable cups of coffee and glasses of wine keep me sane, and your unwavering belief in my ability to reach The End keeps me tapping for long hours on the keyboard.

A NOTE FROM THE PUBLISHER

Thank you for reading this book. If you enjoyed it please do consider leaving a review on Amazon to help others find it too.

We hate typos. All of our books have been rigorously edited and proofread, but sometimes mistakes do slip through. If you have spotted a typo, please do let us know and we can get it amended within hours.

info@bloodhoundbooks.com

Made in United States
North Haven, CT
15 August 2022

22771507R10178